"HE'S A HARD MAN, THAT TEXAS JOHN"

He limped outside to check the extent of the carnage. Hooper had come down off the roof and was checking the bodies. Slaughter helped him. They counted eleven dead men and one on his way. One of these was the Robles *vaquero*. The priest emerged from the church, came across the sun-hammered plaza, and knelt beside the dying man, performing last rites. The bandit expired before the priest could finish.

"Guess I'll never know if Don Francisco was a party to this," Slaughter told Hooper as the black cowboy joined him at the body of the *vaquero*.

"Does it really matter?" asked Hooper.

"It does to me. I aim to be in this country from now on, and if I have to deal with Robles, I'd just as soon do it now as later."

The priest came to stand before them, his features taut with anger. "You have killed many men today," he told Slaughter. "May God have mercy on your soul."

"Men?" asked Slaughter coldly. "I've killed some no-account varmints. I haven't killed any men today."

He turned his back on the shocked priest and went back into the brothel.

Hooper smiled faintly at the look on the priest's face.

"He's a hard man, that Texas John," he said by way of explanation, and then walked away to leave the man of God to stand alone among the *bandolero* corpses.

Gun Justice

JASON MANNING

St. Martin's Paperbacks

GUN JUSTICE

Copyright © 1999 by Jason Manning.

ISBN: 0-312-97191-5

Printed in the United States of America

St. Martin's Paperbacks edition / December 1999

St. Martin's Paperbacks are published by St. Martin's Press, 175 Fifth Avenue, New York, N.Y. 10010.

10 9 8 7 6 5 4 3 2 1

CHAPTER ONE

THE MAN FROM
BITTER CREEK

1880

WHEN BILL GALLAGHER SET HIS SIGHTS ON A FEW HUNDRED head of John Slaughter's cattle, he found out the hard way what just about everyone in southwest Texas already knew—that Slaughter was the last man you wanted to trifle with.

Gallagher considered himself a hardcase, and some folks claimed he had killed thirteen men in his short and sordid career as a longrider. It was a rumor that Gallagher himself thought it was in his best interests to cultivate. He called himself "the Man from Bitter Creek." He didn't actually come from a place called Bitter Creek, or anything even remotely close, but he liked the sound of it. Though he sported twin .45 revolvers holstered on his hips, Gallagher's weapon of choice was a sawed-off ten-gauge shotgun. For someone who had gotten the better of thirteen men, he wasn't much of a shot, so the scattergun was a good choice for him. And, too, he'd found out that there were not a lot of men who could look down the twin barrels of his shotgun and keep their nerve.

"You'll see just how hard a man that bastard John

Slaughter is when I catch up to him," he told his partner in crime, Frank Boyd.

"Well," drawled Boyd, a laconic fellow who made a habit of seeing dark humor in all things, "I sure as hell hope that's the case, seeing as how Slaughter has gotten the better of you two times already. Reckon maybe third time's the charm?"

Riding stirrup to stirrup alongside Boyd, with a trio of other dusty, scurrilous no-accounts coming along behind them as they crossed the arid sagebrush plain of southeastern New Mexico under a broiling summer sun, Gallagher looked askance at his sidekick.

"He got the drop on me both times," said Gallagher, his tone of voice sulky and defensive. "First he stole my money, then he stole my cows. And they call *me* an outlaw!"

Boyd smirked. "You never owned a head of beef in your life, Bill. Who do you think you're talking to here? Remember, we go back a long ways, you and me."

"I've sold plenty of cattle in my time."

"That's true, but they didn't *belong* to you," said Boyd, grinning.

"They're mine when I say they're mine. And this here herd we're trailing is gonna be mine. Soon as I kill John Slaughter."

"You mean it'll be ours. I didn't come all this way just to see the scenery."

"You'll get your cut," promised Gallagher. "When have you ever failed to make a profit from riding with me?"

"Never," acknowledged Boyd. "But I might ought to get a bonus on top of a cut this time, seeing as how I've ridden across half of Texas and now more of New Mexico than I ever wanted to see."

"It'll be worth every blister on your sorry ass, Frank. You'll see."

"Yeah, sure." Boyd shifted in his sweat-stained saddle.

He had plenty of blisters and wondered if he shouldn't charge Gallagher a hundred bucks for each one, as a sweetener to add to his cut from the sale of the herd they were about to purloin from one John Slaughter. They had trailed the herd all the way up from the Devil River country in Texas. That meant weeks of sunup-to-sundown riding across the sun-hammered desert. If Boyd hadn't been flat broke he wouldn't have come along. But the saloons in San Antonio did not give away free liquor, nor did the girls in the bordellos there spread their legs for nothing, either. He figured if they could pull this job off he would be sitting pretty for some time to come. And if it all went sour, well, what was the point of living if you had to go through life without whiskey and women?

Being the kind of man he was, Frank Boyd never entertained any serious thought of working for an honest wage. He had nothing but contempt for the cowpunchers on Slaughter's payroll, the ones who were up ahead there where that dun-colored cloud of dust rose up into the sky, dogging over five hundred head of cattle. Only fools labored so long and hard for thirty dollars a month and food. Thirty dollars! Boyd could spend that much in a night on the rowdy side of San Antonio.

He glanced at Gallagher and his gaze lingered on the black sombrero the Man from Bitter Creek was wearing. It was without a doubt the finest hat Boyd had ever laid eyes on. Gallagher insisted that he had killed the leader of Mexican *bandoleros* down on the Bloody Border some months ago, and had taken the man's sombrero as a trophy. It had silver and gold mountings, and Boyd thought it looked damned fine. Whether Gallagher had actually killed the hat's previous owner or stolen the sombrero, the fact remained that it was in his possession and Boyd coveted it for himself.

"Tell you what," said Boyd. "When you and Slaughter meet up, I don't know who's gonna wind up eating dirt.

But if he gets the better of you, I want that hat. You will it to me, Bill, and I'll forget all about the bonus you owe me."

Gallagher laughed harshly. "I don't owe you no damned bonus. And you ain't never getting your hands on this sombrero. John Slaughter is a dead man. He just don't know it yet."

"Yeah, but what if you're wrong?"

"The day I die, this hat is yours. There, does that make you happy? Now quit bitching and moaning like some old woman."

They rode in silence for a spell, Boyd lost in pleasing thoughts of how good he would look in that black sombrero, how all the calico queens in San Antonio would pay attention to him, taking him for a man of substantial means because of the hat. Gallagher was having pleasant thoughts of his own, and they revolved around the image of John Slaughter dying, writhing in agony on the ground, dying by inches with a big bloody hole, courtesy of a shotgun blast at close range, full bore, in his guts.

Gallagher had first met John Slaughter in a San Antonio saloon. An acquaintance had pointed Slaughter out as a man who had money and who seldom passed on a good poker game. Having a high opinion of his own poker skills, Gallagher had figured he could empty Slaughter's pockets, especially since he would be using marked cards. Slaughter had accepted the invite, and the game had commenced in a back room. There were four players, and the other two men, unbeknownst to Slaughter, were Gallagher's cronies who were aware of the scheme and had been promised a share of the winnings. The pots were big and the game went on for hours because Slaughter turned out to be a damned fine poker player in his own right. But in the long run he was losing. Then Gallagher got careless. Not content to rely on the marked deck, he stashed an ace up his sleeve, and when the time was right he employed it to win the biggest pot of the night. Except that when he reached out to scoop up the winnings with both arms, grinning like a cat, he found himself nose to barrel with John Slaughter's six-gun.

"Gallagher," Slaughter had drawled, "you're so crooked they'll have to screw you into the ground when the time comes to bury you."

The grin frozen on his face, Gallagher had very slowly leaned back in his chair, drawing his hands, palms down, across the table to the edge.

"One of those hands drops out of sight," warned Slaughter, "and that burying will take place today."

"Are you calling me a cheat?" blustered Gallagher.

"What would you call a man who plays draw poker with an ace up his sleeve?" Slaughter dropped his hat on the table. "One of you boys put all the winnings in my hat," he said, standing to kick his chair out from behind him, holding the pistol rock steady and aimed at the spot right between Gallagher's eyes. Gallagher fumed as one of the other men obediently raked the pot into the crown of Slaughter's hat. But he kept his hands where Slaughter could see them—even when, at Slaughter's bidding, the pile of cash and coin in front of him was also transferred to the hat.

"Hey, those are my fair-and-square winnings," protested Gallagher.

"Well, I'll be," said Slaughter dryly. "I've never heard anyone call playing with marked cards fair and square."

"You're the thief," sneered Gallagher. "You're taking my stake, too."

"That's the price you'll pay for this lesson." And with that Slaughter took the hat and backed up to the door that led to an alley running behind the Commerce Street saloon. "If you have any objections," he added as a parting shot, "you'll have no problem finding me. Ask anyone. They'll point you in my direction." Then he disappeared into the night.

And Gallagher *had* asked around. Ben Slaughter and his sons—Charley, Billy, and John—were all prominent cattlemen who, between them, laid claim to most of the grass in Frio and Atascosa Counties. John Slaughter was married to a slender beauty named Eliza Adeline, daughter of a business partner named Lease Harris. The couple had a house in San Antonio on Gardner Street, and were there often enough. But no one was home when Gallagher and several of his henchmen came calling a couple of days after the poker game. Not wishing to place his wife and two children in harm's way, and suspecting future skullduggery on Gallagher's part, Slaughter had taken Addie and the kids home to his ranch near Devil River.

Not to be denied vengeance for the humiliation he had suffered, Gallagher went after Slaughter. Faulty information took him to Charley Slaughter's stone house in Friotown. Under the gun, Charley kept his wits about him and prevented an eruption of violence. Patient and intelligent, Charley lacked the rattler-quick temper of his younger brother John, and he tried to reason with Gallagher, who pretended to accept Charley's point that there was nothing to be gained by pursuing a vendetta. Instead, more determined than ever to make John Slaughter pay for what he had done, Gallagher and his hardcase crew rode hard for Devil River. There, the Man from Bitter Creek had a second confrontation with his nemesis.

This one didn't go his way, either.

Slaughter was out on the range, gathering together a herd to drive to New Mexico. As he had told his brothers Charley and Billy, Texas was getting just a little too crowded to suit his taste. Catching Slaughter alone out in the *brasada,* Gallagher tried to bluff his man. After all, Gallagher had several gunmen to back him up.

"I've come to get what's owed me," said the longrider. "You robbed me back in San Antone. Now I'm laying claim to a hundred head of your cattle. I reckon to get ten dollars a head, so that comes to a thousand dollars. It's true, you didn't steal that much from me, but the way I see it, the difference is the price you have to pay for the lesson

I'm teaching you." Gallagher grinned, immensely pleased that at last he'd had the opportunity to throw Slaughter's own words back at him. "Or if that galls you too much, consider it the price of your life."

Slaughter was not a tall man, but as he stiffened in the saddle, prodded to quick anger by Gallagher's words, he sure looked tall. His jet-black eyes flashed with anger, and it dismayed Gallagher more than a little that he didn't appear to be the least bit concerned with the odds that were stacked against him.

"You're not going to touch a single head of my cattle," said Slaughter, and he said it so matter-of-factly and with such confidence that it seemed like God Almighty Himself was making a pronouncement.

Gallagher took a look around, scanning the *brasada,* puzzlement knitting his brow. What was this man Slaughter made of, anyway? Here he was staring death in the face and he didn't look even slightly concerned. It made Gallagher wonder if maybe the cattleman had some men hidden in the brush, covering him. But the longrider didn't see a thing, and chided himself for lack of confidence.

"We'll see about that," he sneered. "I didn't come all this way to go back empty-handed." He knew he had to stand up to Slaughter for the sake of the men who rode with him. If they saw him falter, they would become as useless as udders on a bull. Problem was, the Man from Bitter Creek was feeling a little cowed already, even though Apache torture could not have made him admit as much.

One of the gunmen behind Gallagher started moving his hand closer to the six-shooter on his hip, but Slaughter's cold black eyes fastened on him. "Don't do that." It was all the cattleman said. He didn't have to say anything else. Didn't have to do anything else. He kept his hands on the saddle horn. Still, the hardcase had a sudden revelation concerning his own mortality and took his hand away from the shooting iron.

Slaughter turned his attention back to Gallagher. "As for

you coming all this way, that's a real shame. You shouldn't have wasted your time."

"Now, listen here . . ." started Gallagher, but hesitated, because it was obvious that John Slaughter could not be bluffed. So it was time to either start making smoke or back down. That wasn't how Gallagher had envisioned this confrontation. He had figured Slaughter would take one look at him and his men and bend like a willow in a hurricane. But there was no bend in Slaughter, he could see that now.

Slaughter waited politely for Gallagher to finish his sentence, and when it was clear that the longrider wasn't inclined to finish, he said, "And you've wasted enough of my time, too. So go away, and don't let your shadow fall on my range again."

Bristling at this curt and contemptuous dismissal, Gallagher teetered on the brink of making a play. But then he recalled how unpleasant it had been staring down the barrel of Slaughter's Colt pistol back in San Antonio, and decided it was too soon for an encore. So he savagely reined his horse around and rode away, taking his frustrations out on his mount, and followed by his henchmen.

Thinking back on those two experiences with John Slaughter rubbed Gallagher raw. Now, riding with sidekick Frank Boyd across the arid New Mexican plain, he felt a sudden urge to finish this business once and for all. It really had nothing at all to do with a poker stake or cattle on the hoof, not anymore. Slaughter had stolen Gallagher's self-respect, and had shot holes in his reputation, to boot. Now, for certain, Gallagher had to kill the man. It was a simple matter of survival. A gunhawk like the Man from Bitter Creek could not afford to let it get around that someone had walked all over him. If that happened, he was as good as dead. The idea of a showdown with Slaughter scared him. But he didn't have any choice now. Of a sudden he wanted to get this thing over and done with. So without warning to the others he spurred his trail-worn mount into a canter and pulled away. Surprised, Boyd and the others had to catch up.

In short order they had the herd in sight, and Gallagher told Boyd and the others to hang back. He knew they were of no use to him when it came to dealing with the cattleman. They were just here to help him run off the cattle. They hadn't bought into a shooting spree. His business with Slaughter was the kind of thing he had to do himself.

Gallagher rode right up to one of the drag riders, a dark and dusty young cowpuncher as thin as a fencepost and twice as durable. The cowboy had his red bandanna pulled up over his face on account of all the dust kicked up by the hooves of the cattle on the move up ahead.

"I'm looking for John Slaughter," rasped Gallagher.

"He's at the head of the herd, be my guess."

"You go tell that black-eyed son of a bitch that Bill Gallagher has come to kill him."

The drag rider pulled the bandanna down and gave Gallagher the once-over. Then he smiled faintly, just a curl at the corner of the mouth.

"Yes, sir," said the cowboy. "Why don't you wait right here? I'll go tell him what you said. He'll want to see you, so don't you go nowhere."

"Hurry up," snapped Gallagher.

The drag rider spurred his quick and agile cowpony into a stretched-out gallop. Gallagher veered off out of the thickest part of the dust and laid his scattergun across the saddle in front of him. A glance over the shoulder confirmed that Boyd and the others had checked their horses and were waiting to see what would develop. Gallagher drew a long breath and tried to steady his nerves. This was the moment of truth. If he killed John Slaughter, his reputation would be secured. If this went against him, well, he was done for anyway.

Then he saw his man, riding toward him.

Gallagher didn't want to trade words with Slaughter. He

had gone down that road twice before and lost out both times. Feeling the fear welling up inside him, the Man from Bitter Creek dug his big Mexican spurs so deep into his horse's flanks that the animal snorted and leaped into a gallop. In the next instant Slaughter was encouraging his own mount into a gallop, making straight for Gallagher, drawing a Winchester repeating rifle out of its saddle scabbard. Gallagher had clung to the hope that his charge might serve to unnerve the cattleman. Clearly that was not the case. So the longrider closed the distance between them a bit and then checked and turned his horse and brought the sawed-off shotgun to bear. But Slaughter was quick—too quick for him. Guiding his cowpony with knee pressure, the cattleman brought the repeater to his shoulder and with one shot knocked Gallagher's horse down. The outlaw hit the ground hard, staggered to his feet, and pulled the twin .45-caliber revolvers out of their holsters. He began blazing away at Slaughter, firing one gun and then the other, standing his ground. But the range was a little too long for side guns. Slaughter fired three more rounds from the back of his galloping horse. The first bullet plowed through Gallagher's stomach. The second broke his arm. And the third tore through his lungs. With an incoherent sound, somewhere between a roar of outrage and a whimper of self-pity, Gallagher collapsed.

Slaughter reached him, checking his pony hard, just in time to hear the death rattle in the longrider's throat. Impassive, the cattleman sheathed his Winchester and took a look around. Several of his hands were riding toward him. So were four other horsemen that Slaughter didn't recognize. But he knew in a glance that they were not cowboys. He just sat his horse and waited for the riders to converge.

"Did you ride with this scum?" Slaughter asked Frank Boyd.

"I don't deny that," replied Boyd. "But I don't want no trouble." His hooded eyes swept past Slaughter and the four trail hands arrayed behind him. "All I want is that there hat of Bill's. See, he willed it to me."

"Take it, but nothing else, and then go back where you came from."

Boyd nodded. Dismounting, he retrieved the fancy sombrero, admired it for a moment, then tossed his hat away and put the sombrero on his head. It was, he was pleased to notice, a perfect fit. Then he climbed back into his saddle. He spared the herd of longhorns a quick, covetous glance. But those cows, he knew, might as well have been the Crown Jewels of England, because he wasn't going to get his hands on them. At least he had gotten something out of the deal.

"Well," he said, with a smirk at Slaughter, "we'll be on our way."

"That's a good idea," said Slaughter.

"They tell me you're quitting Texas and staking a claim out in this country. Would that be true?"

"It is. What do you care?"

"Nothing," drawled Boyd. "Just thinking I'll stay in Texas from now on." He glanced at Gallagher's corpse. "You gonna bury him?"

"Yeah. But you're not invited to the funeral."

"I don't cotton to funerals, myself," said Boyd, and then he and his three partners turned their horses and rode away.

Slaughter watched them go for a moment—and decided that he need not worry about them any further. "Dig a hole," he told one of the cowboys, and rode back to the head of the herd.

CHAPTER TWO

KING OF THE PECOS

THE DAY AFTER HE KILLED BILL GALLAGHER, SLAUGHTER found his brother Charley in a temporary camp on the banks of the Seven River. It was nearly noon and already breathlessly hot. Charley was stretched out in the shade of a wagon tarp that was attached at one end to the wagon he had brought all the way from Frio County in Texas, while the other end was staked into the parched and rocky New Mexican soil. Charley had come in advance of Slaughter and the herd with the intention of finding a promising ranch site. Accompanying him was Tiburio, a young Mexican handyman who had worked for all the Slaughters at one time or another, ever since he had been caught by John trying to steal a horse. Instead of hanging the lad, which was the usual fate of horse thieves, Slaughter had taken the scrawny orphan home and fed him. He was not what anyone would call a hard worker, but Tiburio had a way about him that just convinced most people that the world was better off with him in it, even if you couldn't come up with one real solid reason why that was so. He had become intensely loyal to the Slaughter family that had more or less adopted him. Though a miserable shot, Tiburio did have talent when it came to knives, and he was the only man Slaughter had ever met that mules actually listened to. Even the most obstinate knobhead would do what Tiburio told it to do.

When Slaughter rode into the camp, he dismounted, tied his horse to a wagon wheel, and, hearing Charley snoring away under the wagon tarp, kicked his brother's booted foot. Charley sat up quickly, brandishing a six-gun that had been hidden under his leg while he indulged in the siesta.

"Oh, it's you," he said, and put the gun down and ran a hand over his face. "What kept you?"

"A herd of cattle can slow a man down a bit. Lucky for you I wasn't an Indian."

Charley grinned. "Funny you should mention Indians. Had a run-in with five of them day before yesterday. I was out taking a look around and they came out of nowhere, as Indians are inclined to do, and started shooting at me. Take a look at my rig! Put a bullet hole right through the cantle. Ticked me off something fierce. That's a damned fine saddle. I shot one and outran the rest. See that blazed sorrel over yonder? Fastest horse I've ever known. I call him Telegraph."

Slaughter glanced at the saddle, then at the picket line where six mules—the wagon team—and two horses, the sorrel Charley was so proud of and a piebald mare, were tethered. He made no comment about his brother's brush with hostiles. The Slaughter brothers were not ones to make a big issue about close calls. They had all survived too many of them to get very worked up about such events.

"Where's Tiburio?"

Charley looked around. "Damned if I know. Probably gone fishing. River is over that way. What do you think about this country, John?"

Slaughter stepped on a scorpion that he had spotted crawling out from under the blanket his brother was sitting on, grinding the deadly critter under a bootheel.

"Haven't seen sign of a white man for fifty miles in any direction," continued Charley. "I think we could make a go of it right here."

"Hate to be the one to tell you this, Charley, but we're standing on Chisum land."

"Chisum!" Charley got to his feet and put on his hat and emerged from under the wagon tarp, eyes narrowing against the sun's blinding glare. "Damn it to hell, John. Does that man lay claim to all of New Mexico? Who does he think he is? 'King of the Pecos,' indeed!"

"Well, my guess is your river here runs into the Pecos, and the Pecos belongs to Chisum, as does all the land for as far as a cow will wander from its banks in a single day. Got any coffee?"

Charley gestured at the rock-rimmed cook fire, where a blackened coffeepot stood on smoldering coals. "Help yourself. Tiburio made it this morning, so you'll have to scoop it out with a spoon."

Sitting on his heels by the fire, Slaughter poured himself a cup of the thick brew while Charley did some pacing in an agitated state. "Well," he said at last, disgusted, "reckon I'll have to keep looking, won't I?"

"Maybe we should look to the west."

Charley stopped pacing and peered at his brother. "Just how far west do you mean?"

"Oh, about as far as Arizona."

"There is nothing in Arizona but Apaches and diamond-back rattlers."

"That's my point."

Charley grinned. "You got a bur under your saddle and its name is John Chisum. You're thinking this pasture ain't big enough to hold two bulls."

Slaughter had spotted a rider coming toward the camp, galloping in from the north across a sagebrush flat and trailing a plume of yellow dust behind him. Knowing it could not be one of his own hands, Slaughter stood up and transferred the coffee cup from his right hand to the left so that his right hand was free in case he needed to resort to his Colt Peacemaker.

The cowboy checked his quick-footed pony when he reached the camp. He was a black man in his forties. His squinty, sun-faded eyes took in the wagon and the picket line and the two men standing near the cook fire. Slaughter sized up the rider and relaxed a little. He had heard that this country was crawling with owlhoots of every kind, but this man was not made from that mold. This one's hands were callused from long years of hard work with lariat and branding iron. His beard was salt and pepper, his skin as tough and brown as old whang leather. But most importantly of all, he did something that only honest men could do—he looked John Slaughter straight in the eye.

"I'm here to talk to a fella named John Slaughter," he announced.

"And who might you be?" asked Charley.

"Del Hooper is my handle," said the cowboy. "I ride for John Chisum. He sent me to find John Slaughter."

"That would be me," said Slaughter.

"Mr. Chisum would like to palaver with you. You'll find him at the South Spring, about ten miles due north of here."

"What does 'the King of the Pecos' want to talk to my brother about?" asked Charley.

"It doesn't matter what," Slaughter said. "I'll accept the invite."

Hooper nodded and took a look at the horizon to the east, where he could see a cloud of dust. "That would be your herd, back that way, ain't it?"

"That's right."

"Well, then. I'll tell Mr. Chisum you'll be right along." With that the black cowboy whipped his lathered pony around and galloped north, back the way he had come, a dust plume marking his passage across the sun-blistered flats.

"I think I had better come with you," said Charley. "No telling what Chisum wants, but I doubt that it's to give you a hearty welcome."

Slaughter smiled. "Pa always said you were the smartest one. So you don't really want to get in between a couple of bulls, now, do you?"

Charley knew his brother well enough to know that Slaughter was telling him that his presence was not required.

"No, not really," he replied. "So I'll just stay here and maybe do a little fishing with Tiburio."

On his way north to South Spring, following Del Hooper's trail, Slaughter reviewed what he knew about John Chisum. Born in Tennessee, Chisum had moved to Texas at the tender age of thirteen. He had gone from being Lamar County's youngest county clerk to a cattle rancher who made good during the Civil War selling beef to the Confederacy. A couple of years after the war he moved a herd from the Concho range in Texas to New Mexico's Bosque Grande. By 1870 he had relocated all his stock to New Mexico. He prospered by supplying beef to the army at Fort Sumter and the Indian agencies in the region, and now it was said he had over one hundred men on his payroll, year-round. In this lawless land, filled to the brim with rustlers and renegade Indians, he needed every last one of them to hold on to what he owned.

In 1878, Chisum had become involved in the Lincoln County War. That conflict arose out of competition between the mercantile firm of James Dolan and Lawrence Murphy, who sought to monopolize the local market, and a store run by a young English rancher named John Henry Tunstall and his partner, lawyer Alexander McSween. With the sheriff and the district judge in their pocket, Murphy and Dolan played a part in the cold-blooded murder of Tunstall, and the war was on. Chisum had backed Tunstall and McSween, and while he had not directly participated in the bloodshed that followed the Englishman's death, he gave aid and comfort to the Regulators, the men who rode with McSween against the Murphy–Dolan outfit. One of the Regulators was a seventeen-year-old kid named William Bonney, also known as Billy the Kid. Bonney and his cronies gunned down the county sheriff, William Brady. In response, the Murphy–Dolan forces trapped a dozen Regulators, including the Kid, in McSween's house. After a five-day gun battle, Bonney and a few others staged a daring and successful escape. McSween, however, was killed, and with his demise, and the arrival of federal troops dispatched by the territorial governor, the war came to an end. Charged with the murder of Sheriff Brady, Billy the Kid had embarked on a career outside the law that was already legend. It was rumored that the Kid was an occasional guest of John Chisum's, and that while he rustled cattle from other stockmen, he never touched one of Chisum's Jinglebob cows.

Slaughter reached the South Spring as the day was winding down and the setting sun put on a show for him, gilding strips of purple clouds low in the western sky with a rich gold. Chisum's ranch house was a plain adobe structure. When Slaughter rode up, he saw a Mexican man checking all the heavy-timbered window shutters from the outside and lighting a couple of storm lanterns on the cedar-pole gallery that ran the length of the long house. Telling the man to inform the *padrone* that John Slaughter had arrived, the Texan stayed in his saddle. A moment after the Mexican disappeared inside, a tall, dark-haired man with a thick mustache and a piercing blue gaze stepped out, looked Slaughter over, and then said, "Climb on down and come in, Mr. Slaughter. You're welcome here." Then he went back inside, leaving the door open.

Dismounting, Slaughter tethered his horse and stepped into an airy room with big Mexican rugs on the square-beam floor, a stone fireplace, and sofas and chairs of dark, heavy wood and cowhide or horsehair upholstery. Chisum had gone to a cabinet and was pouring them both some tall whiskeys. As he handed one glass to his guest, Chisum said, "I hope Tennessee sour mash suits you. It reminds me of home."

"After a day like this, snakehead whiskey would suit me just fine."

After they had both cut the dust, Chisum gestured at the furniture and Slaughter eased his saddle-sore frame into an armchair while Chisum moved over to the spacious fireplace.

"I hear you had a little trouble yesterday," remarked Chisum.

"It was no trouble, really."

"You killed a man."

"I killed a thief and a murderer. He needed it. Word gets around."

"I like to keep informed about what goes on around these parts."

"Then you know I'm moving a herd across your range."

"That's not all I know. I also know that in Texas it is the custom to pick up unbranded cattle along the trail and throw them in with your own stock." Chisum smiled thinly. "Hell, I've put my brand on plenty of mavericks in my time. The problem is, I calculate you've got maybe two hundred head of my beef in your bunch."

"You'll find no Jinglebob brands in my herd."

"I know you heard what I just said."

"I was listening close."

"Then I take it you're not going to volunteer to cut my cows out of your herd."

"You want to come show me which cows you're talking about?"

Chisum fixed his piercing gaze on Slaughter, but when Slaughter refused to flinch, another thin smile crossed the weathered face of the King of the Pecos. He slacked a long frame into a chair facing his guest, stretching his legs out and crossing them at the ankles and contemplating the toes of his boots.

"I don't even know how many cattle I've got," he said. "Somewhere between eighty and a hundred thousand head. I don't think I want to break into a sweat over a couple hundred beeves."

Slaughter nodded. He knew full well that, had he been so inclined, John Chisum could have gotten his cows back, one way or the other. That he wasn't going to press the issue didn't have a whole lot to do with the fact that he had himself put his mark on many a maverick. As he had said, that was common practice. No, it was because the King of the Pecos had decided to be a friend rather than an enemy. He was willing to spend a couple hundred head of Jinglebob cows to stay on Slaughter's good side. Question was, why?

"I'm moving on to Arizona," said Slaughter. "My brother Billy is bringing up another herd soon. It's been a long hot push and I'm thinking I'd like to winter my cows along Seven River and make Arizona next spring."

"How many head, all told?"

"Fifteen hundred or so."

"Do me a favor. Keep it at fifteen hundred."

Slaughter had to smile. "You can have my word on that."

Chisum finished off his dose of ninety-proof nerve medicine. "I've heard about you, Mr. Slaughter. From down Frio way, isn't that right?"

Slaughter acknowledged that this was so.

"From what I've heard, your word is good. So I'll accept it, and you are welcome to winter your stock on my range."

"I'm obliged."

"You play poker, by any chance?"

"I've been known to."

"Good. Then you'll stay for supper, after which we'll break out the pasteboards and I'll see if maybe I can't win enough of your money to pay for the two hundred head you've made your own."

"I'll pay my hands a bonus with the money I take from you, Mr. Chisum."

It was Chisum's turn to laugh. "Call me John. And I'll call you Texas John. Just to keep things straight."

"That should work."

Over a supper of steak, baked potatoes, stewed carrots and a fresh loaf of bread, all produced by a plump and genial woman who turned out to be the wife of the Mexican man Slaughter had met earlier, Chisum drew his guest into speaking of his past. That was not a topic that Slaughter ordinarily addressed, but he felt at ease with Chisum. It seemed to him that they had a lot in common. After supper they smoked a cigar and had another drink, and then played some poker. Del Hooper dropped in, and when Chisum told the black cowboy to take care of Slaughter's horse, Slaughter didn't raise an objection. He hadn't slept under a roof since leaving the Devil River country, and the prospect was not unpleasant. Chisum expected him to stay the night, and he wasn't going to argue.

By the end of the evening Chisum had lost some money, and though he griped about what poor manners Slaughter had for emptying his pockets after emptying his range, he didn't really mind. The King of the Pecos knew how to read a man, and he had a strong hunch that Texas John was going to make his mark on this country, so it behooved him to learn everything he could about the man.

He learned, for instance, that Slaughter's father Ben had left Hinds County, Mississippi, to join in the Texas fight for independence against the dictatorship of Santa Anna. Ben got to Texas too late to fight, but having liked what he had seen of the land, he moved his family west in 1839. Sons Charles and William had been born in Mississippi, and in 1841 Minerva Slaughter gave birth to a third son, John, in Sabine Parish, Louisiana. When John was three months old, Ben moved his family on across the Sabine River into Texas. "I don't like to admit I was born in Louisiana and not Texas," Slaughter confessed to Chisum, "so if you don't mind, let's keep that between you and me."

Five years later, Ben Slaughter was on the move again. East Texas was filling up in a hurry, and besides, there was incessant quarreling over land titles. He found what he was looking for on the central Texas prairie. The Slaughters put down roots near the bustling frontier town of Lockhart. The rolling hills of Caldwell County had rich soil, good grass, plenty of creeks and springs. It was here that John Slaughter grew to manhood. Here Minerva provided her husband with five daughters in a row—Mary, Minnie, Martha, Delilah, and Elizabeth. John got a little book learning at the common school in Lockhart, but he much preferred the lessons of the great outdoors. The Texas frontier was constantly menaced by Comanche raiders, and in order to survive, John had to become an expert horseman, excellent shot, and tracker par excellence.

In 1847 Ben Slaughter joined the Texas Mounted Volunteers. Another fight with the Republic of Mexico was brewing, and Ben wasn't about to miss this one. Surviving that scrape, he did his share of Indian fighting, too, and by 1859 had moved westward once more, this time to Atascosa County to try his hand at raising cattle. They lived in a windowless shack made of elm poles and covered the earthen floor with antelope and steer hides. This far west, the Comanches were a real danger, and Ben and his boys slept with their boots on and their guns in their hands. They even enlisted in a company of state militia commanded by neighbor John Tom, and saw action against the Indians in a running fight at San Miguel Creek.

When the War Between the States broke out, all three of the Slaughter boys signed up to fight for the Confederacy. Charley and Billy fought the Yankees at the Battle of Sabine Pass with Ragsdale's Battalion of the Texas Cavalry. John fought Indians along the frontier and earned a reputation as a fearless soldier. After the war, the Slaughters pursued cattle ranching with a vengeance. There were plenty of mavericks—unbranded wild cattle—in the thick-

ets of mesquite, blackbrush, and brazil that dotted the land.
All a man had to do was pop them out of the brush, slap
a brand on them, and get them to market.

John's base of operations was Friotown, established in
1871, a town that soon boasted a courthouse, three general
stores, two hotels, and two saloons, all built of stone and
cypress logs culled from the woodlands along the nearby
Frio River. Chisum noted that Slaughter spoke fondly of
Friotown and the people there. People like Aunt Jennie
Waldren, who ran one of the hotels, and Old Bob, who
operated a saloon in the cellar of his mercantile. And there
was the Methodist circuit preacher, Andrew Jackson Potter,
who delivered fire-and-brimstone sermons with as much
vigor as he sang "When the Roll Is Called up Yonder," and
who knew how to use the Spencer carbine he carried with
him at all times. Then there was the saddlemaker, Doc
Neatherlin, who had crafted Slaughter's saddle. The
custom-made rig had a tree made of green elm, and a horn
that was extra big in the Mexican style, the whole built for
comfort and durability.

During those years John and his brothers expanded their
holdings and pushed more and more cattle up the Chisholm
Trail—and, later, the Western—to the Kansas railheads like
Abilene and Dodge City. Sometimes Mexican buyers came
to the Slaughters, and now and then the boys consented to
move a herd south of the border, too. But that was always
a risky business, for the border teemed with desperadoes.
Before long, John was the biggest cattleman in Atascosa
County, adjacent to Frio County, where his brothers had
their homes. But like his father Ben, John didn't cotton to
being hemmed in, and Texas was filling up now that the
Comanche threat had been diminished. So he cast his eyes
westward. John Chisum and Charles Goodnight had proven
that New Mexico was suitable cattle country, and it didn't
take much to convince Slaughter that he should sell out in
Texas and accept the challenge.

"Texas John," said Chisum, as he bade his guest a good

night, "I believe you are man enough to make do out here. You're welcome to winter your herds along the Seven. And if there is anything I can do to help out—this side of donating any more of my cattle—I'd be glad to do it."

Slaughter thanked him and turned in. He didn't bother telling Chisum that he had no intention of sitting idle all winter while his cattle grazed on the banks of the Seven River. He wanted to scout out Arizona. And he wanted to go back to Texas one more time, to get his wife and children and bring them west.

CHAPTER THREE

AN IRONCLAD
GUARANTEE

WHEN CORA VIOLA HOWELL FIRST LAID EYES ON JOHN Slaughter, she was helping her mother get their wagon loaded onto a Colorado River ferry.

At age nineteen, Viola knew how to handle a team of mules. Her brother James, only ten years old, wasn't much help, and her mother just did not possess the aggressiveness one needed when dealing with temperamental stock. Since her father had to get their seventy head of cattle across the river, it was up to Viola to handle the team. Standing up in the wagon box, a slender wisp of a barefoot girl in a faded blue gingham dress, her long chestnut-brown hair half covering her face, Viola commenced to laying the leather on the backside of the mules and shouting at the top of her lungs, using language that made her mother's ears burn.

To Viola's everlasting chagrin, John Slaughter picked that moment to make an appearance, riding out of the cottonwood trees that lined the river. He checked his horse and watched her convince the mules to pull the heavily laden wagon onto the ferry. Completely mortified, Viola sank down onto the bench beside her mother and tried not to appear as though she even knew Slaughter was present.

But she did know, and more than that, she could not resist looking at him, for some reason. He was so handsome, she thought, with his black hair and neatly cropped beard and his sun-darkened skin. And he seemed awfully interested in the wagon. Or was it—could it be—dared she hope it was she herself that had caught his eye? He cut such a dashing figure, sitting straight in that fancy Mexican saddle! He sure looked better than any man she had seen in the Montana gold camps. And there hadn't been any man at all anywhere near the Nevada farm her father had tried to make a go of after giving up on his dream of finding the mother lode— except for an occasional Indian or horse thief passing through.

When the ferry was halfway across the river, Viola looked back to see that the handsome stranger was helping her father push their cattle across. It was quickly apparent that the black-haired man was a top hand. The seventy head that had given Amazon "Cap" Howell so much grief for so many miles seemed like putty in the stranger's hands. He effortlessly bent them to his will, and the river crossing that had worried her father so was accomplished with all the ease of a stroll in the park. Cap Howell was both relieved and immensely grateful. He invited the stranger to share their camp that night and John Slaughter was quick to accept.

Howell was a naturally garrulous man. He was a big talker but not a big doer, so his dreams tended to exceed his limitations. By the time the evening was over, Slaughter knew the man's life story. Howell had earned his nickname, Cap, as a Mississippi riverboat pilot, but a string of mishaps and a wreck or two, while not entirely of his doing, earned him a reputation as a jinxed skipper. During the War Between the States, Howell's service to the Confederacy was principally spent as a prisoner of the Federals. Faced with no prospects at war's end, Howell joined many of his fellow Southerners yondering westward, hauling his meek and uncomplaining wife along with their young daughter in a rickety wagon and making for Montana. Viola grew up in one goldfield after another. Finding no hold, Cap then tried his hand at farming in Nevada. When that didn't pan out, either, the luckless Howell decided that maybe his true calling was stock raiser. Gathering up close to a hundred scrawny cattle, he pulled up stakes yet again and decided to go to Texas to reap the bounty of the burgeoning beef industry there. Indians had run off twenty head, and ten more had expired on the trail because a map Howell had foolishly purchased from a confidence man had turned out to be completely worthless. The con man had sworn convincingly that every watering place in the Southwest was clearly and accurately marked on the map. Such was not the case.

"You would have lost cattle," said Slaughter, "had you let them drink their fill before crossing the river."

Howell was embarrassed. He would have done just that had this man not come along and advised him to keep his thirsty beeves away from the river until it was time to move them across.

"Do you know Texas, sir?" asked Howell, quick to change the subject.

"I was born there," said Slaughter.

Excited, Howell leaned forward. He sat across the campfire from the cattleman, while Viola helped her mother wash the supper dishes in a basin on the wagon gate. James was sitting with his back to a wagon wheel, whittling on a stick with his clasp knife while an old yellow dog, the boy's pet and constant companion, slept beside him. Slaughter had never heard a dog snore so loudly.

"Then tell me, please, all you can about her," Howell implored. "I am told that Texas cattle are bringing better than twenty dollars a head at the Kansas stockyards. I hear anyone with some grit and determination can have a herd put together in no time. All he has to do is get them up the trail to the railhead and he is set for life."

Slaughter was lighting a cheroot with a burning splinter of wood plucked from the campfire. Drawing the smoke to life, he glanced in Viola's direction—and saw her look quickly away. He felt sorry for the girl. And for her mother and her brother, too.

"It isn't that easy," he told Howell. "You have to have plenty of cow savvy to make a go of it. And if you do manage to put a herd together, you'll be lucky to get it to trail's end."

"Lucky," echoed Howell, and sighed. "I'm not what you would call a lucky man, Mr. Slaughter."

"You've got to deal with tougher river crossings than the one we made today. If you don't get an early start, you'll find all the trails pretty well grazed out. And when you get to the Indian nations you have to handle the tribes that expect tribute, and if you don't pay them—and sometimes even if you do—they may try to run off some of your beeves. Then, if you make it to Kansas, the grangers there—and there are more and more of them every year— will make life as hard as possible for you. See, they figure their stock is put at risk on account of the spotted tick fever you sometimes find in a Texas herd. They've got a quarantine line now, drawn straight across Kansas, and no Texas cow is allowed east of it. That put some cowtowns out of business in a hurry. It's just a matter of time before the Texas cattle trade is done for."

Slaughter paused to read Howell's crestfallen face, realizing that he had just wrecked the man's dreams. He reminded himself that by so doing, perhaps he had saved that slender, brown-haired girl from some misery in the long run.

"That's why I'm moving my operation out of Texas," continued Slaughter. "That and I cotton to elbow room."

"What do you have your sights set on?" asked Howell. Slaughter was clearly a man who knew what he was doing, and if he was moving to greener pastures it occurred to

Howell that he might do well to know their location.

"Arizona. I've got a herd down on Seven River. Wintered it there and moving on soon."

"Seven River? Where might that be?"

"Down in the Pecos country. John Chisum's range."

"I've heard of Chisum. You two are friends?"

Slaughter smiled faintly. "Sometimes we manage to be."

"You're a long way from the Pecos."

Slaughter nodded, and a bleakness settled over his features. "I went to get my family in Texas. Wife and children. Got them to Tucson, but my wife had contracted smallpox back in Texas. She died."

"Oh, dear," murmured Viola's mother.

Viola stood there staring at Slaughter, her heart going out to him. He didn't show it, but she could sense how much the man was hurting. Her father, of course, had no idea what to say, and an uncomfortable silence descended on the camp, broken only by the crackling of the fire and the snoring of the old yellow dog. So Viola took it upon herself to break the stultifying impasse.

"And what of your children, Mr. Slaughter?"

He smiled, grateful for her intercession. "They are well. I hired a Mexican lady in Tucson to take care of them."

"Thank God," she said. "What are their names?"

"Addie and Willie. My daughter is six years old. My son is just over a year old. And, if you don't mind, miss, I'd just as soon you called me John."

"Then you must call me Viola in return," she said.

Her mother glanced at the expression on Viola's face and said, "Oh, dear," very softly before going back to her dishwashing.

Much to Viola's delight, John Slaughter stayed with them the next day, helping her father with the cattle. Slaughter's excuse was that he was going in their direction anyway, and besides, the Apaches had been making trouble of late. Cap Howell was thankful for his help and glad of his company, because he wanted to know all that there was to know about a stockman's prospects in Arizona Territory. Slaughter was happy to oblige. It was his aim, he said, to supply beef to the army outposts and the Indian agencies in Arizona, just as John Chisum was doing here. In addition, there was a lot of mining being done in Arizona these days, particularly in the Tucson area and a town south of there called Tombstone. Once word got out about all the gold and silver being found there, folks would be flocking to Arizona from all over. And the boomtowns would need beef, too. Just about the only thing a stock raiser had to worry about were the Apaches and the lawless element. Slaughter figured the army would take care of the former, sooner or later, though he was quick to admit that the Apache was a most formidable opponent, and the terrain was conducive to the hit-and-run tactics those Indians employed so effectively. You just never knew when or where an Apache might attack, and once the damage was done, they had an uncanny knack for seeming to disappear into thin air.

"They've been fighting for centuries," said Slaughter. "The Navajos, the Comanches, the Spanish, then the Mexicans, and now us. Fighting is the only life they know. The name 'Apache' comes from the Navajo—means 'enemy.' And the Apache is the worst enemy you could have."

"There are always risks," replied Howell, thinking that maybe Slaughter was trying to talk him out of Arizona now. "That's true in every worthwhile venture." Placing himself, not to mention his family, in harm's way was a concern for him, but one that had always been subsumed by the desire for fame and fortune. "I would sell ice in hell whether the devil liked it or not, if I thought there was profit to be made from it."

Slaughter nodded. Howell's bravado revealed the man's true character, and he worried about the other Howells and their futures. Particularly Viola's, for some reason. He couldn't figure out why, but she was on his mind all the time. That was all the more remarkable because he hadn't

thought anything could pierce the fog of bitter grief that
had cocooned him since his wife's passing some months
ago.

"I'll tell you what I think," he told Cap Howell. "I think
you should throw in with my herd and try Arizona on for
size."

Howell beamed. It was just what he had been thinking—
only he lacked the nerve to make the suggestion himself.
He was so blinded by his dreams of finding that elusive pot
of gold in Arizona that he failed to even consider the possibility that Slaughter might have some ulterior motive for
making the offer. And when his wife pointed it out to him,
Howell just shrugged it off.

"So what if he is interested in Viola?" he responded.
"She could do a lot worse, you know."

When Slaughter reached the Pecos country with the Howells, he learned that John Chisum had left word with his
brother Charley that he was wanted on a murder charge.

Slaughter rode straight to South Spring to get all the
details.

"Your problem has a name," Chisum told him. "General
Lew Wallace."

"The territorial governor. What's he got against me?"

"Too many bad men in this part of the country. So many
that it has come to the attention of those big augurs back
in Washington. They've got a U.S. Marshal assigned, but
he can't find men who are so tired of living that they're
willing to put on a deputy's tin star. The politicians have
put the pressure on the general, and Wallace got together
a list of all the killings committed in the territory in the
past couple of years. Warrants were issued for every man
who killed someone on that list. And that Gallagher feller,
his name was right there on top. Make you feel special at
all, Texas John?"

"That was a fair fight. Gallagher shot at me first."

"I believe you, I surely do. But you'll have to convince the governor, not me."

"What kind of man is he?"

"One who cares about his reputation, and holding on to his post. Fancies himself a novel writer. Working on some book about the Roman Empire."

"How come the Roman Empire?"

Chisum shrugged. "Damned if I know. Oh, and that's not all the bad news. Word about your outfit has gotten out."

"What about it?"

"The wildest bunch of cowpunchers this side of the Mississippi. That's what they say. You reckon that's a fair assessment, Texas John?"

"Maybe. I don't much care what a man has done in the past, long as he does what I tell him to do and works hard enough to earn his pay and then some. They haven't given you any trouble."

"That's true, they haven't. I'm not the one complaining. And your crew isn't the only one the general wants to clean out. A fellow named Shedd and another name of Pat Coghlan have herds down along the Seven River. Somehow General Wallace has gotten it into his head that all the thieving and killing that's been going on in these parts is being done by Texas cowboys like yours. So the plan is to clean out the cattle camps."

"My boys haven't killed anybody. Leastways not on this push."

"I understand that, Texas John, but the fact remains that in a matter of weeks, maybe even days, there will be soldiers down here with orders to check every herd, and if you can't prove with a bill of sale that you own the cattle you've got, then you'll be arrested."

Slaughter thought it over, a scowl digging furrows between his eyebrows. "Well," he said at last, "I have no such proof. Most of my cattle were wild ones chased out of the brush. Mavericks. I've got no damned bill of sale."

Chisum poured the sour mash, topping off his guest's glass and then his own. "Texas John," he said, "I've got some advice and I hope you'll see fit to take it, from one friend to another."

"And what might that be?"

"Dust out of here, soon."

Slaughter knocked back the whiskey, gasping as it burned his throat, and nodded. "I don't want it said I can't take good advice. I'm leaving for Arizona in the morning."

Chisum extended a hand. "If there is anything I can do for you, you know where to find me. I expect I'll be hearing about you out in Arizona."

Slaughter shook hands with the King of the Pecos and took his leave. He was only a couple of miles from South Spring when he saw a rider coming after him. Checking his horse, he waited until Del Hooper caught up.

"Mind if I ride along?" asked the grizzled black cowboy.

"How far?"

"Like I told Mr. Chisum, I've long had me a hankering to take a look-see at that Arizona country."

"Pecos John didn't send you, did he?"

"No, sir. I am my own man. I go where and when I please. I believe there was a war fought to give me that right." Hooper peered speculatively at Slaughter. "You ain't still fighting that war, I hope."

"No, I'm not. And when I did fight, it didn't have anything to do with slavery. Never owned a slave in my life."

Hooper grinned. "Then I reckon we might get along okay."

"We'll get along if you do what I tell you to do when I tell you to do it."

"I'll take orders, long as I get paid to take 'em."

"You're hired. Let's ride."

They neared the Seven River camp of Slaughter's outfit about an hour before sundown. When he saw the Stars and Stripes flying above the sagebrush, Slaughter pulled up short. There were bluecoat soldiers in his camp. He muttered a curse.

"Maybe you ought to head back to South Spring," suggested Hooper. "Lay low for a spell. Mr. Chisum, he done told me what all's going on. You don't want to wind up in jail, Mr. Slaughter, 'cause you may be a long time getting out once you're in."

"I'm not a criminal," said Slaughter grimly. "I'm not going to run and hide from anyone or anything—least of all the United States Army."

Riding into camp, Slaughter found his trail hands surrounded by a detachment of cavalrymen. Most of the horse soldiers were still in the saddle, ringing the camp; two had dismounted, and one of these was searching the chuck wagon. The other was an officer, who had been talking to a couple of Slaughter's cowboys. Clearly the latter weren't being very cooperative—the officer looked plenty annoyed when he turned on Slaughter.

"I'm looking for one John Horton Slaughter of Texas," said the cavalryman. "Would that be you?"

"It is. Who might you be?"

"Lieutenant Byron Dawson, First United States Cavalry. My orders are to confiscate your herd and place you under arrest, Mr. Slaughter."

Slaughter looked across the camp at the Howell wagon. Cap and his family were standing there watching events unfold, and at the word "arrest" Viola started forward, but Howell put an arm around her shoulder and detained her. The old yellow dog was barking up a storm at the horses of the nearest mounted soldiers, darting between their legs and generally making a nuisance of himself, unmindful of young James, who tried without success to call him back to the wagon.

The discontent among Slaughter's cowboys was both visible and audible. Fiercely loyal to their boss, they did not cotton to the idea of letting the soldiers carry him away in shackles.

"You're going back to Fort Stanton with me, Mr. Slaughter," said Dawson. "Those are my orders and I intend to carry them out—one way or another."

Slaughter sized the lieutenant up. He knew a Civil War veteran when he saw one. Dawson was no shavetail fresh out of West Point. He was a fighter, and not one to bluff.

Over near the Howell wagon one of the horse soldiers was cussing the yellow dog that was in the process of spooking his mount. The horse was snorting and sidestepping and the cavalryman had finally had enough. He drew his pistol to get off a shot at the dog, but the antics of his mount delayed him.

"All right," Slaughter told the lieutenant. "My men won't make trouble on account of my arrest, and I'll go quietly. But if your man over there shoots that dog, all hell is gonna break loose. That's an ironclad guarantee."

Dawson was incredulous—but one look at Slaughter's face and he could not doubt that the man was in deadly earnest.

"Put that pistol away, private!" snapped Dawson.

The horse soldier did as he was told. Slaughter turned to Hooper.

"Del, put a loop over that yellow dog."

Hooper unlimbered his lariat, urged his cowpony forward, and tossed a loop over the dog with one deft throw. It was obvious to him that the mutt belonged to the Howell boy, so he tied the other end of the rope to Cap's wagon, touched the brim of his hat to Viola and Mrs. Howell, and smiled at James as the boy dropped to his knees and put his arms around the dog's neck. Then he steered his horse back across the camp to rejoin Slaughter.

"As for the herd," Slaughter told Dawson, "it stays right here. That's a dry haul to Fort Stanton and we've got a long push to Arizona ahead of us. You move my cows now and I'll lose a good many head somewhere along the way on account of it."

"That's assuming you go to Arizona at all, Mr. Slaughter."

"Oh, I'm going. And nobody this side of God is going to stop me. You can leave some of your men here to keep an eye on things, if you want, and I give you my word that my men won't try anything. But I don't want my cattle worn out before they even get turned west."

"I hope for your sake you can prove that they *are* your cattle," said Dawson.

Slaughter nodded. He dismounted, walked over to some of his cowboys and had a few words with them. Then he turned back to Del Hooper.

"My brothers, Billy and Charley, are over in Tularosa. When they get back I'm relying on you to convince them to stay out of this. I mean all the way out. I don't want to see them in Fort Stanton. Make that clear to them."

"It's as good as done," said Hooper.

Slaughter nodded at Dawson. "I'm ready."

Dawson motioned to a sergeant, who dismounted and put shackles on Slaughter's wrists. While the iron was being clamped down, Slaughter glanced across the camp at Viola again. She was distraught, that was plain to see, and wanted to go to him, but her father prevented it.

"I'm sorry I have to do this, Mr. Slaughter," said Dawson. "You strike me as an honest man, not an outlaw. If that's any consolation."

"It isn't," said Slaughter grimly.

CHAPTER FOUR

A WEDDING IN TULAROSA

WHEN CAP HOWELL TOOK HIS DAUGHTER VIOLA TO FORT Stanton so that she could visit the incarcerated John Slaughter, the last thing he expected to happen was his daughter agreeing to become the Texas cattleman's wife.

Slaughter was being held under guard in a back room at the post sutler's store. The fort's commanding officer, a Captain Purington, was very cordial and helpful, writing out a pass which would allow Viola to see the prisoner. One of the guards ushered his daughter into the room, and Howell bided his time in the store, looking at all the goods and thinking about how he would soon be able to afford to buy his wife Rachel and his daughter all the nice things their hearts desired. All he had to do was strike it rich in Arizona.

When Viola emerged about an hour later, she was beaming. Cap could not recall having seen her quite this happy before. He had expected her to be upset; after all, it was obvious to nearly everyone that she had strong feelings for John Slaughter. There were a lot of soldiers hanging around hoping to get just one look at her as they left the post in their wagon, but Viola paid them no attention whatsoever. She had eyes for no one but Slaughter. And Slaughter was in serious trouble. So why, wondered Cap, was she so all-fired happy? When they had put the fort behind them and were joined by the two cowboys from Slaughter's outfit who had been waiting beyond the gate, Howell could stand the suspense no longer.

"You look awful content with all creation, girl," he said. "I take it Texas John is doing okay."

"Oh, yes," said Viola dreamily. "He'll be free in a few days and then we can all go to Arizona."

"Free?" asked one of the cowboys riding alongside the wagon. He and his partner had tagged along to make sure the Howells had no trouble with bandits or renegade Indians on the trail to Fort Stanton. "Mr. Slaughter told you that himself, miss?"

Viola smiled. "Yes! The governor has decided to drop the charges against him."

"What about all the beeves those so-called cattle inspectors took away?" asked the cowboy.

Viola shook her head. "John is not going to stay here and fight it out with the governor over who has title to those cattle."

"But they took near to half the herd, miss. It ain't like Mr. Slaughter to let somebody steal a single calf from him. He once tracked a man for three months, all the way down into Mexico, on account of that feller had made off with ten scrawny mossbacks."

"John knows when to cut his losses," said Viola.

"Hell, Luke," drawled the second cowboy, grinning at the first, "you know we'll likely pick up a hunnerd or two head of unbranded cows along the way."

"Well, that's true enough," allowed Luke. "A cow without a brand belongs to the man who finds it."

It was this kind of thinking, mused Howell, that had gotten John Slaughter in the bind that he was in now. But Howell made no comment on the subject. Texans had a different way of looking at things, and it usually wasn't wise to criticize their points of view.

"But what I can't figure out," he said as he laid leather across the rump of one of the mules in the team to get its attention, "is how come Texas John is off the hook with the governor."

"All the newspapers are giving Governor Wallace a good going-over," explained Viola. "The editors are claiming that he is using the army to throw honest men in jail and steal their cattle. And somebody got word from Texas about what kind of man Bill Gallagher was, and nobody can blame John for shooting him."

"So we're going to Arizona after all," said Howell, cheering up.

"Yes, Pa. John is ready to make a new start. And that new start includes me."

Cap Howell squinted at his daughter. Only then did he have a hunch why Viola was looking so radiant. "Just exactly what are you saying, girl?"

"He asked me to marry him as soon as he is free. And I said I would."

Howell glanced at the two Slaughter cowboys. They were clearly pleased with the news. And he didn't have any objections to it, either. But his wife—well, that was a horse of a different color. He could hear her now. Rachel Howell was a quiet woman as a rule, an obedient and uncomplaining wife who had not thought it her place to argue with her husband—even though he had dragged her all over the West, going from town to town as he pursued one ill-fated enterprise after another. She had never once objected. It had been very hard on her. He was well aware of that. But she firmly believed it was the obligation of a dutiful wife to support her man and his endeavors, to sacrifice and suffer if need be. Yet as soon as Rachel learned that her daughter and John Slaughter were in love with one another, her attitude changed dramatically and she became uncharacteristically vocal in her opposition to the match.

Howell breathed a deep, long-suffering sigh as he whipped up the mule team. He knew what his wife would say. She would argue that Texas John was much too old for her daughter. He already had two children, and Rachel certainly wasn't old enough to be a mother, nor was it right that she would have to take on the responsibility of raising another woman's offspring. And though she would probably not go so far as to say so, Cap was sure his wife had another reason for objecting to John Slaughter as a son-in-law. He was a violent man with questionable principles. He had killed men. He had in all likelihood stolen cattle that belonged to others. He was certainly not the kind of man she had envisioned as a husband for Viola.

Considering his options, Cap Howell decided his best course of action would be to lay low and not take sides. He figured Viola and Texas John would end up getting hitched. His wife, bless her heart, would put up a valiant fight, but she didn't have a prayer of prevailing against her daughter and the Texan she loved.

The wedding took place in the picturesque little town of Tularosa, located in a fertile basin hard by the stern heights of the Sacramento Mountains. Founded by the Spaniards, Tularosa's population was largely Mexican. It had an old adobe church, but John Slaughter and Viola Howell were married in a wagon yard.

Pushing his herd westward, Slaughter sent a rider ahead to locate the Tularosa justice of the peace. The ceremony took place out-of-doors, since most of Slaughter's outfit was in attendance. Many of the town's inhabitants were also present. The wagon yard was encircled by a high adobe wall and dozens of local children and young men sat on top of the wall to watch the wedding. Tularosa was a sleepy town, and even the marriage of two strangers passing through was a big event. In no time at all a fiesta was under way, following the brief ceremony. With the exception of a herd guard, the Slaughter cowboys were given leave to cut loose. Howell would have enjoyed participating, too, but Rachel insisted that he return with her to their wagon, where Howell had to sit and listen longingly to the distant music and laughter drifting through the evening air. To make matters worse, his distraught wife gave him the silent treatment.

Meanwhile, Slaughter and his new bride retreated to the home of Tularosa's mayor. A widower, the *alcalde* had graciously offered his small adobe home to the newlyweds and packed himself off to stay with his sister and her family. There, while the revelry continued unabated late into the night, man and wife consummated their marriage.

At daybreak they bade Tularosa goodbye. Bleary-eyed, pasty-faced cowboys pushed the herd westward for Arizona. Slaughter said so long to his brother Charley, who had decided to stay in New Mexico and try his luck at ranching and politics. Billy had gone back to Texas to do the same there.

Cap Howell was elated to be Arizona-bound. It didn't bother him that they were trailing cattle through some of the most lawless country in the United States. Slaughter's outfit was a tough bunch. Texas John had known he would require the services of men as handy with a shooting iron as they were with lariat and branding iron. Men like Tom Cochran, Wake Benge, and Tad Roland were, suspected Howell, wanted for something somewhere. But Slaughter didn't give a damn about that. Dealing with hardcases didn't faze the Texan. Howell was frankly glad to be in such company. He felt a lot safer knowing the Apache raiders and would-be rustling gangs would think twice before tangling with this outfit.

They had no trouble with two-legged varmints, but nature threw plenty of obstacles in their path. The Rio Grande crossing was a difficult and dangerous one due to severe flooding. And then they had to cross the Jornada del Muerto, a burning wasteland that Howell thought was aptly named. They had to cross ninety miles of alkali flats before finding their first water hole. But Slaughter and his men got the cattle through.

The suffering of man, horse, and longhorn seemed altogether worthwhile when they reached their destination a few weeks later. Slaughter had done some scouting in these parts the year before, losing himself in the vast solitude of untamed Arizona following the death of his first wife, and he had already picked out a likely spot to start his cattle empire. There were two valleys in Puma and Cochise Counties full of good graze, and Slaughter intended to make a large chunk of one of them his own.

Here in these valleys—the San Pedro and the Sulphur Springs—Spanish missionaries and soldiers had attempted to establish themselves more than one hundred years earlier. A *presidio* had been built, and a land grant called San Bernardino had been issued by the viceroy in Mexico City. In the 1820s, an enterprising lieutenant in the Mexican army tried to run cattle in the valleys, but he and his *vaqueros* were eventually ousted by rampaging Apaches. So there were plenty of wild cattle in the brush. Slaughter had learned all this on his previous visit, and Cap Howell realized then why Texas John had not raised a ruckus about losing nearly five hundred head to Governor Lew Wallace's cattle inspectors.

Less than ten years earlier the great Chiricahua war chief Cochise had roamed this country. Cochise had tried to live in peace with the encroaching whites, at least at first. Then his brother was captured by the bluecoats, accused of theft, and executed. From that fateful moment to his dying breath Cochise was an implacable foe of the white man. He joined his father-in-law, Mangas Colorado, in fighting a pitched battle against federal soldiers at nearby Apache Pass. The Chiricahuas were defeated, and a year later Mangas was caught and killed. For ten years Cochise had wrought vengeance with brilliant hit-and-run raids throughout southern Arizona. Nearly a hundred white people lost their lives as a result. Finally, hounded mercilessly by soldiers, his band greatly diminished in numbers by years on the fugitive trail, Cochise had laid down his weapons and agreed to lead his people onto the San Carlos reservation. At least the Chiricahuas were allowed to remain on the land their forefathers had called home. This was more than many tribes could say.

Slaughter figured he could wrangle a contract to supply the San Carlos Indian Agency with beef. But that wasn't the only convenient market. The nearby boomtown of Tombstone, located on the western side of the Dragoon Mountains, held promise in that regard.

A prospector by the name of Ed Schiefflin had ventured into the Dragoons against the advice of soldiers garrisoned at nearby Fort Huachuca. "All you'll find out there is your own tombstone," was the dire warning issued, but Schiefflin would not be deterred. He spent weeks in a line of black hills that rose to the east of the San Pedro Valley and finally located two rich veins of silver. Schiefflin took some samples to Glove for assaying. The assay looked promising, and Schiefflin found two partners, one of them his brother Al. Schiefflin called his claims Tombstone and Graveyard in honor of the warnings he had received from the Fort Huachuca soldiers. In no time at all the three men had made several more strikes, all in the heights that would come to be known as Loma de Plata, or Silver Hill.

Just as soon as Schiefflin recorded his claims in Tucson, word got out about the discovery, and before long prospectors were flocking to the black hills, while a town called Tombstone sprang up in the valley below. In a year's time the settlement had over two thousand inhabitants and five hundred structures—most of them tents and makeshift shacks that testified to the transient nature of the western boomtown and its denizens. Aside from the countless miners who came to try their luck, there were gamblers, merchants, prostitutes, saloon keepers, doctors, lawyers, and a variety of artisans, all looking to profit indirectly from the riches being extracted from the hills.

This was perilous country. The nearest established town was seventy-five miles away. Apache renegades often jumped the reservation to indulge in a bloody raid, while bandits were prone to venture across the nearby border with Mexico. And for a while the only law Tombstone knew was the law of the gun, the knife, and the fist. It quickly earned a well-deserved reputation as one of the roughest and most dangerous towns on the frontier.

By the time John Slaughter arrived in the area with his herd of longhorns, Tombstone had survived several tumultuous years and was taking on a more permanent look, with lumber and carpenters being imported from great distances, the former from the Chiricahua Mountains a day's ride to the east and the Huachuca Mountains nearly as far to the west. The sound of construction under way was a constant din. The mines were going strong and there was every indication that Tombstone had a bright future ahead of it. John Slaughter was counting on that.

Leaving his bride and crew and herd between the San Pedro River and the Chiricahua Mountains, Slaughter rode south for Tombstone, hoping to drum up some business. He had no idea the kind of trouble he was riding into.

CHAPTER FIVE

A VISIT TO TOMBSTONE

THE TOWN OF TOMBSTONE WAS LOCATED ON AN ELEVATED table of sagebrush desert called Goose Flats, with the Tombstone Hills to the south and west and the Dragoon Mountains eight miles to the east. Slaughter arrived from the south and found himself on Fifth Street, up which he traveled until he turned west of Allen, which was lined for several blocks with businesses. The street bustled with riders and wagons and people on foot. There were a good many saloons and several hotels along here—the Alhambra and the Oriental and the Crystal Palace looked like popular watering holes, while the Cosmopolitan Hotel down near Fourth Street appeared to be a more-than-adequate hostelry by frontier standards. Slaughter noticed that the bars and gambling dens were confined to the north side of the street, with the more respectable businesses lining the other side. Curiosity turned him up Fourth Street and then west again on Fremont. There he found what he was looking for—a newspaper office. In a small adobe-and-timber structure located diagonally across the street from a livery called the O.K. Corral was the Tombstone *Epitaph*. Slaughter left his horse at the corral and crossed back over Fremont to enter the office.

A slight, bald-headed man with a dark, luxurious mustache and bushy black eyebrows was setting type on the Washington press that dominated the back section of a long room. Seeing that he had a guest, the man came forward through a gate in a low railing that separated the room into halves. Wiping his hand on the ink-stained canvas apron he was wearing, he extended it to Slaughter.

"My name is John Clum. How can I be of service to you, sir?"

Slaughter shook the proffered hand. "I'm looking for the editor."

"Then you are in luck. I'm the editor. Printer and typesetter, too, and I am generally left to clean up the place." Clum flashed a broad, easy grin. "I don't believe I know you, sir. Are you just arrived?"

Slaughter nodded and introduced himself. "I've come from Texas with a herd of cattle. I aim to settle down around here, and I'm looking for buyers."

"You and your beeves are most welcome, Mr. Slaughter! Most welcome. The restaurants and hotels here will pay top dollar for beef. And you should try the San Carlos agency, as well. The Apaches there are starving much of the time." Clum frowned. "I was the Indian agent there for a while, until I got fed up with the negligent way in which the government treated their Apache wards. I moved on to Tucson, owned a newspaper there, dabbled a bit in the law. And now I am here. And there is no better place to be, Mr. Slaughter. Mark my words, Tombstone is destined for great things. The only obstacle is the lawless element. You may have to fight to hold on to your herd, sir—and anything else of value that belongs to you."

"I'll do what has to be done."

Clum cocked his head to one side. "Do you have any experience in law enforcement, by any chance, Mr. Slaughter?"

"I rode with the Texas Rangers for a spell."

Clum's eyes lit up. "You have the cut of a man who can

take care of himself, an honest and law-abiding man who doesn't spook easily. Perhaps you would be interested in—"

"Mr. Clum, I came here to raise stock, not wear a tin star."

"Of course. Well, it was just a thought."

"Don't you have any law around here?"

Clum smiled wryly. "A deputy sheriff and a city marshal."

"I take it you don't think too highly of either one of them."

Clum shed his apron. "Tell you what, Mr. Slaughter. I could use a drink and I'm betting you could, too. You look to have had a long and dusty ride. Why don't we wander on down to Allen Street and I'll tell you all you need to know about Tombstone?"

"That suits me. It's why I'm here. Figured a newspaperman would know everything that's going on in these parts."

As they walked together down the west side of Fourth Street, Slaughter found out that John Clum had a love affair going with the town of Tombstone. It was there in his eyes, and in his voice when he greeted people he knew. That seemed to be just about everyone on the street. Reaching Allen, they crossed Fourth and proceeded down the north side, past the Cosmopolitan Hotel to the Oriental Saloon. The glass-inset doors were open and they stepped inside. A tall, slender man sporting a pearl-studded shirt, silk cravat, and handlebar mustache was behind the long L-shaped bar.

"Afternoon, Frank," said Clum. "I'd like for you to meet Mr. John Slaughter of Texas. John, this is Frank Leslie. Otherwise known as Buckskin Frank."

Leslie nodded at Slaughter. "Name your poison, friend."

"A shot of anything that wasn't made in the back room an hour ago."

Leslie laughed and poured Slaughter a glass of Kentucky

bourbon. Then he drew John Clum a beer. The editor led Slaughter to a table in the corner. The saloon wasn't crowded at this time of day. Several men who looked like hardrock miners were "bucking the tiger" at a faro table in back. A steely-eyed man with russet-blond hair and mustache and wearing a black frock coat was running the table.

"Buckskin Frank used to be a bartender on the Barbary Coast in San Francisco," said Clum. "Then he scouted for the army with the likes of Tom Horn. He is a crack shot. When asked to prove it, he'll shoot the flies off the ceiling. And I don't believe he has missed a fly yet." Clum nodded at the man presiding over the faro game. "Frank is a good man to have on your side, and there's another. Wyatt Earp. He and his brothers Virgil and Morgan came to Tombstone about a year ago. Wyatt made a name for himself as a deputy in Dodge City."

"I've heard the name."

"He worked for Wells Fargo for a while, too, riding shotgun. Now he's doing pretty well for himself operating the gambling concession here at the Oriental. Well enough to invest in a couple of mining ventures. His brother Virgil used to be a constable over in Prescott. They are good men, as steady as they come. With men like them—and I dare say like you, John—we can make Tombstone a town where women and children are safe on the streets. Unfortunately, that is not the case today."

Clum gulped his warm beer and peered over the rim of the stein at Slaughter. "There are some men I could point out that you would do well to keep an eye on. I would say steer clear of them, but you don't strike me as a man who walks around trouble."

Slaughter smiled. "Since we're on a first-name basis here, you might want to call me Texas John. This has happened to me before, and it seems to work out for the better."

"Texas John it is, then."

"And you're wrong about one thing. I'll go far out of my way to steer clear of trouble. I've got a ranch to build.

And even more important than that, I've got a new wife and a couple of kids to look after."

"Congratulations. Your children are with you?"

"No, they're in Tucson right now. I'll be headed that way to register my brand and fetch them home. So if you know of any trouble brewing, I'd be obliged to know about it in advance."

"Where is your herd now?" asked Clum.

Slaughter told him.

"Sounds to me like that's the old San Bernardino land grant. The man who owns it lives in Benson, and my guess is he'd be willing to sell it for a fair price."

"I'll give him that."

"But if you ranch there you'll have trouble, sure enough. There's the McLaurys to the west of you, the Clantons to the north and Galeyville not far to the east. That's where you'll find a lot of the rustling gangs who work these parts."

Slaughter knocked back his bourbon shot and settled back in his chair to fire up a cheroot. "I'm listening," he said.

Clum started out telling him about the Clanton clan. Newman Clanton, better known as "Old Man," had moved from Missouri to California and then to Arizona, arriving in the Gila River area a dozen years ago and staking his claim to a water hole on the trail between Phoenix and Yuma. About four years later he moved east along to Gila to try his hand at ranching in the vicinity of Camp Thomas. He operated an inn at Camp Thomas for a while. But his principal activity was buying and selling rustled stock, with the help of three of his five sons. The oldest had decided not to participate in his father's underhanded schemes, while another had died some years ago. Brothers Ike and Phin and Billy were all tough hombres, said Clum. They frequented Tombstone and were not to be trusted.

As bad as the Clantons were, there was a group of rustlers and cutthroats known as the Cowboys who were the real scourge of the territory.

"No one knows for sure how many of them there are," said Clum. "Best guess would be thirty or forty. They range from the western part of New Mexico into these parts. The country in between is full of mountain ranges with dozens of hidden canyons, many of them with good grass and sweetwater springs. The Cowboys conduct raids deep into Mexico, hitting the haciendas down there and bringing the stolen cattle across the border to sell to the likes of Old Man Clanton, who turns around and sells them to the army or the railroad crews. The leaders of these hellions are believed to be Johnny Ringo and Curly Bill Brocius."

"Ringo," said Slaughter. "I heard about him back in Texas."

"Well, I hate to be the one to tell you this, my friend, but many of the rustlers hail from Texas. Ringo was born in Missouri, and when he was a youngster his folks pulled up stakes and headed for California. Along the way his father accidentally blew his own head off with a shotgun. Ringo grew up in California, but by the age of twenty he was in Texas riding with Scott Cooley in the Mason County range wars."

Slaughter nodded. "He was wanted for murder, as I recall. They caught him, but he broke out of a Lampasas jail cell. They caught him a second time, but by then the murder charge had been dropped. Seems the man he killed was a murderer himself. After that, Ringo left Texas. I didn't know he had come here."

"Unfortunately, he has. Spends a lot of time in Galeyville, over in the Chiricahua Mountains. If you ever meet him, you won't recognize him for what he is. He looks and behaves like the perfect gentleman. All the women love him. But he's a cold-blooded killer and maybe the best hand with a gun in the territory. I tell you all of this because Ringo is a good friend of Ike Clanton's. So if you have a run-in with the Clantons, which I wager is likely to happen sooner rather than later, you may have to watch out for Johnny Ringo."

Slaughter went back to the bar and had Buckskin Frank Leslie refill his glass with bourbon. Leaving hard money on the mahogany, he returned to the table and Clum.

"You need to understand," said the *Epitaph*'s editor, "that Ringo and Brocius and their boys are tolerated by many people around here, befriended by some. The small ranchers and farmers feel it is in their best interests to be hospitable when the Cowboys show up at their door. In return, the Cowboys leave them and theirs alone. I've had people tell me that Curly Bill and some of the others are really decent, honorable men who are loyal and generous to their friends. But big ranchers like you and Henry Hooker over in the Sulphur Springs Valley are fair game."

"I see," said Slaughter, judiciously sipping the bourbon. "You mentioned that the Clantons sell beef to the railroad."

"That's right. But I'm certain the Southern Pacific would rather do business with you, Texas John. The SP has a main line running through Lordsburg and Tucson, north of here. Now it's putting down a spur from Tucson to Benson, twenty miles to the northwest of us. Sooner or later Tombstone will be connected by an iron road to Tucson and the main line. The Arizona and Mexico Railroad and Telegraph Company was recently organized, and plans are afoot to build a line from Benson to Charleston and then here to Tombstone. What all this means is that there will be a lot of hungry railroad crews around here for some time to come."

"It sounds like I got here at just the right time. If I can get a contract with the army, the Indian agency, and the railroad—and sell beef to the miners here in Tombstone—I should do all right."

"No doubt you will prosper, if you can deal with the likes of the Clantons and the Cowboys."

"I will if I have to."

Clum settled back in his chair, carefully considering his next words.

"May I ask your political persuasion, Texas John?"

"I don't have one of those."

"Well, you being from Texas, I'm assuming you fought for the Confederate cause."

"That's true, I guess, though all along I thought I was fighting for Texas."

"One assumption leading naturally to another, I also assumed your sympathies would lie with the Democratic Party. I don't know too many Southerners who have anything nice to say about Republicans."

"Politics is not my game."

"There is one other thing you should be aware of. The small farmers and stock raisers around here are primarily from the South. They are predominantly diehard Democrats. They stand four-square against the railroads and the big ranchers. They stand in the way of progress. At the moment, the law here is in the hands of the Democrats. And since the Cowboys go hand in glove with the farmers and small ranchers, the law—such as it is—is sympathetic to people like Old Man Clanton and Johnny Ringo. I am sure now you're beginning to see how things shape up."

"What about you, John?"

"I am Republican. A New Englander, by the way. So, at the very least, if you run into trouble with the likes of the Clanton clan, you might think twice before turning to the law for assistance."

"Well, that's okay," said Slaughter. "I live by a few simple rules. If you try to steal one of my cows, you're dead. If you try to steal one of my horses, you're dead. And if you come after me or mine, you're dead. I don't see any good reason to bother the law about such things."

"Fair enough. I would like to announce your arrival in the *Epitaph*, Texas John, and make clear you have beeves to sell, if that suits you."

"Suits me right down to the ground." Slaughter knocked

back the rest of the bourbon, stood up and extended a hand. "Thanks for all the information, John. I appreciate it."

"If you ever reconsider wearing that star, let me know."

"I won't be interested."

Slaughter left the Oriental and paused for a moment on the boardwalk to give the hustle and bustle of Allen Street a long, careful perusal. From what John Clum had told him, he had a sense that Tombstone was a powder keg waiting for a spark. There was bound to be bloodshed. He could feel it coming. But it was none of his concern. All he wanted to do was raise and sell beef, love his new bride and his children, and build a future for himself. This sure seemed like a place as full of possibilities as it was full of perils.

He bent his step for Fourth Street, eager to be on his way back to the herd. There was much to do.

When Slaughter was gone, Clum got up from the table and moseyed over to the bar, where Buckskin Frank was leaning on the mahogany reading the day's edition of the *Epitaph*'s rival, *The Nugget.*

"You've got some nerve, Frank," said Clum, only half in jest, "reading that in my presence."

"Yes, I do," agreed Leslie cheerfully, "but then you knew that."

"One of these days everyone is going to have to choose sides. You know what I stand for. Law and order and progress. Statehood. But I'm still not quite sure about you, Frank. You—or Texas John Slaughter, either. What do you think of him?"

"I think he's an hombre. The kind you want to make sure you don't cross."

"I wonder how long it will take the Clantons and the Cowboys to find that out," mused Clum. He pushed his empty stein at Leslie. "Pour me another one, Frank."

CHAPTER SIX

TROUBLE ON THE BORDER

THE SAN PEDRO VALLEY WAS A HUNDRED MILES LONG AND ringed by mountain ranges. Since the great southern herd of buffalo did not come this far south, the grama grass was rich and in abundance. So was the water. Cottonwood trees marked the locations of numerous springs and creeks. Mexican old-timers in the area, however, insisted that the land was cursed. Yes, it looked like a verdant paradise in the midst of a burning desert, but in this case looks were deceiving. The Jesuits had built a mission there, and used the Indians to mine a king's ransom in silver from a mine at Taopa. But then the Jesuits were expelled by the Spanish crown. The silver was hidden, but the few who knew exactly where met untimely deaths under mysterious circumstances, with the result that the whereabouts of the hidden fortune remained a secret. The abandoned mission was destroyed by flood and fire.

Then there was the Mexican soldier-adventurer Ignacio Perez, who had built the first San Bernardino Ranch. It was said that two treasure hunters convinced Perez that a parchment map in their possession revealed the location of the Jesuit treasure. But the two treasure hunters simply vanished one day. Their camp was found, undisturbed, and their mules as well, but of the men there was no sign. No one ever knew what happened to them. Not long after, the Perez family was forced to abandon San Bernardino because of incessant Apache raids.

The ruins of the first ranch remained, an adobe wall enclosing three acres; a number of buildings had once stood there, but now only crumbling walls remained, mute testimony to the ruined dreams of those who had earlier sought to tame this land. John Slaughter, though, could not be deterred by ominous folklore. He rode to Benson and gave his promissory note to the man who owned the sixty-five-thousand-acre spread. Then he went to Tucson and registered his ownership of the property as well as his Z brand. Not far north of the ruins of the old hacienda was a splendid sweetwater spring. Hiring a number of Mexican locals to do the construction work, Slaughter had several modest adobe buildings erected nearby. One would be for him and his family; the others would house his crew. As for Slaughter's cowboys, their principal task was to keep close guard on the longhorns.

Slaughter himself was often away, traveling to acquire contracts with the Southern Pacific Railroad, the army at Fort Huachuca, and the San Carlos Indian Agency. He used these business trips to acquaint himself with his neighbors. One of these was Henry Clay Hooker, whose Sierra Bonita Ranch lay to the north of the San Bernardino. Hooker had settled there seven years earlier and prospered. His spread, like Slaughter's, afforded plenty of grass and ample water for livestock. He had sold off the longhorns of his initial herd and replaced them with purebred Herefords from the Midwest. When Slaughter showed up, Hooker gave him a warm welcome, and the two soon became fast friends. Hooker told Slaughter how he dealt with the constant Apache menace—he never begrudged the renegades a few beeves, but he did not tolerate any threats or violence against himself or his men. As a consequence, the Apaches had so far left the Sierra Bonita alone.

Hooker suggested that Slaughter look south of the border to find shorthorn cattle, which brought a higher profit than the lanky longhorns he had trailed from Texas. But Hooker warned his new neighbor that many perils awaited a *gringo*—especially a *gringo* with a lot of "adobe dollars," or silver coin—in Mexico. Apart from numerous bandit gangs prowling the malpais, one could not always trust the *hacienderos*. These proved to be prophetic words.

Slaughter realized that there was no time to waste in acquiring more cattle, so he made immediate plans to buy Mexican beeves. The word spread quickly, and a few weeks later two *vaqueros* from the *ranchero* of Francisco Robles appeared at San Bernardino and informed him that their *padrone* had several hundred head of cattle for sale.

"I'll buy all the young stuff your boss is willing to part with," Slaughter told them. "But only two-year-olds. I won't take older cattle."

"And you have money to pay for all these cattle, *señor*?"

"I'll pay cash on the barrelhead."

"It will be a pleasure doing business with you, Señor Slaughter."

"We'll see."

"Come at once. The cattle will be waiting for you."

Slaughter decided to take two men with him. One was John Battavia, but everyone knew him as Old Bat. An ex-slave born in Louisiana, Old Bat had wandered into Texas a free man at loose ends following the Civil War. Billy Slaughter had hired him as a camp cook. Old Bat had been with John Slaughter's second herd, the one Billy had pushed into the Pecos country, and he had decided to stay with Texas John rather than return to Texas with Billy. Old Bat had already proven himself to be a dependable and fiercely loyal employee. He was completely devoted to Slaughter, and Slaughter trusted him without reservation. As far as Slaughter was concerned, Old Bat's one and only shortcoming was his fife-playing. The graying black man considered himself a talented musician, but anyone who had the great misfortune of hearing the god-awful sounds he tortured out of that fife would testify to the contrary.

The second man Slaughter took with him was Del Hooper. The black cowboy was an expert tracker and a fearless fighter, quite apart from being a top hand. Since he could not spare his outfit to push Mexican cattle north, Slaughter counted on hiring some *vaqueros* in the border town of Aqua Prieta.

That proved to be easy enough to do. There were plenty of out-of-work Mexican cowhands on the border. Slaughter selected six men and told them they would be paid only after the cattle he was about to buy arrived safe and sound at San Bernardino. If for any reason the cattle didn't make it, the *vaqueros* wouldn't be paid. Slaughter didn't pay up front because he knew that to do so would nearly guarantee waking up to an empty camp the next morning. Most of these *vaqueros* were out of work for a good reason. But he figured that they were adequate for the job at hand. With these men—and Old Bat and Del Hooper, too—he pressed on to the Robles *hacienda*.

The *hacienda* was an adobe fortress that had withstood for many years the depredations of Apache raiders and Mexican marauders. Francisco Robles was of old stock—courteous, refined, educated. But beneath the cultured veneer was a true *brasadero*, hard as nails and tough-minded. One could not maintain a *ranchero* in the lawless Sonoran Desert without being as hard and uncompromising as the land itself.

Inside the exterior wall of the *casco* lived over a hundred people—the vaqueros and their families, the men who worked the irrigated fields of crops, and those who watched over the vast herds of Robles sheep. The *ranchero* was a self-sustained community. There was a small church and a school for the children. There were dozens of small adobes within the *casco*. All of the people here served Don Francisco. In many cases their forebears had served the father of the current *padrone* and his father before him. Robles was lord of all that he surveyed, and when he emerged from the *casa principal* to greet Slaughter and his men, who waited with a number of Robles *vaqueros* in the dusty, sun-hammered plaza of the *casco,* there was a steely arrogance in the way the wiry, gray-haired *haciendero* carried himself that Slaughter was quick to detect.

Don Francisco greeted his guest effusively. "Señor Slaughter, I have heard a great deal about you. You are always welcome in my home. You have had a long and arduous journey. Please, come into my humble home and let us get to know one another better. If we are going to be neighbors, then we should also be friends, do you not agree?"

"Better friends than enemies," said Slaughter, in fluent Spanish.

"Enemies? But there is no reason for us to be enemies, *señor.* Come, I have some excellent cognac which I think you will find very much to your liking."

"Tell you what, Mr. Robles. Let's take care of our business first and then have that drink."

Robles gazed at the Texan for a moment, taking the measure of the man, and then shrugged indifferently. "But of course, if that is what you wish."

"So where are the cattle you want to sell?"

Robles pointed. "In corrals beyond the wall. Come with me and I will show you."

Slaughter dismounted. Handing the reins to Del Hooper, shielded from view between his horse and the black cowboy's mount, he murmured under his breath, loud enough only for Hooper to hear and speaking now in English, "Keep your eyes open. And keep the men in their saddles, Del."

Hooper made no acknowledgment, but Slaughter knew he had heard and understood. He joined Robles and together they walked across the plaza to the southern wall of the *casco.* The *haciendero* led the way up a ladder to the top of the thick adobe wall. Slaughter followed. From the

top he could look down into a row of large holding pens
filled with shorthorn cattle. Robles made a grandiose ges-
ture.

"There you are, *señor*. Before you are three hundred of
the finest cattle to be found in all of Sonora." .

Slaughter took a moment to carefully survey the stock.
Robles watched him out of the corner of his eye, trying to
read the expression on the Texan's hard, stoic features.

"That may be true," said Slaughter at last. "But they
don't suit me."

"I do not understand, *señor*. We had an arrangement, I
thought."

"Yes, we did. I told your man I would only accept two-
year-olds. This is not young stuff. You've rounded up all
your culls. I'll make no money off these cattle—assuming
any of them made it back to San Bernardino."

Robles smiled. "You are wrong, *señor*. These are very
good cattle. And you will pay me for them, as promised."

Slaughter glanced back at the plaza. About a dozen of
Don Francisco's *vaqueros* had gathered around his mounted
men. They had slowly, casually converged from different
parts of the *casco*, and there was nothing particularly men-
acing about their attitudes, at least at first glance. Someone
less perceptive than Slaughter would not have thought
twice about them being there, assuming that curiosity about
the newcomers had drawn them out. But every last one of
them was armed—a knife and a pistol the usual arma-
ment—and Slaughter knew exactly why they were present.

Robles had drawn him into a trap. The *haciendero* had
told his men to surround Slaughter's crew without raising
an alarm. Like a pack of wolves they had moved in on their
prey, and at Don Francisco's signal their pistols would begin to speak.

Thing was, Old Bat and Del Hooper were no fools, and
neither were the Aqua Prieta *vaqueros*, for that matter.
They could all sense that something was not right. And all

Hooper and Old Bat were waiting for was a signal from their boss.

All Slaughter had to do was figure out a way to even up the odds.

Turning his attention back to Robles, Slaughter bristled at the smug contempt evident on Don Francisco's dark, aquiline face. The *haciendero* held out a hand, palm up.

"I will thank you to hand over my silver. Whether or not you take the cattle makes no difference to me. But either way you are going to pay me for them."

"Well," drawled Slaughter, "looks like you got me dead to rights."

"You are smarter than most *gringos*. Most would be too proud to see reason, as you have done, *señor*. They would fight, and then they would die."

"I don't aim to die just yet," said Slaughter.

He reached under his long gray duster—then lashed out with his left hand to grab the lapels of Don Francisco's short green *chaqueta*. Jerking Robles toward him, Slaughter's right hand emerged from under the duster. In it was a Colt Peacemaker. Slaughter jammed the barrel of the six-shooter under Don Francisco's chin and pressed hard, bending the *haciendero*'s head back.

"Now, you son of a bitch," breathed Slaughter, "let's see how proud you are. Tell your men not to fire. First shot and my trigger finger is guaranteed to twitch, and then I'll end up blowing your goddamn head off."

He watched the anger and the fear—and the fierce pride—swirling in Don Francisco's dark eyes, and for one stomach knotting instant he thought Robles would call him, and death be damned. Down in the plaza the *vaqueros* were drawing their pistols. On pivoting horses, Hooper and the rest of Slaughter's crew were doing the same. For an instant there was a standoff, with everyone hesitating to be the one who fired first. Men on both sides were shouting. Slaughter could sense that they were a tick's hair away from a bloodbath. And it all depended on Don Francisco Robles, and whether the *haciendero*'s desire to live outstripped his pride. Slaughter wasn't at all sure which way it would go. He had met men before whose pride had been strong enough to kill them.

But Robles chose to live. He barked a stern command to his men down in the plaza, and his *vaqueros* backed away from Slaughter's crew, holstering their pistols.

"Now climb down the ladder, nice and easy," Slaughter told the *haciendero*. "Wait for me at the bottom."

Robles did as he was told, and stood at the bottom of the ladder trembling with rage. Slaughter kept him covered all the way down, and then descended the ladder himself. Prodding Robles between the shoulder blades with the barrel of the Colt, he walked close behind the *haciendero* using the man for cover as he reached Del and Old Bat and the hired *vaqueros*. Then he climbed into the saddle.

"You're gonna lead us out, as far as the gate," he told Robles, his side gun still trained on the man. "If I see anything I don't like, I won't hesitate to shoot you in the back of the head. Then my men and I are going to ride out of here. You keep your cattle, I'll keep my silver. And no one will be worse off for what happens—unless you make the mistake of coming after me."

Robles made no reply, but stiffly turned and headed for the *casco*'s main gate. Slaughter put his horse into a walk, trailing along behind, and his men followed. The procession was watched by Don Francisco's *vaqueros,* some of whom drifted toward the gate as well, but kept their distance. Many of the other inhabitants of the *hacienda* also watched, and Slaughter figured it had to be truly galling for a man like Robles to be held under the gun like this. Not that Slaughter really cared if Don Francisco's feelings were hurt. It just made him wonder if Robles would be able to let bygones be bygones.

They reached the main gate without incident. Two sentries posted on the walls on either side of the gate carried rifles, and Slaughter told Robles to order them down from their vantage points. He did not fancy a bullet in the back as he passed through the gate. Nor did he want to take Robles out of the *casco*. The people here were intensely loyal to their *padrone*, and their lives depended on him. Slaughter doubted they would just stand by and let a *gringo* take their lord and master away.

As the sentries put down their rifles and descended from the wall, Robles glowered at Slaughter.

"You have made a very bad enemy today, *señor*," said Don Francisco icily. "One does not survive long in this land if he has a forgiving nature. I do not, I assure you. One day you will regret having met me."

"I already do," replied Slaughter coldly, and spurred his horse into a gallop, passing through the gate and leading his men down a narrow road between the cultivated fields. Del Hooper lingered until all the hired *vaqueros* were out of the *casco,* then brought up the rear, rifle in hand, twisting in the saddle to keep an eye on Robles and the sentries until he felt the range was too long to worry about getting shot in the back.

A few miles from the Robles *hacienda,* the grizzled black cowboy brought his mount alongside Slaughter's.

"We going home now, boss?"

"We're going back to Aqua Prieta. I came down here for cattle and I'm not giving up on finding someone who wants to sell some to me. Not yet."

Hooper nodded. "You reckon that Robles feller will let this business drop?"

Slaughter glanced at him with a crooked smile. "What do you think?"

Hooper pursed his lips. "Well, to tell you the truth, I reckon we'll have to do a spot of killing if we want to get out of Mexico alive."

"I expect you're right," said Slaughter.

CHAPTER SEVEN

SHOOTOUT AT AQUA PRIETA

AQUA PRIETA WAS A COLLECTION OF ADOBE HUTS BUILT around a plaza and hemmed in by dusty, brush-covered hills. The town had gotten its name from the bitter black water of nearby springs. Drinking water for the community was hauled from the White River a mile or so to the west. Directly across the plaza from an old church, a long adobe building sporting stone arches housed a cantina, a brothel, and an inn—if you could call a room lined with broken-down, vermin-infested bunks an inn. The building had once served as a customs house—back when the Republic of Mexico had been naive enough to believe it could actually control border commerce. Of course, that had proved to be an impossible task. This country was a smuggler's paradise. Men like Concho, also known as the Whiskey Fox, carried mescal by the wagonload into the United States, and a half-Mexican, half-Irish gunrunner named Pedro O'Rourke made sure the Apaches had plenty of rifles and ammunition when they decided to jump the reservation. O'Rourke had run circles around the U.S. Cavalry for years. There were many more like Concho and O'Rourke on the border.

When he reached the border town, Slaughter told the hired *vaqueros* what he had in mind and gave them an opportunity to back out or stay on his payroll. Most of them stayed on, and he paid them enough to give them the wherewithal to sample the liquor and the ladies that Aqua Prieta had to offer. Then he set about finding another source for cattle, informing the town's *alcalde* and several other leading citizens of what he was wanting. He had no idea how long it would take—perhaps days, maybe weeks. But however long it took, he needed cattle to fulfill his end of the bargain struck with the army, the Indian agency, and the Southern Pacific Railroad. He stood to sell every head he could get his hands on for at least twice what he paid for them, and he would make more off Mexican shorthorns than on the lanky longhorns that had not yet recuperated from the long, hard drive west from the Pecos country.

Once the word had been put out, all Slaughter could do was sit back and wait. He spent a lot of his time in the shade of the stone arches that ran the length of the old customs building, watching the lazy course of Aqua Prieta's life. He wrote a letter to Viola, explaining the delay but not going into the details of Don Francisco Robles's deception, for he did not want to worry her. At first he tried to prevail on Old Bat to deliver the letter, but Bat refused. He wanted to stay—insisted on it, in fact—for precisely the same reason Slaughter wanted him to go. They both knew it was dangerous to linger on the Bloody Border. There was plenty of riffraff drifting through Aqua Prieta, and some of them evinced a predatory interest in the news that a wealthy Anglo rancher with plenty of silver was in town. Slaughter carried the money in a special belt worn under his shirt, and he didn't complain that Del Hooper and Old Bat had become his constant companions. Like his own shadow, they were always there whenever he turned around. Slaughter himself took to carrying a sawed-off shotgun everywhere he went. It was the same weapon Billy Gallagher had brought from Texas when the late and unlamented gun-hawk had made the fatal error of seeking a showdown with his old nemesis.

On the morning of the sixth day of their sojourn in Aqua Prieta, Old Bat entered the room in the back corner of the old customs building which Slaughter had made into his accommodations. The room had previously been used for storage by the owner of the adjacent cantina, and there were barrels and crates piled up in the corners, a single door, one small window with timbered shutters, a hardpack floor, and a rickety table with one chair. Slaughter was still sleep-ing, lying on his blankets, his head on his saddle. When Old Bat came in, the door tipped over the chair Slaughter had balanced against it. Even before the chair hit the ground, Slaughter was sitting up with scattergun in hand, aimed at the intruder. When he recognized his visitor, Slaughter lowered the sawed-off shotgun and drew a long, calming breath, trying to smooth out his nerves.

"Are you tired of living, Bat? Is that the problem?"

"No, suh, I ain't. That's why I'm here to tell you that it's time for us to make tracks for the border."

"How come? You homesick?"

"I done told you why, boss. 'Cause I ain't tired of living. A sheepherder come into town a bit ago. Says a passel of bandits are holed up at his place across the river a few miles west of here. They showed up late yesterday. The sheep man, he managed to slip away and come to warn us. See, he heard them bandits talking. Appears they plan to ride in here and kill us and take your silver."

"How many are there?"

Old Bat smirked. "Too damned many. Come on, let's get while we still can."

Slaughter pulled on his boots. "How many did you say?"

The ex-slave heaved a sigh of resignation. "About twenty, or so says the sheep man. Reckon a sheep man knows how to count. And twenty is way too many matched up against three. You'll notice I said three, on account of you and I both know them Mexican cowboys you hired are gonna make themselves right scarce soon as they get a sniff of trouble. So that leaves you and me and Del."

His boots on, Slaughter stood to put on his hat and duster and strap on his gunbelt. He went to the table and broke open the sawed-off shotgun to check the loads in both barrels. Then he fished some shotgun shells out of his saddlebags and stuffed them in his pockets. Old Bat watched every move he made—and he didn't like the look on John Slaughter's face.

"I'll go saddle the horses," he said, and started to leave.

"You do that. Put them behind this building."

"You mean we ain't leaving right away?"

Slaughter grinned at him. "You had your chance when I asked you to deliver my letter to Viola."

Old Bat grimaced. "I was afraid you were gonna say something like that."

"I'm not going back without cattle. That's what I came down here for."

"I ain't never met nobody even half as hardheaded as you, boss, and I hope I never do."

"It's not likely you'll get to. Those bandits will see to that."

"I don't think that's funny," said Old Bat morosely.

"I wasn't joking. Now go get the horses saddled."

Old Bat took his leave and Slaughter left the room right behind him, circling the long adobe building in the gray half-light of those uncertain moments before dawn. He found Del Hooper under the stone arches, leaning against a wall, a Winchester rifle cradled in his arms. Slaughter plucked two cheroots out of a coat pocket and offered one to the black cowboy.

"Heard the good news yet?" asked Slaughter.

At that moment two of the *vaqueros* who had ridden with them to the Robles *hacienda* came boiling out of the cathouse door. One of them was hopping on one leg as he pulled on a boot. They saw Slaughter and Hooper, and the man who had just gotten his footwear on began to mumble something that Slaughter assumed could have been a half-baked apology—and then he and his companion made haste in the opposite direction.

"Yep, I sure have," drawled Hooper, watching the two *vaqueros* depart. "And as you can see, I ain't the only one."

Slaughter struck a match, lit Hooper's cheroot, then his own. He leaned against the wall and the two men watched the sun rise. Finally Slaughter spoke.

"What galls me," he remarked, "is people who try to take what don't belong to them."

Hooper just smiled and didn't say anything. He knew that in his own unique way, John Slaughter was trying to explain to him why it was that they weren't doing the sensible thing. That being to run for their lives.

A short while later Old Bat joined them, informing Slaughter that the horses were saddled and ready, waiting behind the old customs building. By then the day was only half an hour old, but Slaughter could tell that the word had spread through the border town. There were very few people in the plaza or on the streets. A priest crossed the open space, making for the church across the way; he glanced at the three men waiting under the stone arches and quickened his step, disappearing into the *iglesia*, firmly shutting the heavy wooden doors of mountain mahogany. A cat appeared, purring as it curled its long tail around their legs. Old Bat looked at it and said, "Just be glad you ain't black." The cat mewed softly at him and then went around the corner of the building, on the prowl for its breakfast.

An hour after sunrise Slaughter heard a sound very much like distant thunder. But the sound never stopped, only grew gradually louder. He knew what it was.

"Here they come," he said. "Del, there's a ladder in the cantina leading up to the roof."

Hooper nodded and was on his way. Slaughter turned to Old Bat. "Better get down to the corner of the building."

Old Bat nodded. He sported a couple of old Colt Navy

revolvers in his belt, and now he checked the loads with steady hands. Slaughter had never seen the ex-slave in a scrape, but his instincts told him that Old Bat would keep his nerve and perform well when the lead-slinging started.

The thunder grew louder, then reached a crescendo as twenty riders galloped into the plaza. They checked their horses at the signal of the man in front—a dark, squarely built man with a sweeping mustache and broad Indio features, bandoliers crisscrossing his barrel chest. His beady eyes swept the buildings fronting the plaza, then settled on Slaughter, who was still leaning against the adobe wall of the old customs house. The *bandolero* turned his horse in that direction, his men spreading out as they followed his lead. Checking his horse in front of the stone arches, the leader cocked his head to one side and leered at the Texan.

"I think maybe you are the man I have come to see," he said.

"I think so, too," replied Slaughter in fluent border Spanish.

"You are expecting me? That sheepherder . . ." The man clucked his tongue and shook his head. "You cannot trust an honest man."

Some of the other bandits laughed. Slaughter let his steely gaze slide off the leader to one of the other riders.

"I remember you," he said. "You ride for Robles."

The *vaquero* made no reply. Slaughter then turned his attention back to the leader.

"So are you here for yourself or for Don Francisco?"

"I am here for your silver, *gringo,* and what happens to it from now on will not be your problem. You will not have any problems after today."

Slaughter took the stub of his second cheroot of the morning from between his teeth and dropped it on the ground. Pushing away from the wall, he crushed the cheroot under a bootheel, then looked up bleakly at the bandit leader.

"What's your name?" he asked.

"What does it matter to you, *hombre*?"

"I like to know the names of the men I kill."

The grin on the bandit leader's swarthy face grew taut. "My name is Ortega!" he shouted—and pulled a pistol from his belt.

Crouching, Slaughter brought the sawed-off shotgun up and cut loose with both barrels. Ortega and his horse went down. Switching the empty scattergun to his left hand, Slaughter moved sideways, out of the eye-burning powder smoke, drawing his Colt Peacemaker as the guns of the bandits began to speak. He heard bullets smack into the adobe of the wall behind him. Ortega, badly wounded, was getting to his feet, stumbling over the neck of his dead horse. Snarling with rage, he advanced on Slaughter, firing his pistol. The bullet missed Slaughter by a hair, tugging on his duster. Slaughter stepped forward and fired into Ortega's face. This time the bandit leader did not get up.

Slaughter sought cover behind the base of one of the stone arches just as another *bandolero* spurred his horse through the arch. He got off one shot at the Texan, and his bullet put another hole in Slaughter's duster but left its wearer unscathed. Slaughter shot the man out of his saddle, then darted for the nearest door, one that led into the Aqua Prieta brothel, using the riderless horse for cover. One strong kick opened the door and he barged in. A woman screamed bloody murder. Bullets chased him inside. He slammed the door shut and pressed his back against a wall and took a deep breath as more hot lead splintered the old timbers of the door. Scanning the room, he saw an older woman huddled with two younger ones in a corner. The former wore a faded scarlet wrapper trimmed with fur. The other two—and Slaughter thought they looked entirely too young to be making a living in a bordello—wore hardly anything at all.

"You idiot!" raged the older woman. "You will get us all killed."

"Beg pardon, ma'am, but you're the idiot for still being here. Now take your girls out the back way." When the woman hesitated, he put some steel in his voice. "Git, I said!" he rasped, and as an afterthought added, "And don't even think about taking my horses."

As the three women left the room through a curtained doorway, Slaughter moved to the single shuttered window, pushed one shutter open with the long barrel of the Colt, and took a look outside. The bandits had scattered. Some were still mounted, trying to shoot from horseback on pivoting ponies. Others had dismounted. Slaughter drew a bead and coolly shot another *bandolero* out of the saddle. Then he saw Old Bat moving across the stone arch directly in front of him, Colt Navy revolvers blazing. Just then the ex-slave got hit high. The impact spun him around. Slaughter muttered a curse and went through the door. He shouted at Bat to get the man's attention, then flinched at a sharp lancing pain in his leg, whirling to gun down the bandit who was crouched against the wall of the old customs building and preparing to take a second shot at the Texan. He never got that chance. Slaughter's bullet splattered his brains and blood all over the peeling adobe. Slaughter helped Old Bat through the door into the bordello and shut it against the hot lead that sounded like hail beating against the walls. From overhead came the sharp report of Del Hooper's Winchester. Slaughter leaned against the wall and reloaded his Peacemaker, feeling hot blood leaking down the back of his right leg below the knee. Old Bat sat on the floor, breathing hard, the smoking Colts in his lap, his sleeve soaked with blood.

"How bad are you hit?" asked Slaughter.

"Not too bad. I'm still kicking, ain't I?"

Slaughter limped to the window and fired out into the melee of blood and powder smoke, emptying the Peacemaker again. Then he turned and ripped Old Bat's bloody sleeve off and saw that the *bandolero* bullet had cut a deep gouge in the ex-slave's arm. He slapped the hot barrel of the Colt Peacemaker against the wound. Old Bat jumped and let out a yelp of pain.

"Damn, boss. That hurts! Give me some warning next time."

"Should slow the bleeding some," said Slaughter, and, kneeling there beside Old Bat, he reloaded both the Peace-maker and the scattergun. Just as he finished, the door cracked back on its hinges and a bandit rushed in, pistol blazing. Slaughter and Old Bat fired simultaneously, all three Colts speaking at once, and the impact of the three bullets picked the Mexican up and hurled him back outside. Slaughter got up, kicked the dead man's legs out of the way, cut loose with both barrels of the scattergun at another bandit rushing toward him, and then shut the door.

"Hope he'll know to knock next time," said Old Bat. "Ol' Saint Peter won't abide nobody trying to barge through them Pearly Gates."

Slaughter returned to the window. The shooting had suddenly diminished. Del Hooper's Winchester barked again, then once more. The sound of horses at the gallop faded away. Slaughter rested his weight against the adobe wall and listened for a spell, trying to get his breathing back to normal.

"Looks like you took one in the leg, boss," said Old Bat.

Slaughter nodded. He could feel his boot filling up with blood. "That's okay," he said, his voice raspy, his throat very dry, a copper taste on his tongue. "I got another one." He noticed his hands were trembling slightly. That was how it always happened. He was rock steady in a scrape. Only when it was over did his nerves start to unravel a bit.

A few minutes later he limped outside to check the extent of the carnage. Hooper had come down off the roof and was checking the bodies. Slaughter helped him. They counted eleven dead men and one on his way. One of these was the Robles *vaquero*. The priest emerged from the church, came across the sun-hammered plaza, and knelt beside the dying man, performing last rites. The bandit expired before the priest could finish.

"Guess I'll never know if Don Francisco was a party to this," Slaughter told Hooper as the black cowboy joined him at the body of the *vaquero*.

"Does it really matter?" asked Hooper.

"It does to me. I aim to be in this country from now on, and if I have to deal with Robles, I'd just as soon do it now as later."

The priest came to stand before them, his features taut with anger. "You have killed many men today," he told Slaughter. "May God have mercy on your soul."

"Men?" asked Slaughter coldly. "I've killed some no-account varmints. I haven't killed any men today."

He turned his back on the shocked priest and went back into the brothel.

Hooper smiled faintly at the look on the priest's face.

"He's a hard man, that Texas John," he said by way of explanation, and then walked away to leave the man of God to stand alone among the *bandolero* corpses.

CHAPTER EIGHT

———◆———

APACHE RAIDERS

WHEN THE TWO COWBOYS CAME RIDING IN OFF THE RANGE, one of them bleeding from a gunshot wound in the arm and both of them with that dazed, hollow-eyed look of men who have stared death in the face, Tom Cochran had a gut feeling that his life had gotten a whole lot more complicated— even before the pair of San Bernardino riders uttered the dreaded word "Apache."

Cochran was a wiry, sandy-haired young man who had once ridden with William Bonney, and who had helped the legendary Kid avenge the death of the English rancher Henry Tunstall during the bloodshed that had come to be known as the Lincoln County War. For that reason it could be expected that Cochran was no stranger to trouble and knew how to handle himself in a tight spot. In fact, this attribute went a long way toward explaining why John Slaughter had agreed to put Cochran on his payroll back in New Mexico, even though the latter had a warrant out with his name on it. Such warrants did not count for much with Slaughter, since he had been the subject of similar attention by the authorities in New Mexico.

Cochran was grateful for the second chance Texas John had given him, and had done his utmost to demonstrate that

Slaughter's faith in him had not been misplaced. It was a tribute to Cochran's success in this respect that Slaughter had named him *segundo* when the cattleman took off for Mexico to buy cattle and took Del Hooper with him. As *segundo,* Cochran was responsible for making sure San Bernardino was in perfect working order when Slaughter came home. It was a big responsibility.

It was made even bigger by the fact that Cochran felt obliged to see to Viola Slaughter's welfare, too. To an extent, all of Slaughter's outfit felt protective toward the boss's wife. None of them wanted to answer to Slaughter if harm came to his young bride. Problem was, Viola insisted on getting involved in the Apache business.

According to the two cowboys, about eight or ten Chiricahua Apaches had jumped them and run off about six beeves. It was the first time the Indians had preyed on Z brand cattle, and Cochran cursed his sorry luck that it had happened on his watch, while Slaughter was away. Texas John had made his sentiments clear: In the event of Apache thievery, there had to be a quick and firm response.

"You know what has to be done," Viola told Cochran after the two cowboys had told their story.

"Yes, ma'am. I'll get right after them."

"No one has lost his life yet," she said. "John would want to keep it that way."

"I know that, ma'am." Cochran wanted to know how a person was supposed to tangle with renegade Apaches and get stolen steers back without shedding some blood, but he didn't pose the question to Viola. Fact remained that Slaughter didn't want the hostiles to get the notion that they could purloin San Bernardino stock with impunity. But at the same time he didn't want to start a blood feud with the Chiricahuas.

Cochran got together five men he knew had plenty of nerve and were better-than-average shots, and he was about to head out when he learned that Viola was planning to ride along. He saw the young Mexican Tiburio appear with a pair of horses—one for himself and the other for Viola. She emerged from the modest adobe ranch house wearing a brown serge riding suit, her chestnut-brown hair pulled back in a ponytail, a Winchester repeating rifle in one gloved hand, a quirt in the other.

"Jesus H. Christ," muttered Cochran under his breath, and walked across the dusty hardpack from where he and the other riders had gathered in front of one of the bunk-houses, reaching Viola just as she climbed into the saddle. "Beg pardon, ma'am, but just what in God's name do you think you're doing?"

"Why, I'm coming with you, Tom."

Cochran winced. "The hell you say."

Viola smiled tolerantly. "Whose cattle did those Apaches steal?"

"Mr. Slaughter's, of course."

"And who am I married to?"

"Well, to Mr. Slaughter, but—"

"Then those cattle also belong to me, don't they? I'm sure you've heard John say that everything that belongs to him is also mine."

"Well, yes, ma'am, but—"

"Tom, I was born on a Mississippi riverboat and grew up in a Montana gold camp. I know how to look out for myself."

Cochran grunted his skepticism. "Not against Apaches, you don't. Nobody does. You just can't ride with us, and that's all there is to this. It's too risky by far. You know what Mr. Slaughter would do to me if I let you come along? Why, he'd skin me alive. Those are true words and you know it, ma'am."

"I'm sorry to hear that. I would feel better if I were riding with you. But since you won't let me, I will just have to go on with Tiburio."

"Now, hold on just a minute . . ." began Cochran, but Viola did not wait around to let him complete his protest, and a heartbeat later Cochran was gaping at Viola and the young Mexican as they rode away from the ranch. "I'm done for," he muttered—then ran back to the other men gathered near the bunkhouse. "Luke, get everybody who can ride and come after us!" With that he leaped into his own saddle and led all but one of the men after Viola. He wondered if he could get away with hog-tying Viola and dragging her back to the ranch. That being, as he knew, the one and only way he was going to be able to keep her from going after those Apache cow thieves. He concluded that no matter what he did, John Slaughter was going to make him rue the day he had been born.

Late that afternoon they arrived at the spot where the Apaches had jumped the herd and stolen the beeves. It was obvious by the tracks that the hostiles were heading due north into the rugged Chiricahua Mountains. Cochran had heard that there were a handful of renegades up in those mountains who had refused to abide by treaty obligations to reside on the San Carlos reservation. No one could say for certain how many Indians were up there, but none doubted that they were desperate and dangerous individuals. They had been known to slip down out of their hiding places and waylay the occasional traveler or make off with some livestock. Even after Luke joined up, bringing an additional ten men, Cochran could not feel too sanguine about his chances of protecting Viola if they managed to catch up with the Apaches.

He didn't like it that he had to bring so many riders with him, either. It would be hard enough to slip up on the hostiles with just a few men. When they reached the mountains, he opted for a daring scheme. He and two other men would ride on ahead. The rest of the party would follow along a few miles behind. The hope was that the Apaches would turn on Cochran and his companions. Then the trick would be to hold them off long enough for the rest of the San Bernardino riders to come up. With any luck, the Indians would see the advance party and assume they had come alone in search of the stolen cattle. If the Apaches

could be caught by surprise, they might, in their haste to
flee, leave a trail Cochran and his bunch could follow to
the renegade hideout.

It was a dangerous gambit, but Cochran had no shortage
of volunteers when he asked the others who wanted to ride
with him. He picked Tad Roland and Wake Benge. He
knew both men were crack shots and tough hombres. Both
Tad and Wake had spent some time on the owlhoot trail.
"So I know you're long on gumption and short on sense,"
he told them, grinning.

"Yeah," said Roland. "That's right. We're just like you,
Tom."

Cochran didn't hold out much hope that his scheme
would work. He thought it more likely that their Apache
prey would see right through the ruse. Like as not they
would simply vanish deeper into the mountains. As much
as he felt it was his duty to account for the stolen beeves,
Cochran didn't think he would mind all that much if he
had to go home empty-handed. At least that way Viola
Slaughter would stay alive.

But his plan did work.

On their second day in the mountains, as Cochran and
his two companions passed through a narrowing canyon, a
shot rang out from high up on the slope to their left, and
Wake's horse went down screaming. A flurry of gunfire
followed as Apaches on both sides of the canyon started
shooting. Cochran jumped clear as his horse was killed. The
Indians wanted to make sure that the *pinda lickoyi*—the
white men—did not get away. Quick-thinking Tad Roland
slid out of his saddle, turned his horse around, and creased
it, firing a shot with his side gun so that the bullet lay a
bloody groove across the pony's flank. The horse lit out at
a hard gallop, back the way they had come. Cochran
doubted it would stop running until it reached the rest of
the San Bernardino riders. And when they saw it they
would come running. Only question was whether he and
Tad and Wake would be alive when the others got here.

The three men scrambled for cover in the rocks, returning the Apache fire with repeaters and handguns. The problem was finding a good target to shoot at. Just about the only thing Cochran saw was a puff of smoke marking the location of an Apache, and shooting at smoke was a waste of ammunition because after he fired an Apache usually moved. Cochran figured there had to be at least ten of the hostiles. They would try to work their way down the rocky slopes, edging ever closer, and then in a sudden charge would fall on the Slaughter cowboys and finish them off—assuming any of the white men were still alive. So Cochran and his partners had to keep shooting to try to slow down the Apache descent. They had brought plenty of ammunition. It wasn't that they would run out of that. Running out of time was the real danger.

Crouched among the rocks in the breathless heat of the canyon bottom, the trio of San Bernardino riders grimly held on, trying to keep the Apaches at bay long enough for help to arrive. Wake Benge took a bullet in the leg, and Tad Roland killed an Indian at point-blank range when the Apache broke cover and lunged at him. Then another one jumped Cochran just as the cowboy was reloading, and Cochran had to grapple with the hostile, rolling around in the dust until he got the upper hand and used the Winchester like a club, breaking the repeating rifle's stock against the broncho's skull, and dodging the Indian's knife at the same time.

Then the rest of the San Bernardino riders showed up, catching all of the Apaches down near the canyon bottom, charging up into the rocks after them, guns blazing as the Indians tried to flee. Spotting Viola, Cochran saw the young Mexican Tiburio get her off her horse and wisely lead her to shelter among some boulders. He ran to them.

"Well," he said, "so much for no killing."

"I'm just glad that you are unharmed," said Viola.

Cochran grinned. "Thanks, ma'am. I'm as happy as can be about that, too."

In moments the shooting had died down, and Tad Roland showed up to tell them that several Apaches had been killed and the rest scattered. Luke Smith had been hit high in the shoulder. Cochran was eager to be after the renegades. He ordered Tad and one other man to stay behind with the wounded. And he tried to persuade Viola to do the same. That was an exercise in futility, as he had known deep down that it would be. In no time they were hot on the trail of the Apache bronchos.

By midafternoon they had located the Apache hideout, a collection of half a dozen *jacales* among some dusty scrub junipers on a high table of land where a spring trickled out of a limestone ledge. At Cochran's orders the San Bernardino men encircled the camp and closed in. Some of the bronchos acted like they were going to put up a fight, but their leader, Yanozha, put a stop to that. There were women and children in the encampment, and Yanozha did not want them to come to harm. In return, Cochran and his boys held their fire. Yanozha approached Cochran and Viola and gravely laid his rifle on the ground. Then he drew a revolver from the belt around his waist and laid that down, too. Stepping away from the weapons, he bleakly surveyed the ring of grim cowboys and then curtly ordered the other bronchos to lay down their arms.

"Well, ma'am," said Cochran, pointing to a brush corral where five Z brand cattle were held, "there's your property, less one."

Viola nodded. But her attention was riveted to the women and children of the renegade camp. "These people are in a bad way, Tom."

"Yes, ma'am, looks like it. Living a life on the run isn't easy." He smiled wryly. "You can take my word for that."

When she had established that Yanozha spoke fluent border Spanish, Viola asked Tiburio to translate for her, and turned to the Apache leader.

"My husband is the *padrone* of San Bernardino," she

said. "His cattle are marked with the Z brand. Those cows that you have stolen belong to him."

"They are on Apache land," said Yanozha. "We take what we want when it is on our land. That is our right."

"Not anymore," said Viola, and Cochran was surprised by the stern authority in her voice and demeanor. It was hard to believe, watching her now, that she was just a nineteen-year-old slip of a girl. "The San Bernardino belongs to my husband. If the Apaches want to cross his land, that's fine. If the Apache needs some beef so that their women and children do not go hungry, that's okay, too. But when the Apache tries to kill one of our people, then there will be trouble."

Yanozha stared at her for a moment, inscrutable. "You did not come here because of the cattle?" he asked.

"We came here because one of our men was shot. My husband will not tolerate that."

"Where is your man? How is he called?"

"His name is John Slaughter. He does not want to make war on the Apaches. But he will if the Apaches make war on him."

Yanozha surveyed the San Bernardino cowboys arrayed around the encampment.

"My people do not wish to live on the reservation," he said pensively. "There the Chiricahua Apache is treated like a dog. We would rather die here, free in our mountains, than go to San Carlos."

"We will not tell the soldiers where to find you," promised Viola. "But in return you must not shoot any more of our people."

Yanozha nodded. Viola thought she could see the distrust in the Apache leader's eyes. But who could blame him for being leery of a white person's promise? The Spanish and then the Mexicans had made a sport of cheating and tricking and hunting down Apaches. They had lured entire bands into massacres. They had offered bounties on Apache

scalps. The United States government had not behaved
much better. From what Viola had heard, the Apaches on
the reservation had been treated with contempt. The government had vowed to keep them fed, but when the
Apaches got any food at all it was often spoiled, and it was
never in sufficient quantity to fill all the hungry bellies.

Little wonder that resentful young bucks occasionally
"jumped" the reservation, embarking on a brief raid, stealing a few head of livestock, striking at remote ranches.
These raids were opportunities to vent frustrations, to al-
leviate boredom. And the whole countryside would be ter-
rorized by the prospect of a handful of Chiricahua
troublemakers on the prowl. The army would send out patrols, and the raiders would eventually be cornered, and
more often than not they would capitulate without putting
up much of a struggle, and allow themselves to be escorted
back to the agency. The ringleaders would spend some time
in chains. The others would be made to swear that they
would remain on the reservation and behave themselves.
The Apache was as honorable as the next man, but a promise given to the *pinda lickoyi* was not one that had to be
kept. After all, the white man did not keep his promises to
the Apache.

Cochran knew that generally speaking you couldn't trust
a man like Yanozha to do what he promised to do. But in
this case, with the bargain Viola had struck, he thought
maybe the Apache leader might see that it was in his best
interests to keep his word. Otherwise the whereabouts of
his band would be betrayed to the yellow-leg soldiers. And,
worse than that, he would have to tangle with John Slaughter's San Bernardino outfit. Neither was a very pleasant
prospect for Yanozha.

So the deal was struck, and Viola led the cowboys out
of the mountains, leaving the stolen cattle behind. Cochran
was immensely impressed by the way Viola had conducted
herself. She had courage and she was smart and, well, she

was just pretty damned amazing. Texas John was one lucky hombre.

As soon as they got back to the ranch, Cochran had another occasion to find out just how remarkable a woman Viola was, for word from the border had arrived in their absence: John Slaughter and his companions had been killed by bandits.

A mescal peddler had been apprehended by an army patrol, caught red-handed in the process of selling his potent merchandise to Yaqui Indians. In a vain attempt to strike a bargain with the bluecoats, the peddler claimed he knew the whereabouts of the *bandoleros* who had murdered the Anglo cattleman John Slaughter. The army dutifully passed the word on to San Bernardino. The bearer of bad tidings was a shavetail lieutenant who regretfully informed Viola that the army had it on good authority that her husband was deceased. Cochran was present when Viola heard the news, and he expected to see tears. But Viola held herself together somehow, graciously inviting the young officer to stay over at the ranch and start back for his post in the morning after a good meal and a night's sleep. Ill at ease, the lieutenant respectfully declined the offer and took his leave, relieved that the unpleasant task was done.

The next morning at daybreak Viola Slaughter started for the border, driving a wagon, intent on locating her husband's remains and bringing them home. Cochran and several other cowboys rode with her. It was a grim and silent procession. Cochran could scarcely believe that Texas John was dead. He'd just assumed that Slaughter was too tough to die. And while he wanted to express his condolences to Viola, he could not corral the right words to get the job done. What could a person say at a time like this? His heart went out to her.

Late in the afternoon of the second day they spotted a cloud of dust on the horizon that could only be one thing— a herd of cattle on the move. It turned out to be Slaughter and Old Bat and Del Hooper and a half dozen *vaqueros* pushing over two hundred head of prime beef.

Only then, as she flew into her husband's arms, did Viola break down and cry. Cochran was glad to see Texas John alive and well—more or less well, since the man had taken a bullet in the leg—and he was glad that Viola had been spared a widow's long anguish. But at the same time he felt a twinge of jealousy. That surprised him, and he gave it a lot of thought, and after a sleepless night of unaccustomed introspection he came to the only possible conclusion. He had fallen in love with John Slaughter's wife! He knew the smart thing to do would be to turn his back on the whole business and ride away—ride as far away as his horse could carry him. If he didn't, then sooner or later there would be hell to pay. But he just couldn't do it. He couldn't bring himself to quit on John Slaughter. The Texan had given him a second chance in life when he had most needed it. Now Texas John was building a solid future at San Bernardino, and he needed all the help he could get. Then, too, Cochran didn't ever want to be far away from Viola. He sensed that it didn't really matter how far he ran, he would not be able to escape his feelings, or the misery that was his fate since he would never be able to have her. So all he could do was stick it out and try to keep his true feelings a secret.

CHAPTER NINE

GUNPLAY IN TOMBSTONE

JOHN SLAUGHTER FOUND OUT ABOUT THE GUNFIGHT IN TOMB-stone's O.K. Corral from John Clum. The editor of the Tombstone *Epitaph* had made a concerted effort to establish a friendship with the Texas cattleman. A year had passed since Slaughter had taken over the San Bernardino range and made it his own. In that time Texas John had fared well, profiting from contracts with the army, the Southern Pacific, and the San Carlos Indian agency. He and Henry Hooker were the most prosperous ranchers in the area. It was clear that Slaughter was here to stay. From the first, Clum had had a hunch that the Texan would succeed. And of course the newspaperman had judged Texas John to be a man worth having on the side of law and order and progress. So a few days after the shootout occurred, he rode out to San Bernardino to carry the news.

"Texas John," said Clum, "there has been some killing in Tombstone. It is the beginning of a war that I've known for a long time was coming."

Slaughter poured them both whiskeys and took one glass to his guest before sitting on a horsehair sofa beside his young wife, Viola.

"What kind of war are you talking about, John?" asked the cattleman.

"Between the law-abiding citizens of Cochise County and the Cowboys." Clum leaned forward. "I've heard you've had a run-in or two with the Clantons and the McLaurys. Is that true?"

Slaughter shrugged. "Nothing much to speak of, really. I found a few of my cattle in a stock pen down near Charleston. The Clantons were running irons, changing my Z brand to a Box Slash mark. They denied it, of course. But I took my cows back and warned them about making off with my stock. Far as I can tell, they haven't since."

"And one day," said Viola, "when John and I were riding into Tombstone, we happened to meet Ike Clanton on the road. I thought for a moment that he intended to draw down on my husband, but John lifted the shotgun he had resting in his lap, and Mr. Clanton behaved himself and rode on by."

Clum nodded. "You can't trust a Clanton any more than you can a rattlesnake. Well, now young Billy Clanton is dead. So are Frank and Tom McLaury."

"Who did for 'em?" asked Slaughter.

"The Earp brothers. With some assistance from Doc Holliday."

"Doc Holliday," murmured Slaughter. "Well, that doesn't surprise me one bit."

He had heard a great deal about Georgia-born John Henry Holliday—and not much of it was good. Holliday had graduated from the Pennsylvania College of Dental Surgery in 1872 and headed west for his health, as he had been stricken with tuberculosis at an early age. But Holliday preferred gambling to pulling teeth, and made a fair living as a cardsharp. He had been in Dallas, Texas, in 1875, when a violent altercation with a local saloonkeeper prompted him to hastily pull up stakes. The following year found him in Denver. The year after that he met Wyatt Earp and a prostitute called Big Nose Kate Elder in the raw frontier community of Fort Griffin, Texas—two people with whom his name would be associated for the rest of his life. In 1879 he shot and killed a man in Las Vegas, New Mexico—by all accounts in self-defense. But his reputation as a dangerous character was exceeded only by that enjoyed by Johnny Ringo. The thing with Holliday was that he was dying, and he knew it. He had no fear, since as far as he was concerned it would be better to die by the gun than by coughing his lungs out bit by agonizing bit. To make matters worse, Holliday was an alcoholic. He had a quick temper. And he was also a crack shot. All that mixed together made for a deadly combination. Considering himself a true friend of Wyatt Earp, Holliday had come to Tombstone with his traveling companion, Big Nose Kate. Word was that his relationship with the fiery Kate was a tempestuous one.

"It was Doc that got the ball rolling," said Clum. "Not to say he didn't have just cause. He was over in Tucson doing a little gambling when he heard that Ike Clanton was making threats against the Earp brothers. Now, you have to understand that Virgil Earp has quite a bit of law enforcement experience, and he is serving as Tombstone's city marshal these days."

"I'm told he owes his present position to you, John, now that you're the mayor."

"I don't deny I campaigned for him. What else could I do? Sheriff Behan is entirely too cozy with the Clantons and the McLaurys and the Cowboys. In past months Virgil, with the help of his brothers Wyatt and Morgan, has been making life difficult for the rustling gangs. He's made a great many arrests. The Clantons had come to the conclusion that the Earps had to go, one way or the other. So when Doc Holliday heard that Ike was talking about killing an Earp, Doc made haste back to Tombstone. He found Ike at the lunch counter in the Occidental and cursed him, calling him out. But Ike wasn't heeled. Wyatt and Morgan Earp showed up. Seeing that he was in a bad fix, Ike beat a hasty retreat. Doc went out after him, but the Earps detained him, and Virgil threatened to arrest him if he didn't cool off. The law comes first for Virgil Earp, and he won't hesitate to arrest a friend to keep the peace. I must confess he even arrested me once." Clum chuckled. "The charge was reckless riding on a city street."

Clum went on to explain that after the confrontation at the Occidental, Wyatt went to the Crystal Palace to run the faro game there for a couple of hours. When he finally left the Palace he found Ike Clanton waiting for him outside. This time Ike was armed. But he didn't make a play. "I wasn't fixed when Doc came at me," he told Wyatt, "but I will be in the morning. It's time we settle things between us." Wyatt advised Ike to cool off, and said he didn't want a fight because there was no profit in it. Then he walked away, but Ike followed him all the way down the street to the Oriental, and stopped Wyatt there to say, "I will be ready for you in the morning." Then he walked on.

"Ike Clanton must have been drunk," decided Slaughter. "The Earps and Doc Holliday are gunmen. Ike isn't. He'd have to be drunk, or a bigger fool than I took him for, to challenge four gunfighters."

According to Clum, Wyatt collected his faro winnings at the Oriental and went home. Doc Holliday retired to his hotel room and the gentle attentions of Big Nose Kate. But Ike Clanton returned to the Occidental and bought into an all-night poker game with Tom McLaury, Sheriff Johnny Behan, and Virgil Earp. At daybreak Virgil got up to leave. Ike followed him outside and asked him to carry a message to Doc. "Tell that son of a bitch that he's got to fight me now." Virgil warned him against making such talk and went home to bed.

Ike prowled the streets of Tombstone as dawn came. He was spoiling for a fight, and Clum assured Slaughter that there were a number of witnesses ready to testify to that fact. Clanton told a number of people that Doc Holliday and the Earp boys had insulted him the night before and that as soon as they showed themselves on the street, the fight would take place. After hitting a couple of saloons, Ike fetched his rifle and went to the boardinghouse on Fremont Street where Doc and Kate were staying. Kate was up early, and saw Clanton roaming around outside. She hurried upstairs to awaken Doc and tell him about Ike, but Doc just rolled over and went back to sleep.

Shortly after noon Virgil and Wyatt Earp were on the streets again—and soon learned that Ike Clanton was on the prowl, hunting them with a Winchester rifle and a six-shooter. The two located Morgan and agreed that Ike needed to be placed under arrest. Both Wyatt and Morgan were on the city payroll as deputy marshals. Wyatt branched off to search Allen Street. Virgil and Morgan took Fremont. They found Ike coming out of the Capitol Saloon.

"I was standing on the corner of Fourth and Fremont," said Clum, "and saw the whole thing. Virgil and Morgan walked right by me, pistols drawn and held down by their sides. Ike was looking the other way, and he didn't see them coming. At the last instant he must have heard them, because he turned quickly. Not quickly enough, however. Virgil pistol-whipped him and jerked the Winchester out of his hands. Ike fell, and they hauled him to his feet and dragged him off to the police court at the Mining Exchange Building."

Clum followed them into the police court and arrived in time to see Virgil leave in search of the judge. Wyatt arrived a moment later and cursed Ike Clanton as a "damned dirty cow thief."

"Clanton said that if he had a gun he would fight both Wyatt and Morgan on the spot," continued Clum. "Morgan offered him a pistol, but there was a deputy sheriff present, and he put a stop to that. Judge Wallace arrived and fined Clanton twenty dollars for carrying a concealed weapon. Ike paid up and walked out."

Leaving the court, Wyatt ran into Tom McLaury, who was on his way to the Mining Exchange Building, having heard that his friend Ike Clanton had been arrested. Wyatt confronted McLaury, a heated exchange resulted, and Wyatt pistol-whipped McLaury to the ground. Clum conceded that witnesses were fairly certain McLaury wasn't armed at that time. But Wyatt later insisted that the man was carrying a concealed pistol yet refused to draw. Wyatt left McLaury bleeding on the ground and went to Hartford's Saloon to buy a cigar.

"I think by then Wyatt had had enough," said Clum. "I know the man well and I can assure you he is slow to anger. I know he tries to avoid trouble whenever possible. But Ike Clanton wandering around Tombstone all day shooting off his mouth was more than Wyatt could stand. And when Wyatt Earp loses his temper—well, things can go from bad to worse in no time at all."

While Wyatt was enjoying his cigar, Frank McLaury and Billy Clanton rode into Tombstone. These two arrived at the Grand Hotel, where Ike had been staying. There they learned what had transpired and went in search of their brothers. They found Ike at George Spangenberg's Gun Shop, and were joined there by Tom McLaury and a friend of both the Clantons and the McLaurys, a young member of the Cowboys named Billy Claiborne. The five men walked together to the Dexter Livery and Feed Stables and spent some time there talking things over. During this interval, Virgil and Doc Holliday converged on Allen Street and met Wyatt there. The latter had been standing on a street corner a half block away from the Dexter Livery, keeping an eye on things. A few minutes later they saw the five Cowboys cross Allen Street and enter the O.K. Corral. Billy Clanton was riding his horse, and Frank McLaury was leading his.

Sheriff Behan arrived on the scene and asked Virgil Earp what the trouble was. Virgil replied that Ike Clanton and Tom McLaury had made threats. "If they leave town, I'll let it go," said the city marshal. "But if they come back out on the street, I will arrest the whole bunch."

"They won't surrender their guns to you," said Behan. "I had better go have a talk with them."

Behan found the five Cowboys in an alley behind the O.K. Corral, moving toward a vacant lot fronting Fremont Street and located between Fly's Rooming House and a private residence. He found Frank McLaury trying to talk sense to his brother Tom and Ike Clanton, both of whom were seething with anger and reluctant to leave Tombstone without settling matters with the Earps and Doc Holliday. They refused to give up their weapons to Behan. Frank told the sheriff he would hand over his guns if the Earps and Holliday gave up theirs.

"By that time Virgil Earp had run out of patience," Clum told the Slaughters. "It was obvious that the Clantons and the McLaurys weren't leaving town. So Virgil told Wyatt and Morgan and Doc Holliday that he was going in to disarm the Cowboys. He handed Doc the shotgun he was carrying and Doc hid it underneath the long gray coat he was wearing.

"Behan was still talking to Ike Clanton and, according to him, the men were planning to ride out. He also says that Ike and Tom McLaury were unarmed. Then he saw the Earps and Holliday coming down Fremont Street toward the vacant lot, and he hurried out to intercept them. He told Virgil he was not going to allow any trouble, and that Ike Clanton and the others were in his custody. But the Earps just walked right past him."

Reaching the lot where Ike and his four companions were gathered, the Earps and Doc Holliday arrayed themselves across the side facing Fremont Street.

"You sons of bitches have been looking for a fight," said Wyatt Earp. "Now you can have it."

"Boys, throw up your hands," said Virgil. "I'm here to disarm and arrest you."

Tom McLaury held his coat open. "I haven't got anything."

Billy Clanton held his hands out in front of him. "Don't shoot me. I don't want to fight."

But Frank McLaury dropped his hand to the six-shooter at his side. The Earps went for their pistols. Billy reached for his, too, while Tom McLaury whirled to his horse to pull a Winchester carbine from the saddle scabbard. Doc Holliday got off the first shot with a nickel-plated revolver, wounding Frank McLaury. Morgan Earp fired almost simultaneously with Holliday, hitting Billy Clanton. Struck in the chest, Billy staggered and fell against the wall of the Harwood House. Tom McLaury's horse shied away from the sound of the guns and kept Tom from reaching the Winchester just long enough for Holliday to bring the shotgun to bear and fire. The buckshot staggered Tom McLaury, who stumbled out of the vacant lot, around the corner of the Harwood House. He took a few steps and then fell. Billy Claiborne broke and ran, and Ike Clanton ducked into Fly's Rooming House as Wyatt and Virgil drew their artillery and commenced firing.

Fetched up against the side of the Harwood House, Billy Clanton gamely returned fire, wounding Virgil Earp in the leg. Frank McLaury was shooting, too, trying to use his horse for cover. Morgan Earp was hit in the shoulder, falling, and then getting back on his feet. Wyatt and Virgil were blazing away at Billy Clanton, who took another bullet between the ribs and slumped to the ground, his pistol empty, his strength rapidly fading. Frank McLaury's horse got away from him and, gutshot and doubled over, Frank stumbled out into Fremont Street, still trading lead with Doc and Morgan. It was Morgan who hit him again, this time in the head, and Frank McLaury went down for good.

"And then it was over," said Clum. "Billy Clanton and Frank and Tom McLaury lay dying. Ike Clanton and Billy Claiborne had turned tail and run. Virgil was wounded in the leg, Morgan in the shoulder. Doc Holliday was grazed by a bullet on his hip. Sheriff Behan walked up to Wyatt and told him he was under arrest. Wyatt replied that if

Behan was God Almighty Himself he could not arrest him."

The three dead men were displayed in a funeral parlor window with a sign that declared they had been "Murdered in the Streets of Tombstone." The town was sharply divided into those that supported the Earps and what they had done—John Clum among them—and those that believed them to be cold-blooded murderers. Virgil and Morgan were laid up in the former's house, which was barricaded against the possibility of an attack by a pro-Cowboy vigilante committee, while a pro-Earp committee armed themselves and vowed to protect the brothers from Cowboy vengeance at all costs. The funeral of Billy Clanton and the McLaury brothers was a grand affair, with nearly two thousand in attendance. And in the two-day coroner's inquest that followed, no blame was attached to either party; the jury very circumspectly came to the conclusion that the three men had been fatally shot and then went home.

"I was afraid the Cowboys would wreak their vengeance on the town of Tombstone," admitted Clum. "They were friends of the McLaurys and the Clantons and I believe John Ringo and Curly Bill Brocius could have mustered a hundred men. That's why I requested Governor Gosper send troops. But he didn't send them. Fortunately, the Cowboys didn't come. But Ike Clanton filed charges against the Earps and Holliday, and warrants have been issued for their arrest. Their trial starts in a couple of days."

Slaughter nodded. He was aware that John Clum was head of the Citizens' Safety Committee, a group of over one hundred businessmen, mine owners, and other "respectable" folk who had demonstrated a willingness to pick up their guns and resort to vigilantism. Clum and his committee would make certain that the Earp brothers got a fair trial.

"I have no doubt that the Earps will be acquitted," said Clum. "It's clear that Ike Clanton and his friends intended mischief, and that Virgil Earp and his deputies were only doing their duty."

"Well, I don't know," said Slaughter. "Sounds to me like they gunned down an unarmed man in Tom McLaury."

"Tom was going for a saddle gun, Texas John. What would you have done under those circumstances? Waited for him to get off a shot or two?"

"I wouldn't shoot a man who didn't have a gun in his hand. But then I don't have to worry about such things."

Clum leaned forward again, elbows on knees, hands clasped in front of him. "I respectfully beg to differ, my friend. Do not be deceived into thinking that this is the end. No, it's only the beginning. The opening salvo, if you will. The war between the lawless element and the law-abiding people of Cochise County has just now begun in earnest. You're going to have to take sides, Texas John. We need you on our side, the side of right, the side of law and order."

Slaughter's smile was colder than a blue norther. "I've dealt with the Clantons and their crowd. They have learned not to mess with me or mine. I have no quarrel with the Cowboys. Don't try to pull me into this. It is not my fight."

Clum sighed. "I hate to tell you this, but you're dead wrong."

Late that night, Viola awoke to find her husband absent from their bed. She found him sitting in a chair in the moonlight in front of their adobe house, smoking one of his Mexican cheroots. Pulling her wrapper tight against the evening chill, she placed a hand on his shoulder.

"You know Clum is right, don't you, darling?" she asked. "Someone is going to have to clean up Cochise County."

"Let Clum and the Earps do that."

"You don't mean it. The Earps didn't kill those men for the sake of law and order."

"You're right about that. They sure didn't. What they did was as lawless as the worst crime committed by the Cowboys, in my book. As for Clum and his damned Safety Committee . . ." Slaughter grimaced. "I have no tolerance for vigilantes. But I just don't want to get involved, Viola. I care about a few things—you, my children, and San Bernardino. That's all. We have made a good start here. But there is still a lot of work to be done. If I pin on a badge, I'll always be away. And I cannot afford to be gone that much. Not now. Besides, I can't see that either faction— the Cowboys or Clum and the Earps—is in the right."

"Of course you can't," she said, "because neither one is in the right. There is no law in Cochise County. That's my point. Sooner or later someone will have to introduce it. Someone like you, John."

Slaughter adamantly shook his head. "There has to be someone else who can do that job."

Viola bent down and kissed his cheek. "I may be just a tiny bit prejudiced," she whispered in his ear, "but frankly, I can't think of anyone who could do it better than you."

CHAPTER TEN

━━◆━━

THE COWBOYS GET REVENGE

IN SPITE OF HIS INSISTENCE THAT THE CONFLICT BETWEEN THE two factions in Cochise County was none of his affair, John Slaughter was one of the many spectators at the hearing held before Justice of the Peace Wells Spicer. It was Spicer's job to determine whether the three Earp brothers and Doc Holliday would be bound over to a grand jury. The prosecution charged that Ike Clanton and his friends had been on their way out of Tombstone to avoid a confrontation, and that when they were attacked by the Earps and Holliday, both Ike and Tom McLaury had been unarmed. The defense argued that Ike Clanton had made numerous threats against the Earps and that he and his companions had been spoiling for a fight and had been the first to go for their guns.

Slaughter was particularly interested in the rumors that the feud between the Earps and the Clanton–McLaury bunch had its source in the holdup of a stagecoach during which a driver had been shot and killed. Some people believed that the Clantons and McLaurys knew that Doc Holliday and maybe even one or more of the Earp brothers had been involved in the robbery, and that the Earps had provoked a fight in order to silence the Cowboys. Others argued that it had been the Clantons and the McLaurys who had held up the stage and committed murder.

The hearing lasted two weeks. In the end, Spicer ruled that the killings of Billy Clanton and the McLaury brothers had been justifiable homicide.

"I cannot resist the conclusion," said Spicer, "that it was a necessary act, done in the discharge of an official duty. Virgil Earp was authorized to arrest, with or without warrant, all persons engaged in any disorderly act within the town limits. Marshal Earp, however, committed an injudicious and censurable act in selecting James Holliday and his own brother, Wyatt Earp, to assist him in the arrest, considering that both James Holliday and Wyatt Earp had engaged in altercations with Ike Clanton and Tom McLaury previous to the gunfight. Yet when we consider the conditions of affairs incident to a frontier country, namely the existence of a law-defying element in our midst, the prevalence of bad, desperate and reckless men who have been a terror to the country and who keep away capital and enterprise, I can attach no criminality to Virgil Earp's unwise act.

"The evidence taken before me in this case would not in my judgment warrant a conviction of the defendants by a trial jury of any offense whatsoever. I therefore do not bind them over for trial."

As soon as Spicer gaveled the hearing closed, pandemonium erupted. Every man in the courtroom was on his feet, and many of them were shouting. John Slaughter caught a glimpse of Wyatt Earp and Doc Holliday, seated at the defense table, shaking hands as they congratulated one another. Virgil and Morgan, still recuperating from their wounds, were not present. On his way out of the Mining Exchange Building, Slaughter ran into Mayor Clum.

"If you consider the Earps your friends," said the Texas cattleman, "you'll persuade them to get out of Tombstone right away."

Clum handed Slaughter the day's edition of the *Epitaph*.

"I thought you might like to read what Governor Gosper had to say about what we need in Cochise County, Texas John."

Slaughter took the newspaper to the nearest saloon and perused it over a shot of whiskey. Governor Gosper blamed the troubles in Tombstone in large measure on the rivalry between various law enforcement officials. What was needed, said Gosper, was someone new, someone unaffiliated with any faction, someone whose only loyalty was to the law—"a man of courage and character and cool judgment, who can fully comprehend the true nature of the situation and then go forward with a firm and steady hand, bringing the leading spirits of this lawless class to a severe and speedy punishment."

Slaughter grimaced and pushed the paper away.

The Earps did not leave Tombstone. Shortly after the acquittal, they found themselves on a "death list" authored, it was said, by the Cowboys. Along with the three Earps, the list included Wells Spicer, John Clum, Doc Holliday, and the lawyer who had defended him. Intending to visit his son and parents back East, John Clum left Tombstone on an evening stage that was attacked by a large group of masked men. The coach was riddled with bullets. Miraculously, neither Clum nor any of his fellow passengers were injured. The six-horse hitch bolted and the stage outran the highwaymen. There was speculation that the real target of the ambush had been Clum himself—that assassination rather than robbery had been the intent of the attackers.

Wells Spicer received a threatening letter, which he promptly handed over to the *Epitaph* for publication:

Sir, if you take my advice you will take your departure for a more genial clime, as I don't think this one is healthy for you any longer. You are liable to get a hole through your coat at any moment. If such sons of bitches as you are allowed to dispense justice in this Territory, the sooner you depart from us the better.

Spicer added his own statement in response:

> I will say that I will be right here where they can find
> me should they want me.

The Earp brothers moved themselves and their families
to the Cosmopolitan Hotel after suspicious characters were
spotted lurking around their houses. A few days after
Christmas, Virgil Earp left the Oriental Saloon shortly before midnight and bent his steps toward the hotel. Gunfire
erupted from a darkened alley across the street and Virgil
went down with buckshot in his left side and left arm. He
managed to get back on his feet and stumble back into the
Oriental, where Wyatt was still running the faro table. Doctors removed bone fragments from Virgil's shattered arm.
Witnesses claimed they had seen Ike Clanton and two other
Cowboys, Frank Stilwell and Johnny Barnes, fleeing the
scene of the bushwhacking.

In an election that followed a month later, Virgil Earp
was replaced as city marshal. But Wyatt Earp asked for and
received an appointment as a United States Marshal. John
Clum swore that all Wyatt wanted to do was maintain law
and order in brother Virgil's place. Slaughter knew better.
He figured Wyatt Earp intended to use the badge and the
authority it conveyed to exact revenge for the attempt on
Virgil's life. Wyatt gathered a notorious group of gunmen
around him. In addition to the ubiquitous Doc Holliday
there was Turkey Creek Jack Johnson, Texas Jack Vermil-
ion, and Sherman McMasters. These men were paid from
a "citizens' fund" raised by Earp supporters in Tombstone.

Obtaining open warrants, Wyatt and his men set out on
a campaign to round up the Cowboys. They were aided by
some of the men who rode for Henry Hooker. This "posse"
swooped down on the nearby settlement of Charleston, believed to be a stomping grounds for the rustling crowd. A
door-to-door search, however, produced no arrests.

The night of March 18, 1882, was a stormy one, but the
weather did not prevent the Earp brothers from attending

the Tombstone theater, after which they went to Hatch's
Saloon, where Morgan Earp challenged the proprietor to a
game of billiards. The room contained a back door with
four glass panes in it, and it was through this door that
someone fired a shot that struck Morgan in the back. The
bullet shattered his spinal column and tore through his ab-
domen, exiting out the front. Sherman McMasters ran out
into the dark alley in search of the shooter, but found no
one. Morgan died in Wyatt's arms less than an hour later.

A coroner's inquest implicated several Cowboys in the
murder—Pete Spencer, Frank Stilwell, and Indian Charlie.
Wyatt shipped Morgan's body back to their parents' home
in California. Virgil and his wife Allie accompanied the
remains. Wyatt and Doc and McMasters and Turkey Creek
Jack Johnson rode the train that carried Morgan as far as
Tucson. The word was out that some of the Cowboys
planned to waylay the Earp party and finish the feud once
and for all. As the train prepared to leave the Tucson depot,
gunfire erupted. It was a dark evening, and no objective
witnesses could testify with any certainty as to what transpired. According to Wyatt Earp, Ike Clanton and four or
five other Cowboys attempted an ambush. The end result
was that when the smoke cleared, Frank Stilwell lay dead.
Wyatt bid brother Virgil so long, saying, "Got one for
Morg!" As the train rolled out of Tucson, Wyatt and his
"posse" headed back to Tombstone. Warrants were issued
out of Puma County for Frank Stilwell's killers, but Wyatt
and his men were forewarned. They were leaving the Cosmopolitan Hotel when Sheriff Behan confronted them.

"Wyatt, I want to see you," said the sheriff.

Wyatt Earp laughed in Behan's face. "If you're not careful, you'll see me once too often, Johnny. Now go away."

Behan chose discretion over duty and let Wyatt and his
men ride out. The next morning he deputized a posse and
set out in pursuit of the fugitives.

Two weeks later Wyatt Earp, accompanied by Doc Holliday and three other men, showed up at John Slaughter's

house. Their horses were bottomed out. They were dusty and haggard. Their eyes were the eyes of the hunted.

"Nobody knows for sure where you stand, John," said Wyatt Earp. "But I need your help."

"I stand for myself. For my wife, my outfit, my ranch."

Wyatt nodded. "I would not be here if I had a choice. But we have to have fresh horses. And we need some food and some ammunition, if you have any to spare. Sheriff Behan has a posse of Cowboys hot on our trail. And they mean to kill us, not serve warrants."

"I have had no trouble with the Cowboys and I want to keep it that way."

Wyatt's features might have been carved from stone, and his deep-set eyes glittered with a cold rage. "They killed my brother. Shot him in the back like the cowards that they are. What did you expect me to do?"

"Seems to me that Tom McLaury was killed in cold blood, too. And some say you bushwhacked Frank Stilwell in Tucson. And what about that Mexican woodcutter named Cruz up in the Dragoon Mountains? From what I hear, you and your partners rode him down and shot him in the back."

"You are mistaken, sir," said Doc Holliday, with his slow Georgia drawl not quite masking an undertone that was icy and dangerous. "I bade him turn around, which he was kind enough to do, and then I shot him."

"Be quiet, Doc," said Wyatt quietly, not taking his eyes off Slaughter. "Cruz was involved in Morgan's death. He's been in league with the Cowboys for years."

"You've got solid evidence to prove that?"

"I guess you'll just have to take my word for it."

"So when is it going to stop? The vendetta? I hear you had a run-in with the Cowboys over at Iron Springs. You were lucky to get out of that one with your hide."

Wyatt nodded. "True enough. They jumped us. Had us pinned down pretty as you please. It was a miracle that none of us got killed that day."

"Damnedest thing I ever saw," said Holliday. "Wyatt got

up and waded right into those sons of bitches, guns blazing. He killed Curly Bill Brocius and the rest of the Cowboys lost their nerve and made for the tall timber."

"You haven't answered my question," Slaughter reminded Wyatt. "You can't kill all the Cowboys. You've done some damage, I'll allow. You've gotten your blood for blood. And don't waste time telling me you ride for justice, Earp. It's vengeance that you sought."

"We didn't come here for a sermon," said Holliday.

Slaughter fastened a steely gaze on the gunman. Unlike nearly everyone else in Arizona, he was not afraid of Doc Holliday. "A year's worth of sermons wouldn't do you a bit of good, mister. You're no better than the worst of the Cowboys."

"Ease up, Doc," said Wyatt wearily. "Don't pick a fight here. All we ask for is fresh horses and some food," he told Slaughter. "Then we'll go on north to Henry Hooker's place. I reckon he'll let us hole up there, and Behan's posse won't tangle with his outfit."

Slaughter called for one of his men, several of whom were loitering near at hand, watching the riders warily.

"Luke, get these men some fresh mounts. And tell Old Bat to fix them up with some grub."

"What about ammunition?" asked Holliday.

"No," said Slaughter flatly. "You don't need any."

"And why do you say that?"

"Because you're all going to do the smart thing and leave Cochise County, for good."

Holliday started to say something, but Wyatt cut him short with a sharp look.

"I think he might just be right, Doc. We've done about all we can do. We can rest up at Hooker's place for a few days and then ride north for Colorado."

"And what about the Cowboys?" asked Holliday. "Who's gonna take care of them?"

Wyatt Earp glanced at Slaughter. "Won't be our problem. And sooner or later they'll get cleaned out. They'll get what they deserve. It's just a matter of time."

CHAPTER ELEVEN

THE LAST STRAW

Tom Cochran sat on the steps of a porch that fronted a small house on the edge of Tombstone. He judged by the position of the sun in the brassy sky that it was nearly noon, and he tried to curb his impatience. But he'd been trying to do that for hours now, and it was getting increasingly difficult. Viola Slaughter was inside the house paying one last visit to an ailing friend. Cochran had hoped to get an early start—it was sixty miles back to San Bernardino, a long day's journey. Obviously, though, an early start was out of the question now. The cowboy figured if they tarried much longer it would be just as well for them to stay over in town for another night. It just wasn't safe traveling late at night in this country. And Viola's safety was Cochran's first priority.

Viola came to Tombstone several times a year, for she had developed friendships with several of the women who lived here. John Slaughter always sent a rider along with her. This time it was Cochran's turn. He was glad—not because it presented him with an opportunity to sample the amusements that Tombstone had to offer a cowboy. He hadn't so much as stepped foot in a saloon, and he had steered clear of the gambling halls and bordellos, too. No, he was glad because it meant he got to spend time with Viola.

A little while later Viola emerged, and Cochran gave her a hand up into the waiting buggy.

"How is Mrs. Keogh, ma'am?" he asked.

"Not well, I'm afraid, Tom." Viola's smile was laced with sadness. "I honestly don't know if she will live out the year."

"What's wrong with her?"

"If you ask me, she's lost the will to live. Ever since her husband died she just hasn't been the same. They were married nearly twenty-five years. He meant everything to her. I don't think she wants to go through life without him. You know what I mean, Tom?"

Cochran caught himself gazing into Viola's lovely face, and looked away. "Yes, ma'am. I know exactly what you mean. That's a real shame."

"Have you ever loved anyone like that?"

"No, ma'am," lied Cochran, afraid that if he said yes, Viola might want to know more—and of course he was in no position to tell her about his love.

"My feelings for John are that strong," she said. "I mean, I simply can't imagine life without him."

Her words were like daggers plunging into Cochran's heart, and he turned quickly to his horse.

"We had better get a move on," he said gruffly. "Unless you want to stay in town another night and go early tomorrow morning. Might not be a bad idea, ma'am."

"No," said Viola firmly. "I'm ready to get home." Visiting Irma Keogh had reminded her just how precious her time with John Slaughter was, and she wanted to return to her husband's arms as soon as possible. She gathered up the reins and coaxed the big bay in the buggy's traces into motion. Cochran swung into the saddle and rode alongside the buggy as they put Tombstone behind them.

They had traveled for several hours when Cochran spotted three men to the south of the road, riding up out of a ravine about three hundred yards away. Turning their horses toward the road, they angled to cut Cochran and Viola off.

"Who are those men, Tom?" asked Viola.

"Better stop the buggy, ma'am." Cochran checked his horse and pulled the Winchester carbine out of its saddle boot. Bringing the repeater to his shoulder, he took careful aim and squeezed off a shot. The bullet kicked up dust a few yards in front of the three riders, who stopped their horses.

"That's plenty close enough!" shouted Cochran.

The trio sat their horses for a moment. Cochran thought they were talking to one another, but at this distance he could not be sure that was the case.

"Should we make a run for it?" asked Viola.

He took a quick look around. The desert stretched for many miles in every direction. The stark peaks of the Dragoon Mountains rose far to the north. They were a good twenty miles from Tombstone, and about forty miles from the San Bernardino ranch house. This was a lonely stretch of road, with no ranch or town or way station for miles.

"No place to run that I know of," he said at last, admiring her calmness. "We'll have to stand and fight if they mean to make trouble for us."

He looked at her with worried eyes, and she smiled reassuringly at him, then reached down to pick up the rifle that lay beneath her feet.

At that instant the three men started shooting. One stayed put, while the other two fanned out to east and west. Cochran got off one more shot before he was distracted by the sudden death of the big bay in the buggy's traces. Cursing, he swept Viola out of the buggy, wrapping one strong arm around her narrow waist and setting her down on the ground before dismounting himself. Grabbing his saddlebags and canteen, he gave a shout and laid the barrel of his Winchester across the pony's flanks, pulling the trigger and creasing the animal, just as he had seen Tad Roland do when the Apache renegades had jumped them in the Chiricahua Mountains six months ago. The startled horse took off down the road at a gallop. Cochran used a clasp knife to cut the tangled harness, unhooked the traces, and then put his back into tipping the buggy over on its side. Viola's trunk, strapped to the back, broke open, spilling her personal items into the dust of the road. Cochran was sorry that that had happened, but he didn't have time to worry about it. One of the bandits was riding hard to intercept his fleeing horse. The cowboy drew a bead and fired again. The bandit's horse went down, shot through the lungs, throwing its rider. Cochran watched his own horse disappear in a cloud of dust.

"Go home, fella," he muttered. "For God's sakes, go home."

Bullets slammed furiously into the overturned buggy. Viola was trading lead with the bandit who had split off to the west. Cochran yelled at her to keep her head down. Then he saw the bandit whose horse he had just slain break cover and scamper across the road fifty yards to the east. Cochran got off one hasty shot. The bandit fell and crawled into the low brush north of the road. Cochran muttered another curse. The man was trying to get around behind them. He was hit, but how bad? The other two highwaymen had dismounted and were now keeping up a steady fire.

After a while the bandits stopped shooting. Crouched behind the buggy beside Viola, Cochran scanned the brush north of the road. Was the bandit he had shot dead or alive? If alive, where the hell was he? Checking the sun, Cochran calculated that sundown was about an hour away.

"What are they doing now?" asked Viola.

He handed her his canteen, and she accepted it gratefully, taking a long drink. Cochran's mouth was as dry as cotton, but he capped the canteen without drinking when she gave it back to him. The water—all of it—was for Viola.

"Waiting for dark, I reckon," he replied. "If they rush

us now, we'll get one or two of them, maybe. They figure if they hold off until dark they can slip right up on us before we know they're here." He looked at her, afraid that his words had frightened her. "But don't fret, ma'am. I won't let anything happen to you."

She smiled at him again. "Tom, I would not feel any safer if John himself were here."

Cochran was stunned, and didn't know how to respond. He glanced down the road in the direction his horse had taken.

"With any luck," he said, "your husband will be along right soon."

But would it be soon enough? he wondered.

Occasionally the two bandits still in the brush south of the road called out to each other, and they were close enough now so that Cochran could tell that they were Mexicans, even though he could understand little of what was being said. The last hour of daylight crawled by; when at last the murky shadows of dusk had crept across the desert and reached them, Cochran told Viola it was time to move. At his bidding she crawled on her belly into the low brush north of the road, and he followed her. Fifteen yards away from the buggy, they stopped and waited another hour, daring neither to move nor speak. Then gunfire erupted, so close that it made Viola jump. Orange blossoms of flame illuminated the darkness—muzzle flash. The two bandits had closed in on the overturned buggy and then charged across the road with guns blazing. The shooting was followed by cursing and conversation, and then the pair ventured into the brush north of the road, figuring their prey had gone in that direction.

One of the men almost stepped on Cochran and Viola—his bulky shape loomed against the star-speckled night sky. At the last possible moment Cochran rose up and fired into the shape at point-blank range. The bandit cried out and fell backward. His *compañero*, a few yards to the east, whirled and blazed away at Cochran. The cowboy felt the numbing impact of a bullet striking him high and spinning him around. Still he managed to get off two more shots as he went down. Fighting to remain conscious, he heard the sharp report of a Winchester rifle and knew it had to be Viola. Then silence—a silence so complete that it scared him, and he whispered her name hoarsely, the dread rising up in him until she reached his side and spoke his name and touched his face with her fingertips.

"I'm right here, Tom. I'm right here. I—I think they are gone." She cradled his head in her lap and, putting down her rifle, drew his six-shooter from the holster on his hip. Cochran could tell he had been hit just below the ribs on the left side. The bullet had passed clean through his body, and he could only hope that it had missed any vital organs. He wasn't spitting up blood, and he thought his lungs were okay. But he was bleeding badly from the bullet's entry and exit wounds, and he wadded his shirt up in his fist and pressed it against the entry hole. The pain coursed through his body, and he began to shake involuntarily, but he kept quiet, clenching his teeth together to keep them from chattering. Viola's hand was soft and cool and comforting on his cheek.

And then he felt it, a vibration in the ground beneath him, accompanied by a sound like continuous thunder, very faint at first but growing steadily louder, and he knew what it all meant. A large body of riders approaching. More bandits? Or Texas John and the San Bernardino crew? He soon had his answer. As the horsemen reached the overturned buggy, he heard John Slaughter calling out his wife's name. Viola responded, and a moment later Slaughter was with them.

"Viola! Thank God you're alive!"

"I am not hurt, John, but Tom—I think Tom is in a bad way."

"I've been in a lot worse shape," said Cochran.

A shot rang out, and a moment later another rider approached.

"Found one of them over yonder, boss," said the rider, and Cochran recognized Tad Roland's voice. "He was hit, but still alive. I finished him off."

Slaughter nodded. "There's another one right over there, but he's dead. How many were there in all, Tom?"

"There were three of them."

"Have the men spread out," Slaughter told Roland. "Find that third man. Old Bat! Get the hell over here with a blanket."

The ex-slave arrived and covered Tom with a blanket. A fire was built, and by its light Slaughter inspected Cochran's wound.

"Want I should ride into Tombstone and fetch a doctor?" asked Old Bat, for he could see that Cochran's injury was serious.

"No need for that," said Slaughter. "The bullet passed right through. He isn't spitting up any blood that I can see, so I reckon he'll live, if we can stop the bleeding. You get that buggy turned upright and put a horse in the traces."

Cochran watched Slaughter heating the blade of a knife in the fire. "You better not stick around for this, ma'am," he advised Viola.

"Nonsense," she replied. "I'm going to be right here, Tom."

Slaughter fetched a silver whiskey flask from his saddle-bags and offered it to Cochran. "Drink this down, Tom. It won't hurt quite so bad if you do."

Cochran grinned. "You're a damned poor liar, boss."

"And you're a damned good man, Tom. I owe you."

"Just do me one favor. The one that got away—he's the one who put this hole in me. I'd be obliged if you'd find him and return the favor."

"That's as good as done, *amigo*," said Slaughter grimly.

Viola took Cochran's hand in hers. "Hold on tight to me, Tom."

"Yes, ma'am." Cochran kept his eyes locked on Viola's face. The starlight seemed to shine in her eyes. He stayed focused on them as Slaughter ripped open his shirt and applied the hot steel to his already tortured flesh. Cochran's body went rigid. He hissed through clenched teeth at the pain, but managed to keep from crying out. Slaughter put the knife back in the fire to heat the blade again before applying it to the exit wound. That was about all the discomfort Cochran's body would stand for one night. As he faded into unconsciousness he heard Slaughter say, "I think that's done it."

Cochran's last thought was that he had gripped Viola's hand too tightly, and he mumbled an apology in case he had hurt her and loosened his grip. But she tightened her own grip, not letting go of him, and said, "You're going to be fine, Tom, just fine." Her words caught up with him as he spiraled down into painless oblivion—and Tom Cochran blacked out with a smile on his face.

CHAPTER TWELVE

A LESSON LEARNED

WHEN JOHN SLAUGHTER RODE INTO THE BORDER TOWN OF Naco, south of Bisbee, he did something that very few Anglos before him had ever done. He rode in alone. Naco was a dusty collection of cedar-post shanties and adobe huts, and it had earned a well-deserved notoriety for being the stomping ground for the territory's lawless element. No one knew for certain how many people had died violent deaths in Naco. No records were kept about such matters, and while Naco had a cemetery, not all of of the people who had died there found their way to the local bone orchard. In fact, it was just as likely that a man killed in Naco would be dragged off into the desert beyond the town limits and left to the coyotes and turkey vultures. Of course, first the corpse would be stripped of anything of value, and in Naco just about everything except human life had some value. That included gold fillings, clothing, and sometimes even scalps.

So Naco was the last place one would expect a law-abiding man to enter of his own accord, unless he was tired of living. But John Slaughter didn't seem overly concerned as he dismounted in front of a cantina and tied his tall gray horse to a hitching post. Drawing a Winchester carbine from its saddle boot, he paused to survey the town's single street. Here and there stood a few disreputable-looking men, Mexicans and Anglos and breeds, and they were watching him like buzzards. Another man sat in a chair tilted back against the peeling adobe wall of the cantina, but he wasn't watching Slaughter. He appeared to be taking a siesta, his hat pulled low over his face.

"Is your name Geronimo Baltierrez?" Slaughter asked him.

The man lifted the brim of his hat. "Who wants to know?"

"That would be me."

The man looked at the Winchester, then at the long duster that Slaughter wore, and he wondered what other weapons the duster concealed. He figured Slaughter for a side gun at least. But he couldn't know about the scattergun Slaughter had rigged with a sling so that he could carry it under his left arm. The man didn't need to know about the sawed-off shotgun to realize that the stranger was not one to trifle with.

"No, I ain't Baltierrez. I don't even know a Baltierrez."

"Okay. Keep an eye on my horse."

"Keep an eye on your own damned horse, mister."

"No, you watch it. 'Cause if it's gone when I come out, I'm gonna find you and shoot you."

With that, Slaughter stepped inside the cantina. He moved sideways so as not to silhouette himself in the doorway, then paused to let his eyes adjust to the dimness of the interior. There were two men playing a desultory hand of poker at one table, and a third man behind the bar—planks laid across barrels. A mangy one-eyed cat lay curled up at one end of the bar. The floor of the cantina was hard-packed earth, the walls were speckled with dead flies. The place reeked of sweat and mescal.

Slaughter moved to the far end of the bar so that he could see the length of the room and watch the two men at the table as well as the front door. Behind him and to the right was another doorway, this one draped with a tattered blanket. He turned his body slightly so that he could see that doorway out of the corner of his eye.

"What do you want?" asked the bartender. He was a burly Anglo, paunchy and balding, with wisps of long greasy brown hair curled back over his ears. His nose had been broken so many times that it didn't resemble a nose anymore.

"I'm looking for Geronimo Baltierrez."

The two men playing cards lost all interest in their game and looked warily at Slaughter. Clearly they knew the name.

"I don't know anybody named Baltierrez," said the bartender.

"You're lying." Slaughter could see it in the man's eyes.

"You go to hell, mister."

Slaughter smiled and shrugged. "If you don't mind, I'll have a drink first. Whiskey, if you've got it."

The bartender scowled at him, but poured the drink and brought it over. Slaughter laid four bits on the plank. The bartender reached for the money, taking his eyes off Slaughter for a moment. That was long enough for Slaughter to bring the stock of the Winchester carbine around and slam it into the man's face. The barkeep reeled backward, stumbled, and fell, covering his face with his hands and uttering a strangled cry of pain. Slaughter went under the plank and, straightening, leveled the Winchester at the two card players.

"Time for you boys to make yourselves scarce," he said.

The two men hastily took their leave.

Lying on his side, blood leaking between his fingers, the bartender looked up at Slaughter with watery eyes.

"You bwoke my nose, you son of a bitch," he whined.

"If you would learn to be a little more cooperative, people might start leaving your nose alone," said Slaughter. "Now, I'm going to ask you one more time. Where is Geronimo Baltierrez? I know he hangs around these parts a good bit. And you run the only cantina in Naco, so I figure you know exactly who I'm talking about."

"Yeah, I know him."

"So, we're getting somewhere. And where might he be?"

Glaring balefully at Slaughter, the bartender nodded at the blanket-draped doorway. "Back there. With Molena. And when he's with Molena, he doesn't like to be disturbed. He'll put bullets in your kneecaps and then gut you like a fish. And he'll enjoy doing it even more than I'll enjoy watching it." The man spit blood.

"You talk too much for a man with a broken nose," remarked Slaughter. "You stay right where you are. Don't move."

Ducking under the planks again, Slaughter moved to the doorway and slowly pushed the blanket aside with the barrel of his Winchester. He glanced down a short, dark hallway. There was a door at the end which he presumed led outside, and two more doors, one on either side of the corridor. Edging cautiously down the hall, he heard the distinctive sounds of lovemaking—a man grunting, a woman moaning—coming through the door to his right. He went through the door on the left first, and found himself in a storeroom. Turning, he kicked open the other door and went in with the Winchester at his shoulder.

A man rolled quickly out of bed, diving for a pistol in a gunbelt that was draped over the back of a chair. Slaughter's Winchester boomed; the bullet splintered one of the chair legs and the chair toppled over, away from the man, who froze, crouched, beside the bed. He was a small, wiry Mexican with lank black hair to his shoulders. Not yet thirty by Slaughter's calculation, he had led a singularly violent life; he was naked, so Slaughter could see the scars. There were a lot of them, and most of them had been made by bullet or knife blade.

The woman in bed was young, too, a bit on the plump side. She yelped when the rifle spoke and pulled a blanket up to cover her pendulous, dark-tipped breasts.

"Who the hell are you?" rasped Baltierrez.

Slaughter levered another round into the Winchester's breech and aimed the rifle at a spot between the man's eyes.

"I'm the man whose wife you nearly killed a couple of months ago, on the road out of Tombstone." Slaughter used his left hand to pull the duster aside so that Baltierrez could see the sheriff's badge pinned to his shirt. "I also happen to be the newly elected sheriff of Cochise County."

"Slaughter," breathed Baltierrez. He glanced at his holstered pistol, now on the floor beneath the overturned chair.

"Go right ahead," said Slaughter. "Try your luck."

Baltierrez looked at the Winchester, then at Slaughter— and smiled coldly.

"You would like, huh? But then, what chance would I have?"

"None at all."

"You can't prove anything, lawman?" sneered Baltierrez. "I don't know anything about your wife or what happened to her on the road out of Tombstone."

"Sure you do. The two varmints you're known to ride with got themselves killed. The third man got away. That third man would be you and there's not a doubt in my mind on that score."

"I heard about those two getting killed. But I was right here in Naco when that happened. Plenty of my friends here will testify to that."

"We'll see. I'm taking you in, Baltierrez."

"Can I at least get dressed first?"

Slaughter moved sideways to a pile of clothes on the floor, keeping the Winchester trained on Baltierrez. He knelt, picked up a pair of chinos, and tossed the pants to the Mexican.

"Put them on."

Baltierrez pulled on the pants. "And my boots, *señor*?"

"No," said Slaughter. He kicked the bandit's boots over and bent down again to pick up the sheathed Bowie knife that had fallen out of one of them. This he stuck under his belt, then tilted his head toward the door. "Let's get moving."

Baltierrez shrugged, and smiled at the woman. "Do not worry, Molena. I will be back soon."

He left the room and Slaughter followed, the Winchester aimed at his prisoner's spine, held at hip level. They passed through the blanket-draped doorway into the cantina proper, where Slaughter ordered Baltierrez to sit at one of the tables. The bartender was on his feet now, leaning over the planks of his makeshift bar and holding a blood-soaked rag to his face.

"Hey, you," said Slaughter. "Make yourself useful and go get a horse for this man."

The bartender contemplated refusal, but decided that was too dangerous and swallowed his pride. He left the cantina without a word. Baltierrez propped his legs up on the table and leaned back with his hands behind his head. He didn't look the least bit concerned about his predicament.

"Why don't we have a drink while we wait, lawman?" he suggested.

"I'll wait and have my drink when you're in the Tombstone jail," replied Slaughter, keeping one eye on his prisoner and the other on the door to the street.

"I tell you again, you have the wrong man."

"No, I don't. You're a road agent, Baltierrez. You've probably killed a dozen innocent people. You've robbed stagecoaches. You've stolen horses."

Baltierrez sorrowfully shook his head. "I have been falsely accused of such things. Yes, it is true, I trade in horses. But I am a mustanger. I capture them, break them. I do not steal them."

"Tell it to the judge."

A quarter hour passed before the bartender returned. "His horse is outside," he told Slaughter.

"Okay, Baltierrez. On your feet."

Baltierrez got up and stretched and smiled at the barkeep. There was nothing friendly about that smile, though.

"Riley, remind me when I get back to thank you for being so helpful."

Riley took that for what it was—a threat. "Goddamn it, Geronimo, that bastard bwoke my nose."

"I will break something else. Maybe your neck, who can say?"

Slaughter prodded Baltierrez in the spine with his rifle. "Get going."

They moved out into the street. Slaughter narrowed his eyes against the sun's glare. There were more men out on the street now, watching his every move.

"You know, *señor*," said Baltierrez cheerfully, "you may not get out of Naco alive."

"Well, if I don't, you won't." Slaughter took a pair of shackles from his saddle and put them on his prisoner's wrists. Then he mounted up and motioned with the Winchester for Baltierrez to lead the way. The *hombres* on the street watched them ride by, and no one tried to stop them. None of the men wanted to tangle with someone like Slaughter, who had the *cajones* to ride into Naco all by himself, and who had obviously gotten the better of a hardcase like Geronimo Baltierrez.

"Has the jury reached a verdict?"

"We sure have, Your Honor. We find the defendant not guilty."

Leaning in the doorway of the courtroom in Tombstone's Mining Exchange Building, John Slaughter turned abruptly on his heel and walked outside, leaving behind the tumult that erupted after the verdict was given. He'd expected this outcome, had tried to prepare himself for it. And yet a helpless fury burned inside him and he tasted bitter bile.

Jeff Milton was waiting out in the sunshine, a tall, slender, dark-haired man with an easygoing smile that disguised his hard edge. Slaughter had recruited Milton for the position of deputy sheriff of Cochise County because the man had built a reputation for himself in Tucson as a determined and incorruptible lawman who didn't know how to back down from trouble. It had been hard to find a good man willing to take a job like that; most people equated badge-toting in Cochise County with suicide. But Milton saw it as a challenge, and he'd never been able to pass up one of those. He was smart, reliable, courageous, and Slaughter had come to rely on him a lot in a relatively short period of time.

One look at Slaughter's face told Milton all he needed to know about what had transpired inside the courtroom.

"So they let the varmint go," he said, shaking his head.

Slaughter nodded. "No evidence that Baltierrez was there that night."

"Other than the fact that the hombres he'd been riding with for years were killed on the spot."

Slaughter fired up one of his Mexican cheroots as the trial's spectators began to pour out of the building. Most of them steered well clear of him. John Clum, though, walked right up to Slaughter and his deputy, looking very sympathetic.

"Hope you don't take the verdict personally, Texas John. There's no question in my mind that Baltierrez was involved in the attack on your wife. A lot of folks believe that."

"Well, doesn't look like any of those folks made it onto the jury," remarked Milton.

"Hell, he had witnesses that put him fifty miles away that night," said Clum. "What else could they do?"

"Thanks, John, but I do take it personally," said Slaughter.

Clum headed for the office of the Tombstone *Epitaph*. A moment later Geronimo Baltierrez and his lawyer emerged. The Mexican bandit wore a brown wool suit that the shyster had provided him. Seeing Slaughter, the lawyer took Baltierrez's arm and tried to steer him away, but the bandit shook him loose and turned to grin at the sheriff.

"No hard feelings, lawman. You just made a mistake."

"No, I didn't."

"I think you're the one who made the mistake," added Milton.

"I am afraid the jury thought otherwise, Deputy," said the lawyer. "Sheriff Slaughter, I believe you should consider this a lesson learned. Next time make sure you've got the evidence to back up your charge."

"Oh, I've learned my lesson, don't worry about that."

"You know," Milton told the lawyer, "the gold this feller paid you with probably came from the Wells Fargo express him and his *compadres* robbed about five months back."

Baltierrez sighed. "I have not robbed a Wells Fargo express."

"If you had any proof of that, you'd arrest him here and now," said the lawyer smugly. "Come along, Mr. Baltierrez, I'll buy you a drink."

"Make that a quick one," said Slaughter. "And then you better get out of Tombstone, Baltierrez."

"Hold on a minute," protested the lawyer. "You have no call to run him out of town."

"One hour."

"I would remind you that Baltierrez is unarmed," said the lawyer.

Slaughter tossed the bandit's sheathed Bowie knife to its owner. "Not anymore he isn't."

Watching Baltierrez and his lawyer walk away, Jeff Milton said, "I've got a good idea, Texas John. Why don't you go have a drink and I'll tail along behind our friend Geronimo and make sure he leaves?"

Slaughter nodded and parted company with his deputy. He made his way to the Oriental Saloon and had a shot of bourbon. Nearly everyone in the place knew him, but they all gave him plenty of elbow room, assuming—and rightly so—that the verdict had riled him. With a good strong dose of nerve medicine in him, Slaughter strolled over to the jail. Milton found him there some time later.

"Baltierrez bought a pistol and some ammunition at Spangenberg's," reported the deputy. "Then he headed to the livery for his horse and rode straight out of town."

Slaughter nodded. He already had his saddlebags packed—an extra shirt; cartridges for his Colt Peacemaker, Winchester, and scattergun; a sack of coffee; and some strips of jerked beef. He strapped the scattergun on under his left arm, donned his gray duster, and shouldered the bulging panniers.

"Keep an eye on things while I'm gone," he told Milton, and walked out.

Jeff Milton didn't ask Slaughter where he was going. He didn't need to. The law was through with Geronimo Baltierrez, but John Slaughter was not.

CHAPTER THIRTEEN

THE SHERIFF OF COCHISE COUNTY

JOHN SLAUGHTER FOUND THE VANTAGE POINT HE WAS LOOK-
ing for on a high rugged slope deep in the Chiricahua
Mountains, among the red rocks and scrub junipers. From
here, with the aid of a pair of binoculars, he could survey
the woodcutters' camp in the canyon below. These remote
camps were often frequented by Cochise County's lawless
element, so he wasn't all that surprised when the trail of
Geronimo Baltierrez led him here. The camp was a collection of tents and shanties, and it soon became apparent to
Slaughter that one of the tents was being used by a pair of
prostitutes. One of these was a plump, black-haired woman
he pegged as a half-breed. The other was a slender, redheaded girl with skin as pale as alabaster. It was the latter
whom Baltierrez had come so far out of his way to visit.
Apparently Molena, the Naco whore, was not the only
fallen angel the bandit was courting.

The two camp prostitutes had to share the tent, and as
the half-breed woman was presently entertaining company,
Baltierrez escorted the redheaded girl to a nearby shanty
which housed the camp sutler, whose fastest-moving merchandise was mescal and cheap whiskey. Slaughter watched
the bandit and the woman disappear into the shanty, then

settled back and tried to make himself comfortable, chewing on a strip of jerked beef and calculating that there were still a couple of hours of daylight remaining.

He had been trailing Baltierrez for two days, expecting the bandit to make tracks for Naco, or even the border. Instead, Baltierrez had turned east, and for a while Slaughter had wondered if the man was headed for San Bernardino, perhaps to cause more mischief, or maybe even to orchestrate a final reckoning with the sheriff of Cochise County. Instead, Baltierrez had skirted the northern boundary of San Bernardino and moved on into the Chiricahua Mountains. Then Slaughter had thought that the man's destination was Galeyville, the stronghold of the Cowboys. But Baltierrez had come here. Had he made such a journey solely for the purpose of visiting the calico queen with the red hair? At this point Slaughter really didn't care. He was homesick. He missed Viola and the children. It was time to settle accounts with Geronimo Baltierrez.

Slaughter whiled away the time watching the goings-on in the woodcutters' camp. Several wagons were being loaded with lumber, destined for an early morning departure and bound for one of the timber-hungry towns in the area. A couple of drunken loggers stumbled out of the sutler's shanty and got into a fistfight that Slaughter—and onlookers that gathered down below—found amusing, since the combatants fell down more often than they were knocked down. And finally, as the sun sank below the western heights and the blue shadows of night began to collect in the canyon bottom, Baltierrez and his redheaded companion emerged arm in arm from the shanty and made for the prostitute's tent. The half-breed woman had finished with her last customer and was sitting on a three-legged stool beside a fire outside the tent. She and the red-haired woman exchanged a few words and then the former led Baltierrez inside.

Slaughter got to his feet, flexed stiff shoulders, and turned to his gray gelding. The surefooted horse negotiated a steep game trail to the canyon floor. He rode into the camp from the east so that one of the first tents he came to was the one belonging to the prostitutes. The pudgy black-haired woman was hunched over the fire, warming herself with a tattered blanket around her shoulders and a bottle of gin, nearly empty, in her hands. She watched the horseman approach, and as Slaughter neared, she raised her dress to expose a plump calf.

"Hey, handsome," she leered. "I'll show you a good time for two dollars. What do you say?"

Slaughter glanced at the camp beyond. Men were gathered around a couple of blazing cook fires and the mustard-yellow light cast by lanterns escaped from tents and shanties. It was very dark now, the sky a ribbon of indigo blue captured between the rimrock high overhead. Somewhere up there a coyote howled, inciting several dogs in the camp to a frenzy of yapping.

"I've got an idea," said the whore. "Why don't you take me down to Reno's place and buy me a drink? We got a little time to kill, anyway." She threw a thumb over her shoulder, gesturing at the tent. "Alice—she's my partner—is working right now, if you know what I mean."

Slaughter looked at the tent. He didn't want the half-breed woman in the way or, even worse, to raise an alarm. Digging into a pocket, he fished out a ten-dollar gold piece and tossed it to her.

"Why don't you go buy us a bottle and I'll wait right here at your fire?"

The woman grinned. She was missing a front tooth, but that was no great loss, considering the condition of her remaining teeth. "Now, do I get to keep the rest?" she asked.

"Maybe."

She got up and patted Slaughter on the leg. "Don't you go nowhere, honey. I'll be right back."

"Take your time," said Slaughter. "I'm in no hurry."

He watched her trudge off toward the sutler's shanty,

then threw another look around before climbing down off the tall gray. Ground-hitching the horse, he left the Winchester in the saddle boot and reached under his duster to unsling the scattergun. A woman's laughter issued from inside the tent. Slaughter shook his head. Seemed like he was always interrupting Baltierrez when the bandit was womanizing.

"Baltierrez!" he called. "This is Sheriff Slaughter. You're under arrest."

As soon as he had spoken, Slaughter circled the tent—just in time to see his prey cutting a slit in the tent canvas with his Bowie knife. Slaughter waited until the bandit had crawled out and was in the process of standing up before stepping forward with the scattergun held at hip level.

"Drop that pig-sticker, Geronimo."

The bandit whirled, saw the scattergun—and decided not to test his luck.

"What are you arresting me for now, Slaughter?"

"Robbing the Wells Fargo express."

Baltierrez grinned tautly. "You can't prove I had anything to do with that."

"I'm arresting you anyway."

"I don't think so. I'm getting tired of this game of yours."

"Drop the knife."

"I will tell you something, Slaughter, just between you and me. I was there when your wife was attacked. My *compadre*, Miranda, it was his idea. He saw her in Tombstone, found out who she was. You see, we were not going to kill her. Just hold her for ransom. And if you had paid, well, you would have gotten her back alive. Maybe a little worse for wear, if you know what I mean. But alive."

"Either use that knife or throw it down."

At that moment Slaughter heard a sound behind him, followed by a gunshot. A bullet passed so close that it made a sharp cracking noise. He whirled and saw the redheaded whore holding a six-shooter in both hands, pulling the ham-

mer back, intent on firing a second time. Snatching the gun
out of her hand, Slaughter rammed the barrel of his scattergun into her midsection, hard enough to knock the wind
out of her. She doubled over, took two steps back, and sat
down hard. Turning, Slaughter barely managed to avoid the
blade of the Bowie knife as Baltierrez lunged. He used the
woman's gun to strike a hard blow to the back of the bandit's skull. Baltierrez sprawled on the ground. Slaughter
thought at first that the man was unconscious—but then
Baltierrez rolled over, and now there was pistol in his hand.
Slaughter fell back, triggering both barrels of the scattergun, even as Baltierrez fired. Muzzle flash briefly lit up the
night. The bandit missed his target. Slaughter didn't. The
buckshot tore into the Mexican's chest. Geronimo Baltierrez died instantly.

"You bastard!" screamed the redhaired whore. "You
bastard, you killed him!"

Slaughter knelt and checked Baltierrez for a pulse. There
was none.

"Yes, it sure looks that way," he said flatly.

"Are you gonna arrest me, you son of a bitch?"

"Nope. If I did that, then I'd have to put up with you
all the way back to Tombstone. And I'm not in the mood
for that kind of aggravation."

Slaughter retrieved the Bowie knife, put it in his belt,
and headed for his horse. Several men were running up
from the camp. Seeing Slaughter with scattergun in one
hand and pistol in the other caused them to pull up short.

"What the hell happened?" asked one. "We heard some
shooting."

"I just killed Geronimo Baltierrez," said Slaughter, putting foot to stirrup and swinging aboard the gray.

"Geronimo was a friend of mine."

"Good. Then you can bury him."

"Just who do you think you are, mister?"

"I'm the sheriff of Cochise County," said Slaughter, then
turned his horse and rode out of the woodcutters' camp.

*   *   *

"Mr. Arlon Reno, you have been called to testify before this coroner's jury in the matter of the death of one Geronimo Baltierrez which occurred in the County of Cochise on April thirteenth, 1886. Do you understand?"

"I do, Judge."

"What is your occupation at the present time, Mr. Reno?"

"I'm a sutler."

"And where do you currently reside?"

"A woodcutters' camp in Dead Horse Canyon, up in the Chiricahua Mountains."

"Tell us what you know about the death of Geronimo Baltierrez."

"I know Geronimo—that is, Mr. Baltierrez—he rode into camp that day. He wasn't looking for no trouble, I can tell you that. He comes by now and again to pay a call on Alice. Alice, she's a . . . well, she's a . . ."

"A whore," said the judge. "Now get on with your story, Mr. Reno."

The Tombstone courtroom was packed, and somebody in the crowd chuckled—a sound which stopped abruptly when the judge cast a stern look in the general direction whence it came.

"Yes, sir," said Reno. "Well, Geronimo, him and Alice come into my place of business 'round about sundown for a bottle of whiskey, then went back to Alice's tent. About twenty minutes later I heard gunshots. Me and some of the other boys run out to see what was going on. We run on down to Alice's tent and that's when I seen that man there—Slaughter. He come from around back of the tent toting a sawed-off shotgun and a pistol. He said he'd just kilt Geronimo Baltierrez and that if any of us was friends of Baltierrez and wanted to take issue with him on account of the killing, he had plenty of ammunition left over. Then he mounted up and rode off."

"Is there anything else, Mr. Reno?"

"Yes, sir. We went around to Geronimo's body. He'd been hit at close range by a full load of buckshot. We didn't find no weapon of any kind on him, and Alice, she said he wasn't heeled, that Slaughter had kilt him in cold blood and had threatened to do the same to her if she wasn't careful."

"And what did she take him to mean by 'careful'?"

"That she was supposed to keep her mouth shut."

"I understand she isn't here to testify."

"No, sir. She wouldn't come to Tombstone. Said she was afraid of Slaughter and what he might do to her if she testified."

Someone in the crowd snorted. "Ain't you afraid, Reno?"

The sutler scowled. "I want to see justice done. Geronimo Baltierrez was gunned down in cold blood."

"It's widely known what a good citizen you are, Reno," came the voice, and others laughed.

"That's enough," growled the judge. "Is that all you have to tell us, Mr. Reno?"

"Yes, sir, Judge, that's about it."

"Then you are dismissed, Mr. Reno. Sheriff Slaughter, do you swear to tell the truth, the whole truth, and nothing but the truth, so help you God?"

"I do."

"Sheriff Slaughter, you've been called to testify before this coroner's jury in the matter of the death of one Geronimo Baltierrez."

"I know."

"What is your full name?"

"James Horton Slaughter."

"And where do you currently reside?"

"San Bernardino and Tombstone."

"What is your occupation at present?"

"Cattleman—and sheriff of Cochise County."

"Go ahead and tell us all you know with regard to the death of Geronimo Baltierrez."

"I trailed Baltierrez from Tombstone to the camp in Dead Horse Canyon. While he was in the tent with the woman named Alice, I called out to him that he was under arrest. He—"

"What were you arresting him for?"

"The robbery of the Wells Fargo express that occurred in November of last year."

"Did you have a warrant?"

"I did not."

"Go ahead."

"He cut his way out the back of the tent with his knife— a Bowie knife. I was waiting for him. While I was ordering him to drop the knife, the woman, Alice, came out of the tent and took a shot at me with a pistol. She missed, on account of the darkness, I believe. I took the pistol away from her, and that's when Baltierrez jumped me. I pistol-whipped him and he went down. When he rolled over, he had a pistol in his hand, and he fired at me. He missed, too. That's when I shot him dead."

"So the woman and Baltierrez both took shots at you, and at close range, and they both missed?"

"Yes, sir."

"You must be living right, Sheriff."

"I was pretty lucky that day."

"I should say. Anything else you care to add?"

"Not a thing."

"Did you threaten Arlon Reno and those other men?"

"Nope. Didn't have to."

"You're dismissed, Sheriff. Are there any other persons who care to testify under oath in this matter? . . . Very well, the jury may begin its deliberations."

Slaughter sat patiently while the six men of the coroner's jury huddled together. A few minutes later the foreman stood up and informed the judge that they had reached a verdict.

"Well, then get on over here and tell me what it is, George," said the judge.

The foreman did as he was told. The judge listened and nodded and looked at Slaughter.

"It is the verdict of this coroner's jury, having heard the testimony as has been brought before us, that the man known as Geronimo Baltierrez met his death in the Chiricahua Mountains on April thirteenth last from gunshot wounds inflicted by the sheriff of Cochise County in the discharge of his duties." The judge struck his table with a gavel. "This inquest is hereby concluded."

John Clum interrupted Slaughter in the street outside the Mining Exchange Building.

"I'm curious," said Clum. "What evidence did you have that Baltierrez was involved in that robbery, Texas John?"

"Call it a hunch."

Clum smiled wryly. "You had no intentions of bringing him back alive, did you?"

Slaughter fired up one of his Mexican cheroots. "I say, John, you're not trying to muddy my water, are you?"

"Just seem to recall you being pretty hard on the Earps for doing the same kind of thing you did up in Dead Horse Canyon."

"There's a small difference. I haven't gunned down an unarmed man like Tom McLaury."

"Well, some people believe that Baltierrez was unarmed."

"They can believe whatever they want. And you can print whatever you want in that newspaper of yours, John. But as I recollect, the governor once said that what Cochise County needed was for the lawless to be brought to a speedy and severe punishment. And I think that's what you wanted, too, wasn't it?"

"Yes, I suppose so."

"Well, then," said Slaughter, and began to walk away. "You and the governor are going to get your wish."

CHAPTER FOURTEEN

CLEANING OUT THE COWBOYS

IN THE MONTHS THAT FOLLOWED THE KILLING OF GERONIMO Baltierrez, John Slaughter made life hard for the scofflaws of Cochise County.

He did not rely on posses. Having spent some time as a Texas Ranger, Slaughter had adopted that outfit's motto: One fight, one man. He relied on a few good deputies—Jeff Milton being one. And there was Lorenzo Paca, a wily old Mexican who could track better than an Apache. Occasionally Slaughter took one or the other man along with him in pursuit of an outlaw. But more often than not he rode alone on his tall gray gelding. Sometimes he brought his man in alive. Often, though, he dispensed justice out of the barrel of a gun.

Eduardo Moreno was a horse thief of considerable ill repute. He and his associates had operated in Cochise County with impunity for quite some time. So long, in fact, that they thumbed a contemptuous nose at the law. Their base of operations was located in the Huachuca Mountains. They kept the stock they stole in box canyons where springs supplied ample water, but made their camp on a high rocky table with only a single steep trail providing access. The trail was always guarded, and Moreno and his men were said to be crack shots. Little wonder, folks said, that no lawman had ventured into the Huachucas after them. And when Slaughter decided it was time to end Moreno's career, and rode alone to bag the horse-stealer in his lair, there were some in Tombstone who bet serious money that Cochise County would soon be in need of a new sheriff.

Slaughter had asked around about Moreno and his hide-out, and Lorenzo Paca had, too, so when he arrived in the Huachucas, Slaughter knew better than to try to negotiate the guarded trail. Instead, he scaled a two-hundred-foot cliff, arriving at the top just as a new day broke. Moreno and two men were still in their blankets when Slaughter called out for them to put their hands up. The horse thieves came up shooting instead, and Slaughter picked them off with his long gun. A fourth man, who had been on duty as lookout at the top of the trail all night, avoided the fate of his companions by fleeing down into the canyon below and making tracks out of the mountains on one of the stolen ponies.

Leaving the dead men to lie where they had fallen, and making note of the brands on the stolen stock, Slaughter rode back to Tombstone to inform the county attorney that Arizona had three less horse thieves to worry about. The owners of the stolen horses were informed of the whereabouts of their stock. When they returned from the Huachucas they confirmed the killings.

Another horse thief met the same fate, though no one, not even Slaughter, ever knew his name. The man made off with a black thoroughbred, a racehorse that was the pride and joy of the sheriff's father-in-law. Amazon "Cap" Howell had done well for himself at long last, not as a cattleman, but rather as a dairy farmer, providing Tombstone and nearby communities with a precious commodity— milk. When the black racehorse was taken, Slaughter set out after the culprit. Several people reported seeing a young Mexican astride the black, heading for the border in haste. Those same witnesses later saw Slaughter returning to

Tombstone a couple of days later with the black in tow. No one needed to ask what had befallen the thief. Clearly he had made a fatal mistake—resisting arrest.

The Cowboys were still operating in Cochise County. Curly Bill Brocius had been done in by Wyatt Earp in the Iron Springs shootout, and Johnny Ringo had committed suicide. Deprived of the leadership provided by these two characters, the Cowboys were not as active as they had once been, but they were still a nuisance, and still operating out of Galeyville, as lawless a town as any on the frontier. When Slaughter heard that one of the Cowboys, a man named Ed Lyle, was threatening to dispatch the sheriff to Boot Hill, he figured it was time to clean up Galeyville once and for all.

Again he rode alone—straight into Galeyville, where no one wearing a tin star had ever ventured before. That kind of brass threw many of the town's hardcases off stride, so no one interfered when Slaughter strolled into a saloon where Ed Lyle was whiling away the afternoon. Lyle was belly up to the bar, trying to empty a bottle of who-hit-john all by himself. The whiskey emboldened him, and when Slaughter walked up and informed him that he was under arrest, Lyle went for his gun. He was plenty quick, and got the hogleg cleared of the holster and cocked. Slaughter grabbed the gun and thrust a finger under the hammer so that when Lyle pulled the trigger, it was to no effect. Slaughter's rock-hard fist connected with Lyle's jaw a second later and sent the outlaw reeling. Hauling the man to his feet, Slaughter bounced his head off the bar a few times, then dragged the bleeding and unconscious prisoner out into the street and fired his six-gun at the sky in order to get the attention of everyone in the vicinity.

"I'm taking this varmint to Tombstone," announced Slaughter as about two dozen men gathered around—sullen, well-armed men who looked less like law-abiding citizens than any bunch the Texan had ever laid eyes on. "Then I'm coming back here. And every man who's still here when I do had better be able to prove he has an honest job, or he'll be joining this sorry son of a bitch in jail."

He was as good as his word, and a week later, when he visited Galeyville again, this time with Jeff Milton at his side, it was to discover that more than twenty of the Cowboys had departed Cochise County. The rest had faded back into the mountains. The Tombstone *Epitaph* trumpeted the glad tidings—at long last the Cowboys' reign of terror was over. But Slaughter wasn't so sure.

A few weeks later he found out that the Cowboys weren't quite finished after all.

He had bought a small house in Tombstone after winning the election as sheriff, knowing that he would be spending a lot of time in town—much more than he really wanted to. And sometimes Viola brought the children and stayed with him for a spell. But when the Cowboys came calling one hot summer night, Slaughter was glad his family was safe and sound at San Bernardino.

He had spent a long day in court. The Tombstone jail was called the Slaughter Hotel these days because he and his deputies kept it filled with prisoners. The county attorney had decided to free up some cells by dispensing with the cases of the petty criminals being accommodated there at the people's expense, and Slaughter had been hauling scofflaws back and forth between the jailhouse and the Mining Exchange Building for hours. When the last case had been heard, he went to the Occidental and had dinner and a whiskey, then trudged home to his small adobe house at the end of Fourth Street on the edge of town. It was a location that suited him; he had never cottoned to living in the midst of a lot of people, and he wanted to be as far removed as possible from the nightly din that issued forth from the saloons and gambling dens that lined Allen Street's north side.

Throwing open a window to let in what little night breeze there was, Slaughter put his Winchester in a gun rack and laid his scattergun on a table. Unbuckling his gunbelt, he draped it over the back of a rocking chair and then sat down with a glass of whiskey within easy reach on a side table, and the most recent edition of the *Epitaph* open on his lap. The chair was located near the window, turned so that he could look out; sometimes at night, when the moon was full, he could gaze out the window and see the craggy outlines of the Dragoon Mountains against the indigo sky. Sometimes, too, he heard the plaintive howl of a coyote or a wolf, a sound that he was fond of, for it spoke as nothing else could of wild, wide-open spaces.

Slaughter began to read the newspaper, but his eyelids soon grew heavy. The house had two rooms, and he gave some thought to trying to muster enough energy to get up and go to the narrow iron-frame bed in the back room. But tonight he missed Viola even more than usual, and the prospect of going to bed without her did not appeal to him in the least. So he allowed himself to drift off to sleep sitting up in the rocking chair.

Some instinct of danger woke him, and even before he could pry his eyes open he heard an indistinct sound outside the window. Those years of outwitting Comanches on the Texas frontier served him well that night, for even as he opened his eyes and glimpsed the six-shooter aimed at him through the open window scant feet away, he was already on the move, responding to that instinct by lashing out with one arm to smash the glass chimney of the lamp on the side table, extinguishing the flame dancing on the end of the wick and plunging the room into darkness. At the same time he plunged sideways, overturning the chair. An instant later the six-shooter spoke. The gunshot was deafening, and Slaughter heard the bullet splinter the wood of the rocking chair a heartbeat before he hit the floor. The holstered Colt was somewhere near at hand, but the bright muzzle flash of his would-be assassin's gun momentarily blinded him, so he gave up any thought of groping around for his own hogleg. Instead, he gathered himself up and lunged for the long table where he had left the scattergun. Reaching it, he

got the sawed-off shotgun in hand and whirled to fire one
barrel at the window. Glass shattered, wood splintered. He
heard a man shout somewhere outside, and threw down the
scattergun to take his Winchester out of the gun rack on
the wall next to the door.

Rushing outside, Slaughter glimpsed movement at the
corner of the house ten feet to his left, and fired the Winchester at hip level, getting off two shots at a moving shape.
The sound of a man—maybe two men—running along the
side of the house drew him to the corner, but he was not
so reckless that he charged around that corner in haste. His
back to the adobe wall, he listened for a moment. Only
when he heard horses at the gallop did he go around the
corner. Two riders were fleeing the scene, and he sent hot
lead after them. One of the men returned fire, but Slaughter
coolly stood his ground and got off two more shots, knowing it was highly unlikely that the other man would hit his
mark from the back of a hard-running horse in the darkness.
As the pair were swallowed up by the night, Slaughter felt
certain he had hit one of his assailants.

A few moments later men came running, and in no time
at all a crowd had gathered. The city marshal arrived and
Slaughter, puffing on a Mexican cheroot, and with his
nerves already smoothed out nicely from a good stiff shot
of bourbon, told his colleague what had transpired.

"Did you get a look at them, John?" asked the marshal.

"I haven't yet," replied Slaughter.

"Which way did they go?"

"Out of town. Reckon that means they're in my jurisdiction."

The city marshal didn't seem too disappointed. "Yeah,
but maybe not for long. Like as not they'll keep riding until
they're in New Mexico."

"I doubt that. At least one of them is carrying a bullet,
unless I miss my guess."

John Clum appeared and pulled Slaughter aside. "Texas
John, I want you to know that I and the Citizens' Com-

mittee are ready to lend you a hand. All you have to do is
say the word."

"No, thanks," said Slaughter.

"I know how you feel about vigilante justice. But you've
got the Cowboys riled up now. The Earp brothers found
out the hard way what happens next. Now it looks to be
your turn."

"No, I'll deal with the Cowboys."

Clum shook his head. "I do believe you are the most
stubborn man I have ever met, Texas John."

The next morning at daybreak Slaughter rode out of
Tombstone on the trail of the men who had tried to murder
him. Jeff Milton was not available, being down on the border on the trail of cattle thieves, but Lorenzo Paca was
present and accounted for. The old Mexican looked like a
poor sheepherder, but in his case Slaughter knew how deceiving looks could be. Apart from being an expert tracker,
Paca was a tough-as-nails fighter with as much grit as any
man Slaughter had ever known. The Cochise County sheriff
didn't mind at all having such a man to back him up.

In the beginning the trail wasn't hard to follow, and it
soon became obvious that one of the men they were after
was bleeding badly. About five miles out of town the pair
had stopped, and Paca calculated that they had spent a couple of hours there before moving on. He told Slaughter that
the wounded man had lain on the ground and his wound
had been dressed. That explained why they didn't see any
more blood from that point on. The two outlaws were on
the move the rest of the night and all the next day, stopping
infrequently to rest their horses. They were heading east—
for the Chiricahua Mountains, was Slaughter's guess—and
making fairly good time, so that he had to conclude that
either the wounded man was one tough hombre or the
wound itself was not as serious as all the blood they'd seen
earlier had seemed to indicate. "I hit him," Slaughter told
Paca, "but not where it counted."

"I think you will get another chance," predicted the old Mexican.

By day's end they were nearing the mountains, and they had gained some ground on their prey. In spite of that, Slaughter decided to wait until morning before venturing into the mountains. The task of tracking the pair over rocky ground was not going to be easy. And both he and his gray gelding were trail-weary. Paca and his old mule, on the other hand, looked none the worse for wear after the long hard ride from Tombstone. *I must be getting old,* mused Slaughter. But even that was no excuse in this case. Lorenzo Paca had seen sixty years if he'd seen a day, and he looked to be good for another fifty miles without stopping to rest.

They camped in the foothills, near a spring that Paca knew about—he knew about every water source in the territory, with northern Mexico thrown in for good measure. They nighted about two hundred yards from the water—you didn't want to stay too close to a spring in this country; a wolf pack might come along and spook the horses, or a herd of wild horses might show up, or renegade Indians, or even an outlaw gang. So they let their horses drink, filled their canteens, and moved off into a stand of scrub cedar.

The crack of dawn found them on the move again, plunging into the Chiricahua Mountains, and the trail became more difficult for Slaughter to spot. Paca, though, didn't seem to have any trouble in that regard. The Mexican led the way through a labyrinth of canyons. Around midday he stopped and turned to Slaughter.

"The men, they go into this box canyon," he said, pointing. "There is no way out for a man on horseback. You would have to climb out, or come back this way."

"They may just hole up in there. I don't relish sitting out here and waiting on them. Might take till Christmas."

Paca nodded. "*Sí.* There is an old prospector's cabin about half a mile up the canyon. They could be there."

"Will they see us coming up the canyon?"

"*Sí*, they will, I am sure of it."

Slaughter grimaced, then glanced up the steep canyon walls.

"I had to do some climbing back when I was after the Moreno gang. I reckon we better climb this time, too, and try to circle around behind and above them."

They left their horses a hundred yards from the entrance to the box canyon and began the long climb. Paca led the way and made his ascent with the sure-footed agility of a mountain goat. It was all Slaughter could do to keep up with the man. Within an hour, though, they were on a high rib of rock directly above a derelict shack. Two horses were tethered at the side of the structure, which stood on a narrow ledge about fifty feet above the canyon floor. Slaughter figured he and Paca were at least a hundred and fifty feet above the prospector's shack, which was backed up against the cliff.

Paca spent some time studying the sheer rock face below them. "I think we can get down there without being seen," he said finally.

Slaughter was paying some attention to the big rocks around him and replied, "That may not be necessary." He aimed his Winchester at the sky and fired off two rounds. "You men in the cabin!" he yelled. "This is Sheriff John Slaughter. Come out with your hands high!"

Paca unlimbered the Spencer carbine slung on his back. Like its owner, the Civil War–vintage Spencer was old but reliable. The .52-caliber weapon only carried seven rounds, but Paca could make every last one of them count.

"Come and get us, Slaughter!" came the defiant reply, followed immediately by a gunshot. Slaughter spotted a rifle barrel jutting out a side window, but the shooter was unable to get the proper angle and the shot went wide.

"Well, I say, Lorenzo," drawled Slaughter, "they can't get a shot at us from inside that shack."

"But we can't get a clean shot at them, either," observed Paca.

Slaughter smiled. "Maybe we can flush them out. What say you give me a hand with this rock?"

Paca set down the Spencer and joined the Texan in putting his back to a boulder that was about the size of a buffalo calf and poised on the rim. One good strong heave sent the boulder rolling over the edge. It bounced once, twice, then sailed through the air—falling right through the roof of the shack with a rending crash.

Cursing, a man exploded out the front of the cabin, circling to the side where the horses were tethered and firing a rifle up at the rim as fast as he could work the lever action.

"Goddamn you, Slaughter!" he roared. "You killed Buck, you son of a bitch!"

As the bullets sang off the rocks, Paca dove for his Spencer. But Slaughter stood straight and tall, seemingly oblivious to the hail of hot lead. Bringing the Winchester to shoulder, he drew a bead and squeezed the trigger. The man down below sprawled backward, his rifle falling from a dead hand.

They made their way down the cliff, a treacherous descent, and while Paca checked the dead man, Slaughter cautiously approached the cabin. He went in at an angle, a crouching run, rifle ready. But the second fugitive was also dead. This had been the one whose blood they had seen—he had been shot in the leg right below the knee and the wound was wrapped in blood-soaked rags. He lay on a narrow bunk in one corner of the shack—or rather, what had once been a bunk and was now a pile of kindling. The boulder had landed squarely on top of the wounded man. All Slaughter could see was an arm and two legs. He was glad of that.

"He was right," said the Texan when he went out to rejoin Paca, and nodding at the man he had shot. "I killed Buck, all right."

CHAPTER FIFTEEN

❦

SAN BERNARDINO

THE NEXT DAY WHEN THE RESIDENTS OF GALEYVILLE AWOKE, they were confronted by a very unusual sight—a corpse lying in the middle of the street, head resting on a saddle, arms neatly draped over the chest. Many of the Galeyville inhabitants knew who the dead man was—Ed Kelsey, a member of the Cowboys. They also knew that Kelsey and his partner, Buck Long, had vowed to kill Sheriff John Slaughter. So there wasn't much question regarding whose bullet had killed Kelsey, nor as to the fate that had befallen Long.

Slaughter and his deputy, Lorenzo Paca, had carried Ed Kelsey's body to Galeyville to deliver a message, and the dozen or so Cowboys who remained in town understood what they were trying to convey. Within a day or two the majority of them had packed up and departed Cochise County, never to return. The Cowboys were done for. They no longer posed a threat to the law-abiding citizens of Arizona Territory.

On his way back to Tombstone, Slaughter decided to stop off at home for a day or two. He was always heartily glad to be back at San Bernardino. Much had been accomplished in eight short years, in spite of his frequent and prolonged absences, first on trips to buy or sell cattle and now as county sheriff. Encircling the main ranch house, which had been expanded from a modest two-room adobe to a spacious and comfortable home, was an icehouse, a washhouse, a commissary adjoining one of two bunkhouses, and a water supply tank. To the east of these buildings was a large water reservoir encompassed by a rock wall, and beyond this was a schoolhouse standing in the shade of a row of cottonwoods.

There were a number of Mexican families living on the ranch, and some of Slaughter's cowboys had gotten married. Will Watkins, for example, lived with his wife and young daughters in a small house a couple hundred yards south of the reservoir. As the years passed, there were more and more children on the spread, and since the nearest school was fifteen miles away in Douglas, Slaughter had decided it was necessary to build one on his property. As a youngster back in Texas he had been an indifferent student, preferring to roam the *brasada* hills to sitting on a hard wooden bench with his nose stuck in a musty-smelling book. In retrospect he regretted his failure to pay more attention to his studies, and resolved that the San Bernardino children be afforded the best possible education. To this end he employed a Tombstone woman named Edith Stowe as schoolteacher.

South of the ranch house were a barn, corrals, cemetery, and a few irrigated fields where corn and other vegetables were grown. Slaughter's goal was for San Bernardino to be as self-sufficient as possible. Like a south-of-the-border *hacendero*, he was the *padrone* to nearly a hundred people—about two dozen Mexican *campesinos*, thirty to forty cowboys, and just as many women and children. He depended on the sweat of their brow to keep the ranch functioning properly, and they depended on him to provide their food and shelter.

When he arrived home, Slaughter learned from Old Bat that Viola and his daughter Addie, now seventeen years of age, were out riding.

"Not alone, I hope," said Slaughter.

"You know better than that, boss. Tom Cochran, he be with 'em. Whenever you see Miss Viola, you know old Tom's around someplace."

"Well, I'm glad he is. He saved Viola's life once. I know that's the way she sees it, and she feels safe with him. Where's my boy?"

"He be in school," replied the ex-slave. "Though Willie don't cotton to that book-learning."

Slaughter grinned. "He takes after me in that regard."

"He'll be happy as a lark for an excuse to get away from Miss Stowe. She rides them kids plenty hard, and she won't cut Mr. Willie no slack just because he's your flesh and blood."

"Good. I wouldn't want her to."

"I'll go fetch him for you."

"No. It can wait until school is out. Send somebody off to find Del, will you?"

Old Bat nodded. "I'll do it myself. I know right where to find him—the branding ground over on Silver Creek."

Del Hooper was San Bernardino's *caporal,* its foreman, and as such ran the place in Slaughter's absence. Outsiders were somewhat surprised to learn that Slaughter's cowboys—most of whom were Southern-born—didn't seem to mind at all that they had to take orders from a black man. The fact was that Del Hooper had proven himself to be a top hand. He had earned the respect of the other men. On San Bernardino it didn't matter what color your skin was as long as you did your job. And nobody could best Del Hooper when it came to cowboying.

Lorenzo Paca watered his horse and rode on for Tombstone. Slaughter whiled away the afternoon looking through the ranch ledgers. It made him acutely aware of how much time he had spent away from home in past years. Not for the first time he wondered if he had done the right thing in taking the job as county lawman. But then all he had to do to put those second thoughts to rest was recall the attack on Viola, and that strengthened his resolve. He would do what had to be done to make certain his wife and daughter and anyone else could travel through Cochise County without fear. Only then would he take off the tin star and return to the life he wanted to lead. Yes, there were sacrifices he had to make, chief among them the long absences from Viola and his children. But Slaughter had never been one to shirk a task because of the hardships it entailed.

Later that afternoon, Viola and Addie and Cochran returned, and Slaughter went outside to greet them—just in time to see Viola jump a barbed-wire fence on her Kentucky thoroughbred, a recent gift from her father, Cap Howell. The sight made Slaughter's heart leap into his throat. But he could not bring himself to scold her. She was young and carefree—he had to keep reminding himself that she wasn't that much older than Addie. And she was so damned pretty, with her laughing blue eyes so full of life and her long luxuriant brown hair whipped by the wind. She spotted her husband and called out to him in delight and galloped up to the ranch house to leap out of the saddle and fly into his arms. Slaughter felt old watching her, but when he held her in his arms and kissed her warm and willing lips, he felt young all over again.

"Hello, you handsome stranger, you!" she said, beaming.

"God, I missed you, darlin'," he said, his voice husky with emotion. He tore his eyes off her and looked at Addie and grinned. He always grinned when he looked at his daughter—and Willie, too, for that matter. Addie was the spitting image of her mother, and it made Slaughter feel good to know that Eliza lived in their daughter. "How's my gal?" he asked.

Addie jumped down and ran to her father. With one arm around her and the other around Viola, Slaughter couldn't help feeling that the world was not going to get much better. He nodded at Cochran, who had dismounted to take hold of all the women's horses.

"Howdy, Tom. You've got yourself a tough job keeping up with these two. I don't envy you."

Cochran shrugged. "You won't see me complaining." He glanced at Viola. "I'll take care of your horses, ma'am."

She smiled at him. "Thanks for the company, Tom."

Cochran nodded and turned away. It seemed to Slaughter that something had been bothering Tom lately. Cochran had once been a bona fide ne'er-do-well who never seemed to take anything too seriously. But he was plenty serious these days. Yet for Slaughter the thought was a fleeting one, and he turned his attention back to Viola and Addie.

Taking his sweet time tending to the three horses, Cochran paid no attention to the dinner bell—Old Bat beating on the iron triangle in front of the commissary like there was no tomorrow. Having watered, groomed, and fed the animals, he made his way at long last to the bunkhouse. The rest of the boys had finished eating. Cochran didn't care, he didn't have much of an appetite. Seeing that Slaughter was home had ruined it. Tad Roland was cleaning his guns—Tad went through the same ritual every night, whether he had fired his irons or not. Luke was toiling over a letter for back home. Wake Benge and two others were sitting at a table playing cards.

"Here you go, Tom," said Benge. "How about a few hands of draw poker?"

Cochran shook his head and stretched out on his bunk, hands behind his head.

"Come on, now, pard," persisted Benge. "I know you got money to burn. You don't never go to the saloons in Tombstone no more. And from what I've been told, the ladies there ain't enjoyed your company for ages."

"He ain't interested in them," said a cowboy by the name of Clete Hogan. "He got his sights set on one lady in particular and that's all she wrote."

Roland didn't look up from his guns as he drawled,

"Clete, you had better mind your own business."

Clete grinned. He moved to lean against a wall nearer Cochran's bunk and proceeded to build himself a smoke.

"Hell, Tom, I don't know why you're wearing such a long face tonight. You got to spend the whole day with the lady in question."

"Ignore him, Tom," advised Benge.

"Listen," said Clete, "you all know that what I'm saying is the truth. You'd have to be stone blind not to see it. I reckon Tom here is blue on account of the boss is back. See, when Texas John is away, Tom here can make believe he's the big augur. Why, he already thinks he's better than the rest of us, on account of how Miss Slaughter likes his company over ours."

"My God, Clete," said Benge. "You're just tired of living, that's all I can figure."

Cochran swung long legs off the bunk and stood up. Clete watched him, wary now, a sneering smile on his lips. But Cochran didn't even seem to notice Clete. Instead, he looked at the other cowboys. All of them had stopped what they had been doing and were watching him, expecting trouble. Everyone except Roland, who was acting like nothing out of the ordinary was happening. That was because Tad was a good friend. He knew, just like the others, that what Clete was saying was true. And Tad had to know, too, that it was an embarrassing moment for his pard. That was why he was going about his business. Cochran realized the awful truth then and there—that he had been fooling himself, thinking that he had managed to keep his true feelings about Viola Slaughter a secret. All the San Bernardino cowboys knew. Hell, John Slaughter himself would have known by now but for the fact that he was away so much being Cochise County's badge toter. As it stood, Texas John was bound to find out sooner rather than later. That would be bad enough. But worse than that would be when Viola learned the truth. Cochran knew exactly how she would react. She would pity him. And pity was the last thing he wanted to see in her eyes or hear in her voice. The very last thing.

So there was only one thing left for him to do. Because as much as he wanted to avoid Viola's pity, he wanted even more to avoid creating problems for her. Who could say what damage he could do to her life, her marriage? Yes, she was innocent of any wrongdoing. But John Slaughter might always wonder.

Cochran finally glanced at Clete. He knew that Clete resented him, though he had never been certain why. Right then and there he wanted to beat the hell out of Clete, wanted it so bad that he could almost taste it. But what good would that do? Instead, he simply walked out of the bunkhouse without saying a word.

The next morning, shortly before dawn, Slaughter headed down to the barn where his gray gelding was stabled. Cochran was waiting for him there.

"Morning, Tom. I never used to be able to get you up this early in the morning when we were trailing cattle."

"You leaving, boss?"

"Tomorrow is soon enough. No, I thought I'd go see about scaring up some breakfast."

"Mind if I ride along?"

"Not at all. I'd like the company."

Slaughter was sporting a ten-gauge English shotgun, and Cochran knew he was after quail. When he was home, Texas John liked to have quail on toast for breakfast. He insisted on preparing the meal himself, even though San Bernardino's main house now boasted an accomplished Chinese cook. Old Bat cooked the grub for the hands— beans and sourdough biscuits were the ex-slave's specialties—but the Chinaman did most of the cooking for the Slaughter family and their guests. In fact, the kitchen was his private domain—and that claim was never disputed, except when Slaughter brought quail home for breakfast.

They rode for a while in silence. Cochran had a lot on his mind, but he waited until they had started several coveys and Slaughter had bagged his prey. When he had eight birds in the sack tied to his saddle horn, Texas John turned for home.

"I say, Tom, what's on your mind today?"

"I've been thinking," said Cochran, not surprised that Slaughter had been able to tell something was bothering him. "You've had some trouble finding good men to serve as deputies, haven't you?"

"Well, you know what they say. You don't wear a badge in Cochise County unless you're tired of life."

"I'll wear a star."

"You?" Slaughter peered at Cochran. "You're not tired of living, are you, Tom?" he asked, joking.

"Nope. Just tired of cowboying."

"This have anything to do with what happened on the road to Tombstone?"

It seemed to Cochran as good an excuse as any. He had to have a reason, and he sure couldn't use the real one.

"Sort of," he replied. "I know you took care of the man who shot me. But there are still plenty more like him out there, and like you I'd be pleased to see the day when women and children can travel these parts without fear."

"I see," said Slaughter, noncommittal.

"I'm a better than fair hand with a pistol or a long gun."

"Yes, I know you are, Tom."

"And I don't back down from trouble."

"That's true. You never have for as long as I've known you."

"And maybe best of all, I know how owlhoots think. I've ridden the outlaw trail myself."

Slaughter gave Cochran a long and sober look that the latter could not quite fathom.

"You sure that's why you want to be a deputy sheriff?"

Cochran's heart skipped a beat. Why was Texas John asking that question? Was it possible that he knew the truth, as did apparently everyone else at San Bernardino?

"Sure I'm sure. Why else?"

Slaughter shrugged. "Just thought maybe you were getting bored. In the mood to hunt up a little excitement."

Cochran thought it over. "No, that's not the reason. I told you why, boss."

Slaughter nodded. "Good. 'Cause that would be the wrong reason."

They rode on for a spell without a word, and Cochran started to fret. What if Slaughter turned him down? Then he would just have to ride away. Get as far away from San Bernardino as he could. He realized full well that no matter how many hundreds of miles he put between himself and Viola, he would love her as fervently as he did at this moment. That would never end. No other woman would be able to replace her in his heart. And he would suffer all the more for never being able to see her again. But if that was what it took, then so be it.

Even though it would be better to get killed—and getting killed seemed to be pretty damned likely if he was a deputy sheriff of Cochise County.

"Okay," said Slaughter, out of the blue. "You can come to Tombstone with me tomorrow and we'll put you on the payroll and have the magistrate swear you in."

"Thanks."

"But you know Viola won't like it. She won't like to see you go."

That comment was another shock to Cochran's system, though he understood no implications were hidden there, that there was nothing between the lines for him to read.

"Oh, I doubt it'll trouble her all that much," he said in an offhand way.

When they got back to the ranch Slaughter invited him to have breakfast with the family, but Cochran declined, saying he wasn't hungry. He was down by the corrals, watching the horses but not really seeing them, lost in thought, when Viola came to him.

"John tells me you've volunteered to be his deputy," she said.

"That's right, I have."

She was quiet for a moment, pretending to watch the horses, too. Then, at last, she said, "I thought you liked it here, Tom. That you thought of San Bernardino as your home."

In the purest agony, Cochran groped for words. "I—I don't really have a home. I mean, I'm not the sort who really needs one."

"Oh." She looked straight at him then, very earnestly, and he looked away, but not before catching a glimpse of sadness in her blue eyes. "Well, Tom, we'll all miss you terribly."

He just nodded, and she turned and walked away, and not turning to watch her go was the hardest thing Tom Cochran had ever done.

CHAPTER SIXTEEN

———◆———

CROSSING THE LINE

COCHRAN HAD BEEN AT HIS NEW JOB LESS THAN A MONTH when he first heard the name Agustin Chacon.

He was sitting in the office of the Tombstone jail, feet propped up on the scarred kneehole desk, trying to pay attention to the news contained in the most recent edition of the Tombstone *Epitaph*. Problem was, he was bored almost beyond reason. Since pinning on a deputy's star, he had been relegated to keeping the jail and transporting petty criminals. Slaughter regularly called upon Lorenzo Paca to locate or track elusive outlaws, while Jeff Milton was usually far afield, too, these days, charged with bringing down dangerous lawbreakers. Cochran ached for action because he thought that might help get Viola off his mind. He missed seeing her, missed being with her, or at least near her, so much that it hurt. On several occasions he'd had the opportunity to visit San Bernardino, but he had somehow managed to muster up enough willpower to decline.

Watching over a bunch of jailbirds in the Slaughter Hotel was giving him serious second thoughts about staying on as a Cochise County deputy sheriff. Making sure that prisoners got their two meals a day, listening to their constant complaining, and breaking up the quarrels that frequently erupted in the overcrowded cells was worse than any other job Cochran could imagine. Every single day he reached the verge of quitting on Texas John. And not a day passed that he didn't tell himself he ought to haul his freight for California or some other far-distant location. But for some reason—one he could not fully explain to himself—he couldn't bring himself to leave.

Then Chacon came to Tombstone.

The first Cochran heard of it was when Slaughter burst into the office and grabbed some extra shells for his scattergun. It was as clear as mother's milk that trouble was brewing. In fact, Cochran could not remember ever having seen Texas John so solemn.

"What the heck is going on?" asked Cochran.

"Arm yourself and follow me," rasped Slaughter, and marched out.

Grabbing a Winchester repeating rifle and a box of cartridges from the gun case, Cochran did as he was told. It was a cool autumn evening. The sun had bedded down beyond the western horizon an hour ago, and the indigo night sky was alive with stars. It was too early for the half-moon, so the night shadows were deep. Lamplight spilled out of windows to throw patches of gold on the wide, rutted streets of gray dust. Something had set off a half dozen dogs to barking, and from a nearby saloon issued the tinny cacophony of an out-of-tune piano.

Slaughter was moving down the street with long strides full of purpose, and Cochran had to break into a run to catch up with him. It occurred to Cochran that as far as he could remember, John Slaughter had never been leery of facing alone a situation that had the potential for gunplay. So it followed that whatever was happening had to be pretty damned serious, else the sheriff would not have felt the need for someone to back him up. But Cochran knew better than to ask Slaughter a lot of questions. He would find out the details soon enough.

They reached the Mining Exchange Building. Slaughter pulled up and turned to his deputy.

"Chacon has come up from Mexico. I'm told he's in a shanty up that gulch behind this building. I aim to take him in."

"Chacon? I don't know the name. Who the hell is he?"

"He's a killer, and by all accounts he's told everyone up and down the border that he is going to kill me."

"What's he got against you?"

Slaughter drew a deep breath. "My hunch is he's been hired to kill me, and I have an idea who might have employed him. That's why I want him alive, Tom. I'll make him give me the name of the man who's paying him."

Cochran nodded, eyes bright with excitement. This was just the kind of thing he had been hoping for. "Let's go get him, then." He started for the corner of the Mining Exchange Building.

"Hold up a minute, Tom."

"What is it?"

"Don't go acting like a greenhorn and getting yourself killed. From what I've been able to learn, Chacon is the most dangerous hombre in Sonora."

They moved around behind the building and down into the rocky gulch. Cochran saw a dimly lit window up ahead. A hundred yards from the shack, Slaughter grabbed Cochran's arm.

"You go on up to the front of the shack, Tom, and call out. Tell Chacon he's under arrest and to come out with his hands up. I doubt he will without a fight, or maybe he'll try to run. I'll circle around behind. If he tries to get away, I'll be back there to bag him."

"What I don't get is how come he'd challenge you the way he has and then just set himself up like this, like he's asking to be arrested."

Slaughter smiled tautly. "Because Chacon doesn't think anybody would be a big enough fool to brace him. Not even me. He's convinced all he's got to do is come and get me when he's good and ready."

"He doesn't know you very well, then."

"Not yet he doesn't. Give me five minutes."

Cochran hunkered down and kept an eye on the shack as Slaughter vanished into the night making no more noise than an Apache. When he calculated that three minutes had passed, Cochran moved in on the tent. Thirty feet from it, he called out.

"You in there! This is the law. Come out with your hands empty."

The light inside the shack was abruptly extinguished, and Cochran raised the Winchester, only to lower it and break into a run when he heard a shattering of timber, followed in short order by a shotgun blast from back of the shanty. Then Slaughter let out a shout, punctuated by the roar of the scattergun's second barrel discharging its lethal load. This was followed by the tattoo of a horse's iron-shod hooves on stony ground. Cochran saw the shape of a man standing on the rim of a gully and took it to be Slaughter. "That you, Texas John?" Just to be on the safe side, he moved to his right a few steps as soon as he had spoken.

"It's me," said Slaughter, sounding thoroughly disgusted. "That's one slippery son of a bitch."

Cochran peered down into the gully. The sound of the horse was fading rapidly. He couldn't see a thing. It was as black as pitch down there.

"Must have kept his horse saddled and ready."

"He came right through the back wall of the shack," explained Slaughter. "I was watching the window. Surprised me. I triggered one barrel, but just as I did, he fell down, and then he rolled right over the edge into the gully, I reckon."

Cochran went around to the front of the shack and kicked the door so hard it came off its leather hinges and fell flat on the earthen floor. He scratched a sulfur match to life and found the lantern and lit it so that he could examine the interior. There was no furniture, and all Chacon had left behind was a blanket, a knife, and a half-consumed can of peaches. The shack was a derelict, but even in its better days could not have boasted sound construction; the weather-warped planks on dry rotted studs had not posed much of an obstacle for Chacon.

Slaughter called to him from outside. Blowing out the lantern, Cochran left the shack.

"You reckon he'll come back?" he asked Slaughter.

"Who the hell knows about that? He might. And next time, if he's smart, which I think he is, he won't announce that he's coming."

"But it could be that we scared him off for good."

Slaughter looked at him, and Cochran was glad it was too dark to read the expression on the sheriff's face. His last remark was sheer wishful thinking and nothing more. If Chacon was half the hombre that Slaughter said he was, then he wasn't the type to be easily spooked. He had advertised that he was dead set on killing Cochise County's top lawman, and if he was the least bit concerned about his reputation, then he would be back. And reputation meant everything to such men.

"We can start after him in the morning," suggested Cochran as they headed back down the gulch in the direction of Tombstone.

"He'll be crossing the border before daybreak. I don't have jurisdiction down in Mexico, remember."

"So what are you saying, Texas John? You mean we're not going to do anything?"

"We're going to wait. I don't think we've heard the last of Chacon."

"What about finding out who hired him? Even if Chacon does give up, or if you kill him, the man who hired him will just find somebody else."

Slaughter didn't say anything. The answer was obvious. That, too, would have to wait. Cochran realized that Texas

John was right. There really wasn't much they could do besides wait for Chacon to come back. But that ran against the grain. Because next time it might be that they wouldn't know the killer had returned until it was too late—until after he'd put a bullet in his target.

There has to be something we can do, mused Cochran, dissatisfied. He mulled it over all the next day, as he hauled prisoners from the jail to the courthouse and back again. By sundown he had come up with a plan. It was a risky one, but that didn't bother him a whole lot. But it was also outside the law. To catch Chacon he would have to cross the line, like he had done once before. He would have to return to the outlaw trail. His loyalty to Slaughter stemmed from the fact that Texas John had given him the opportunity to put that kind of life behind him. It was no kind of life at all. That gave him pause. But not for very long.

That night he wrote a letter and sealed it with candle wax and left it in the keeping of a barkeep at the Oriental, a man he was pretty sure he could rely on. "Give this to the sheriff before eight in the morning, Bob. It's damned important. Don't let me down." The bartender said he would deliver the letter, and Cochran was riding out of town a quarter of an hour later. The tin star he had worn for the past few weeks was in a drawer in the kneehole desk back at the jailhouse office.

He took the road to Bisbee, and twenty miles outside Tombstone he came to a jumble of big rocks. The road curled around the outcropping to the south. Tying his horse to a greasewood bush, Cochran climbed up into the rocks. The half-moon was on the rise, casting its pale luminescence across the desert floor. A cold wind whispered down from the north. Cochran pulled his coat collar up and settled down to get some sleep, sitting propped up against a boulder with a rifle across his knees.

It surprised him that he was able to sleep so soundly, considering the circumstances. Daybreak roused him. His joints were stiff from the night chill. He clambered up to the highest point of the outcropping and watched the road in the direction of Bisbee. A half hour later he spotted the dust, and a little while after that he saw the stage heave into view. Right on schedule. But then Wells Fargo put a lot of stock in punctuality. Cochran climbed down to his horse. He took a drink from his canteen—his mouth was uncommonly dry. This he put down to nerves. Then he checked his saddle cinch and mounted up.

Ten minutes crawled by before he could hear the stage— the rattle of trace chains, the creak of timber and leather, the drumbeat of horses' hooves. Pulling a bandanna up over his face, Cochran timed it just right—spurring his horse out into the road when the coach and six-horse hitch were less than thirty yards away. The team was moving at road gait, so it took every bit of that thirty yards and then some for the reinsman to work the leathers threaded through his fingers in order to stop the team. He stopped them in lieu of whipping them up in an attempt to roll right through the lone horseman because Cochran had his rifle trained on one of the leaders. The jehu was experienced; he knew that if one of the horses was shot down, then a wreck would inevitably result, sure as night followed day. And usually, in a case like that, someone got killed.

As soon as he was sure the team was slowing to a stop, Cochran swung his rifle up at the shotgunner sitting on the stage driver's left. The Wells Fargo man was wielding a greener, and he appeared inclined to use the weapon, but the fact that the sun was right behind Cochran, blinding him, slowed him down some.

"Put that scattergun aside," said Cochran firmly, "unless you're ready to meet your Maker."

The shotgunner hesitated.

"Put it down!" rasped Cochran. "And tell your partner in the coach to throw his shootin' irons out the window."

The Wells Fargo man thought it over. He didn't want to die, but he didn't want to lose his job, either, especially if the second guard, the one who rode inside, decided to make a play.

"You all by yourself, mister?" he asked Cochran, trying to buy a little time.

"Hell, no. What kind of fool do you take me for? A man doesn't take down a Wells Fargo express alone. Everybody knows that. You've got three long guns trained on you from up in those rocks. If you don't believe that, lift that greener."

"I don't believe you."

"Oh, sure you do."

And Cochran was right. The shotgunner did believe him—because no road agent was desperate enough to hold up a Wells Fargo stage all by his lonesome. Nobody had ever tried it before.

The guard inside the coach apparently believed, too, as evidenced by the fact that he promptly tossed his pistol and sawed-off shotgun out the window and then came out with empty hands raised.

Muttering a curse, the shotgunner up top lowered the hammers on his greener and set it down in the box at his feet.

"No, that won't do," said Cochran. "Toss it over the side, and your pistol, too."

Scowling, the shotgunner obeyed.

"You." Cochran motioned with his rifle to the inside guard, now standing beside the coach. "Haul out the strongbox and put it down beside the road."

The Wells Fargo agent did as he was told.

"Now climb up on top of the coach," Cochran said.

Again the guard complied. Guiding his cowpony with his knees, Cochran rode around to the side of the coach, keeping the three men covered, and took a look inside. It was empty.

"Can we go now?" asked the reinsman. "I ain't never brought a stage in late before and I don't want to start now."

"Not yet." Cochran switched the rifle to his left hand, drew his pistol, and fired two shots at the lock on the strongbox. Then he holstered the side gun, returned the rifle to his right hand, and dismounted to kick the lid of the strongbox open. There were six canvas money sacks inside. He bent down to pick one of them up, keeping his eyes on the three men. From within the sack came the unmistakable sound of hard money.

"Okay, boys," he said cheerfully. "Just making sure you weren't leaving me a decoy strongbox full of river stones. You Wells Fargo people have been known to pull that stunt on occasion."

"You're no greenhorn at this, are you?" said the shotgunner.

"It's not my first holdup, I have to admit."

"But I reckon it's your last. If Sheriff Slaughter don't see to that, Wells Fargo sure as hell will."

"Thanks for the warning. You boys can move along now."

The reinsman was scanning the rocks. "You really got some *compadres* up there, pilgrim?"

"You really want to find out?"

The jehu grimaced and whipped up the team. Cochran kept his rifle trained on the stage until it had passed out of sight. Then he tied the money sacks to his saddle and turned his pony southward.

By the time he'd reached the border, fifteen miles later, the money sacks were gone.

True to his word, the Oriental's barkeep delivered Cochran's letter to John Slaughter before eight that morning. The sheriff had just arrived at the jail. The bartender lingered while Slaughter read the letter—he was curious to know what it was all about, and it was a credit to his integrity that he had not allowed that curiosity to tempt him to the point of reading the letter before delivering it. The expression on Slaughter's face made him more curious than ever. But the sheriff paid him no attention. In fact it seemed as though Slaughter had completely forgotten he was present.

The barkeep finally cleared his throat. "Um, everything all right, Sheriff?"

Slaughter looked up at him blankly, then swung his gaze to the window as he heard the stage roll in. The jehu shouted at the team as he climbed the leathers to bring the coach to a stop. Stuffing the letter in his pocket, Slaughter stepped outside just as the two Wells Fargo guards descended from the stage.

"We've been robbed, Sheriff. Happened three hours back, at the Mimbreno Rocks."

"How much did they get away with?"

The shotgunner wore a pained expression. "I ain't at all sure. We'll have to wire the Tucson office to find that out. But I was told it was a lot. Greenbacks and hard money both."

"Don't worry. I'll get it back."

"Not too sure how many robbers there were. Only saw one. But he said he had three *compadres* with rifles up in the rocks."

"He said that, did he?"

"If you're aiming to put a posse together, we'll ride with you."

"I'll ride alone," said Slaughter, and turned back into the jail office.

He left Tombstone a half hour later, stopping by an old adobe about a quarter mile from town to pick up Lorenzo Paca. They rode hard for the Mimbreno Rocks, then followed Tom Cochran's tracks due south. Four miles from the Bisbee road they came to a rocky creek lined with cottonwoods and cypress. A short search turned up Cochran's blue bandanna, tied to a tree's low-lying branch. At the base of that tree was a pile of stones, and under the stones were the Wells Fargo money bags.

Like Bob the bartender, Paca was intensely curious. Slaughter had told him nothing—in fact, he had scarcely spoken all day.

"Tom Cochran robbed that coach," said Slaughter. "He left a letter for me, telling me where I could find the loot."

"He must be loco," decided Paca. "First, to hold up a Wells Fargo shipment by himself. Second, to tell you where to find the money."

"Yeah, plenty loco. Wait until you hear why he did it. He's after Agustin Chacon."

"Ah." Paca was quick to put two and two together. "So he wants it known that he is a stage robber now. That way he might be able to find Chacon and get close to him—a lot closer than a deputy sheriff ever would."

Slaughter nodded. "That's about the size of it," he sighed.

"Then I was right. He is loco. What are we going to do?"

Slaughter piled the stones back on top of the money sacks, then took Cochran's bandanna from the limb and stuffed it in his pocket.

"We leave the money here, for now. If we turned it in to Wells Fargo, word would get out, and Tom would be as good as dead."

"So we go after him, boss?"

Slaughter was climbing back into the saddle. "No. We don't. I'm going back to Tombstone. Go to the judge and swear out a warrant on Tom. Then we'll put out a lot of paper on him. Plenty of wanted posters. That might just save his life down there where he's going, when you consider the kind of company he's likely to keep."

"But what will you tell the judge? He will want to know why we think it was Tom who robbed that express."

"He'll just have to take my word for it. That will have to be good enough."

Paca nodded. But he looked worried. "How long are you

going to let this money lie here? What if someone else finds it?"

"I can't worry about that. I'll give Tom a month. After that we'll come and get this loot and take it to the Wells Fargo district manager in Tucson. We'll have to tell the unvarnished truth then. But no one must know before that time. If word gets out, Tom is as good as dead. And I probably will be, too."

CHAPTER SEVENTEEN

———✦———

THE OWLHOOT TRAIL

TOM COCHRAN HAD ABSOLUTELY NO IDEA WHAT TEXAS JOHN would do when he learned all the details behind the robbery he had committed. There was the possibility that the Cochise County sheriff would return the stolen money to Wells Fargo right away. Or he might go along with the scheme Cochran had dreamed up to get himself within range of the elusive Agustin Chacon. Then, too, Slaughter might decide to give chase and try to stop him. Cochran decided he had to work on the assumption that the latter was the case. Better safe than sorry.

So he did his best to cover his tracks, using all the old tricks he had learned back in the days when he had ridden the owlhoot trail. Over soft ground he sometimes lassoed a bush and dragged it along behind him to obliterate the tracks. He changed directions often, though he consistently made his way south. When passing over stony ground, he covered his horse's iron-shod hooves with strips cut from a blanket and secured with rawhide saddle ties to the pony's hocks. When he reached a creek, he would ride either upstream or down for several miles before leaving the water. Knowing that John Slaughter was a better-than-fair hand at tracking in his own right, Cochran didn't have real high hopes of throwing the sheriff off his trail completely. And if Slaughter was accompanied by Lorenzo Paca—well, then all the time he took to obscure his trail was wasted. It was simply uncanny how well the old Mexican could read sign.

He continued south for three days after crossing over into Mexico, arriving eventually at a dusty village out in the middle of nowhere. A nearby creek irrigated poor fields where *campesinos* labored over meager crops, and a few small herds of scrawny sheep grazed the sparse foothills of a rugged mountain range west of the village. Cochran was confident that such a place would seldom if ever merit a visit by the *federales,* so he stopped to rest himself and his trail-weary mount.

The only business in town was a store that doubled as a cantina, run by a man who provided the locals with a selection of cheap manufactured goods that he freighted in from the nearest town of any consequence, which was about a hundred and twenty miles to the southeast. The cantina customers sat on rough hewn benches and empty casks at a couple of rickety tables on the morning side of the building, in the shade of a ramada fashioned from shaggy cedar poles. A man was sitting at one of the tables, leaning against the wall, hat pulled down over his face, legs stretched out and ankles crossed. By his garb Cochran took him to be a *gringo.* When the man heard Cochran approaching he lifted the brim of his hat, squinting muddy brown eyes against the day's painful glare, and his features confirmed that he was Anglo.

"Well, I'll be damned," said the man, and his face broke into a broad grin. "Another one of my own kind. We're kinda few and far between in these parts. I'll be damned!"

Cochran kept to the saddle, warily surveying his surroundings. "In more ways than one, probably," he replied.

"How do you mean, friend?"

"I mean I can only think of one reason why you'd be here in this godforsaken place."

"Yep. And that would be the same reason that brings

you, I'd bet." Still grinning, the man nodded. "You're right on the money. I'm worth more dead than alive north of the border. And unless I'm mistaken, you've got paper out on you, too. I can see it in your eyes. You're a wanted man, just like me."

"And just who are you?"

The man stood up and stepped forward to extend a hand. "Bill Stiles is the name. Right now cattle rustling is my game. 'Course, I've done just about everything that's against the law in my time."

Cochran thought about it, then shook the proffered hand.

"Started out with horse thieving back in Arkansas. Hell, I wanted to come west to seek my fame and fortune and I was just too damned poor to own a nag of my own and too damned lazy to walk. So I stole a horse from a man who had plenty of them. But he still raised holy hell 'cause I took one. Irony of it is, that damned horse was a stargazer. Worthless. For every mile between Arkansas and Colorado, that horse threw me at least once. By the way, I didn't catch your name."

"Tom Cochran."

"Well, step down, Tom, and I'll buy you a drink. I hope mescal or aguardiente suits you. They're all out of cognac and champagne here. You don't know how good it is to have a *gringo* to talk English to."

Cochran couldn't see any reason not to take Stiles up on the offer, so he dismounted. Stiles kept talking.

"Well, I got to Colorado in spite of that damned pony. Had nothing but bad luck from the get-go. Finally, one winter, it was either steal or starve. So I held up a general store. Got away with a grand total of thirteen dollars. Yeah, you heard right. Thirteen. So you can see how much attention Lady Luck was paying to me up Colorado way." Stiles stuck his head inside the adobe's doorway and shouted in Spanish. "Frederico! Wake up, you lazy bastard, and fetch my friend and me some mescal, pronto!"

Stiles continued his personal history. "As you can figure out on your own, Tom, thirteen dollars didn't take me far, so I fell in with the Grayson brothers, a pair of real hardcases who had taken up robbing trains. They were both dumber than fence posts, and we got into a shooting scrape with Pinkerton men riding a train we stopped. I didn't think it was a good idea to stop that train, but you couldn't talk no sense to the Graysons. They got themselves killed and I would have, too, if I hadn't curled the toes of one of those Pinkerton agents before he pulled the trigger on me. As it is, I still got a bullet in the leg, but I got away."

A Mexican emerged from the adobe and set cups of mescal on a table, then held out a hand, palm up, into which Stiles deposited a couple of pesos. He knocked back the mescal, gasped, and proceeded with his narrative.

"So before I knew it, I was wanted for horse stealing, robbery, and murder. Murder, even though it was self-defense. That Pinkerton man was going to plug me. They're not in the habit of taking too many prisoners. I headed south. Before I got to the border, though, a town marshal over in Lordsburg tried to kill me, too. As you can see, he didn't get the job done."

"Maybe he was an ex-Pinkerton man," remarked Cochran wryly, and downed the fiery mescal.

"Maybe. So here I am. Now I'm rustling cows. Fell in with a gang that steals stock from the local *haciendas*. Then we run the beeves up to the border and sell them. I mean, hell, look at it this way. These damned Mexicans have been stealing American cattle for years. I'm just giving them a dose of their own medicine."

"Well, that's one way to look at it."

Stiles threw back his head and laughed. "To be honest, I do it mostly for the money."

"No kidding? You make good money?"

"Oh, hell, yes. These boys I ride with, they're damned good at what they do, for Mexicans. We got the big ranchers down here so riled up they went and hired a professional gunman to do away with us. A manhunter by the name of Chacon."

Cochran nearly fell off the bench he was sitting on.

"I take it you know who I'm talking about," observed Stiles.

"I've heard of him. He's supposed to be the best at what he does."

Stiles nodded. "Yeah. If I was on my own, I would worry. But the bunch I ride with have some hard bark on them. I reckon we can handle Chacon when and if he comes for us. But he sure is taking his own sweet time about it, I'll tell you that much. Maybe he won't find us at all. Maybe he ain't all he's cracked up to be."

Cochran could tell Stiles was more concerned about Chacon than he was letting on.

"Maybe he had some other business to attend to first."

Stiles shrugged. "That could be. So what have you done to bring the law down on you, Tom?"

"Robbed a Wells Fargo express."

Stiles let out a low whistle. "Not what I would call easy pickings. Did you have to shoot anybody? Those Wells Fargo agents don't generally give up without a fight, from what I hear."

"Well, they did this time."

Keenly interested, Stiles leaned forward. "And just how much loot did you get away with, *amigo*?"

Cochran smiled faintly. "Why, you know, Bill, that's none of your damned business."

Chuckling, Stiles shrugged. "Just curious is all." He glanced speculatively at Cochran's horse.

"You can stop checking out my rig, too," said Cochran. "I don't have it with me. I put it in a safe place north of the border. I didn't come in with yesterday's rain. Not about to ride down here with money bags tied to my saddle for all to see."

"You mean you don't have any pards to split up that

loot with? You held up a Wells Fargo stage all by your lonesome?"

"That's about the size of it."

"I'll be damned. So what do you aim to do?"

"Lay low for a spell. Then, when things cool down, I'll slip back over the line and get the money and dust out."

Stiles nodded. "Makes sense. You know, you're a smart hombre, Tom, and you've got guts. I got an idea. Why don't you ride with me back to the hideout? It's as good a place to lay low as any you'll find in these parts."

"What about your friends? They might not appreciate my company."

"Don't worry about them. I'll handle all that. I'll tell them you and me are friends from way back."

Cochran considered it. He realized that Stiles wasn't making the offer out of the goodness of his heart. No, the man wanted the loot. And for that reason he wanted to keep Cochran close at hand. Cochran knew how it would play out. Stiles would try to become his friend, his saddle pard, and hope that when it came time to recover the money he would be invited to tag along.

" 'Course I guess I ought to warn you," said Stiles, "it wouldn't be smart to tell my Mexican friends about that money you stole. They might decide they ought to have it for themselves. You know how some people are."

"Yeah, I know. That suits me."

"Then it's all settled. We'll ride out, right after we have some more mescal. Frederico, you lazy pig, get out here!"

Cochran knew he was taking a big chance. But he couldn't just ride on, not now, now that he knew Agustin Chacon was hunting Stiles and his fellow cattle rustlers. It was a happy coincidence that he had met Billy Stiles, and he wasn't going to pass up on the opportunity. Stiles was wrong. Chacon would find him and his *compadres*. It was just a matter of time. *So Chacon will be coming to me,* mused Cochran. *And all I have to do is stay alive long enough to kill him.*

*   *   *

The hideout Stiles had mentioned was located in the mountains west of the village, a twenty-five-mile ride that ended in a hidden canyon. The last half mile or so was difficult going—they had to walk their horses up a steep, rocky draw and then pass through a crevice between towering cliffs, a passage so narrow that at times both stirrups on Cochran's Texas rig scraped stone. Then they descended a treacherous shale slope, winding around clumps of stunted cedar and huge boulders that had fallen from the rugged heights above.

It was along here that they were confronted by a Mexican with a rifle, who stared at Cochran with such open hostility and suspicion that the latter felt there was a better than fifty-fifty chance he was about to be shot—in spite of everything Bill Stiles told the lookout. But in the end the Mexican refrained, and Cochran and Stiles were allowed to pass on. At the bottom of the slope stood an adobe. A spring provided plenty of fresh water, and scrub oak and cedar offered shade from the oppressive summer heat and wood for winter fires. It was a good hideout, decided Cochran—as long as its location remained a secret. But if that secret was found out, the hidden canyon would become a death trap.

There were four men, including the lookout, and all of them Mexicans, with whom Stiles worked. Two were brothers, and the oldest of these, a scar-faced man whose name was Miguel, appeared to be the leader. He was a big man, rawboned and broad-shouldered, who sported a sweeping mustache and a ferocious expression. He looked powerful enough to break a man's spine with his bare hands, as easily as he might snap a twig in two. But he wasn't all brawn—Cochran could sense that Miguel was a smart man, the brains of the outfit, with plenty of cunning. He made the cattle-rustling enterprise work. The others were just cheap labor, and that included Bill Stiles. Miguel listened intently to Stiles as the latter explained how Coch-

ran had come to be there, and Cochran knew that if Miguel
wasn't convinced that he was Stiles's friend—or even if he
was convinced but didn't care for his company—then it
was all over. Still, Cochran kept his nerve. Miguel would
fasten a dark scowl on him from time to time, but he always
met it with a cool and steady gaze of his own. That spoke
to his courage, and Miguel understood this, and ultimately
it proved a decisive factor in the gang leader's decision to
let Cochran live.

For the next three weeks the hidden canyon became Tom
Cochran's whole universe. His life hung in the balance
every minute of the day. He was watched constantly, and
one wrong move would mean instant death. But he didn't
make a wrong move. Instead, he simply bided his time,
concealing the fact that the enforced idleness severely
tested his patience. During the second week Miguel and
Stiles and two others were gone—off to rustle cattle and
then push them up to the border for a quick sale to some
unscrupulous *gringo* who would in turn sell them to a mining camp or an Indian agent. Cochran could only speculate
about that part of the operation. He was not made privy to
any of the details. One man was left behind to keep an eye
on him. Cochran figured he might be able to get the better
of his keeper, but he didn't want to. He was right where
he wanted to be.

After the rustlers had been back for a week, Bill Stiles
prevailed on Miguel to let Cochran accompany him into the
nearby village. Every three or four weeks, Stiles went into
town to pick up a few staples. As far as the villagers were
concerned, he was a prospector. In Cochran's opinion,
Stiles looked less like a prospector than anyone he had ever
met, but apparently the villagers were gullible. That, or
wisely declining to be too inquisitive. Miguel and the other
Mexicans could not show their faces in the village. They
were well-known in the region as criminals with substantial
bounties on their heads. If they had a hankering for whiskey
or a woman, it had to wait until they could swing through

a wide-open border town on the way back from the sale of
stolen beeves.

Cochran wasn't surprised that Miguel let him go with
Stiles. The gang leader had returned from the border with
a wanted poster. Wells Fargo was offering a $500 reward
for Cochran's capture. He didn't find the likeness on the
poster very flattering, but the paper served to convince Miguel that he was genuinely on the run. Cochran didn't particularly want to leave the canyon with Stiles, but he
thought it might seem odd if he turned down the chance.
He half expected Stiles to make his play while they were
gone, to suggest that now was the time that they should
ride north together, recover the Wells Fargo loot, and make
for places unknown. But it turned out that Stiles had more
patience than Cochran gave him credit for. The rustler had
his cut of the recent sale in his pocket, and he was intent
on showing Cochran a good time. Or at least as good a
time as a man could find in a poor Mexican village out in
the middle of nowhere. That meant some mescal and the
tender affections of a young woman who, Stiles knew from
experience, was willing to do just about anything if there
were a few pesos in it for her. Cochran had a drink or two,
but he turned down Stiles's offer to share the woman.

They stayed overnight in the village and late the next
morning set out to return to the canyon, carrying some coffee and sugar and tobacco and flour. Late afternoon caught
them passing through the crevice and then descending the
steep shale slope. Cochran wondered where the usual lookout was. It wasn't like Miguel to leave the entrance to the
hideout unguarded. He mentioned this to Stiles, who
shrugged it off. But Cochran wasn't inclined to take any
chances. As the adobe came into view, he checked his horse
and dismounted. Stiles was ahead of him, and proceeded
on for a moment before realizing that Cochran was no
longer coming along behind him. Twisting in the saddle,

he looked back to see Cochran checking his mount's front left hoof.

"What's the matter?" asked Stiles.

"Looks like he picked up a stone. You go on, I'll walk him in."

Stiles nodded and rode on. Cochran tarried, cautiously surveying the canyon. There was an itch at the nape of his neck—his instincts were telling him that something was wrong. It was too damned quiet. Where were Miguel and the others? Their horses were in the corral, unsaddled. Could they all be inside the adobe?

Cochran was still fifty yards behind Stiles when the latter reached the adobe. Stiles called out to his *compadres,* but there was no answer. Dismounting, Stiles drew his pistol and cautiously approached the adobe's door, kicked it open, and jumped to one side. Nothing happened. Stiles peered inside. There was no one there. He looked back at Cochran, who was by now approaching the adobe, and shrugged.

"I don't get it," said Stiles, mystified. "Where the hell is everybody?"

"They're your friends, not mine. You tell me."

Holstering his pistol, Stiles stepped inside. Cochran paused in the doorway, scanning the interior of the adobe. There was the usual clutter, but nothing out of the ordinary. Except for one thing—Miguel's gunbelt was on the table over there, and the holster was empty. Cochran looked around for a gun or rifle and didn't see a single one. Yet there was no evidence of a fight.

"Damn it," muttered Stiles. "This doesn't make a damned bit of sense. Their horses are in the corral. They wouldn't just walk out of here. So what's going on? I'll take a look outside."

Cochran stepped inside to clear the door for Stiles. "I wouldn't go out there if I was you."

Stiles looked at him, puzzled—and then Cochran saw

the puff of smoke and a spray of blood as a big-caliber bullet struck the rustler squarely in the chest. Stiles was hurled backward to sprawl dying on the floor, his body convulsing. He grunted and wheezed and gasped for a last breath—and then coughed up blood and died.

Cochran pressed his back against the wall to one side of the door, his blood running cold. He had been standing right where Stiles had been a few seconds earlier. The adobe wall was thick enough to stop a round from a buffalo gun—and by the sound of it Chacon was using something about that powerful. He knew it was Chacon. It had to be. The booming echo of the gunshot still echoed off the walls of the hidden canyon. All Cochran had was his side gun; his repeating rifle remained in its saddle scabbard. He scanned the room again just to confirm that all the weapons had been removed. Between them, Miguel and his *compañeros* had carried a small arsenal. Cochran figured Chacon had all the artillery now.

"Hey, *gringo*!" called Chacon. "Throw out your pistol, then come outside where I can see you. I will not shoot, I give you my word."

Cochran glanced at the six-shooter in Bill Stiles's holster, and a desperately risky plan sprung to mind. Would it work? Probably not. Chacon was not the type to make mistakes. But what other options were open?

"All right!" yelled Cochran. "I'm coming out!"

CHAPTER EIGHTEEN

CHACON

GETTING DOWN ON HIS BELLY, COCHRAN REACHED OUT TO take Stiles's pistol from its holster. He couldn't be sure of Chacon's position, or how much Chacon could see of the rustler's body. He could only hope that Chacon was not close enough to see him expropriate the dead man's pistol.

Standing, Cochran checked the gun and put it under his belt at the small of his back. Drawing his own pistol, he broke it open and let the shells fall to the floor. There was no point in giving his adversary another loaded weapon.

"*Gringo!*" called Chacon. "I am sometimes a patient man. But this is not one of those times."

Cochran tossed his empty pistol out the door. "Okay, here I come. Don't shoot!"

Realizing he might be as dead as Bill Stiles in a matter of seconds, Cochran steeled himself and then stepped through the door into the bright, slanting sunlight, hands raised, wondering if Chacon's word was worth anything.

A minute dragged by—the longest minute of Tom Cochran's life.

Then Chacon appeared from behind a boulder about eighty yards away and started walking toward the adobe.

He was dressed in black—black boots, black chinos, black *chaqueta,* and black sombrero. His spurs and hat band were silver and caught the sunlight. His *chaqueta* was buttoned at the top and flared open to reveal a white muslin shirt. His angular face sported a thick, well-groomed mustache. He carried a pearl-handled Remington revolver on his hip, and in his hands was a Springfield .45-70 sidehammer rifle, the Trap Door Model. This was the weapon that had fired the bullet that had ended the career of Bill Stiles. Cochran wondered if the bullet in it now would end his.

Chacon stopped twenty paces away and, standing hip-shot, tilted his head to one side and gave Cochran a long look. "I do not think I know you, *señor.*"

"We nearly met once before. In a dry gulch on the outskirts of Tombstone, about a month ago."

Chacon's eyes narrowed. "You are not John Slaughter." It wasn't a question.

"No. But I used to be his deputy. That was before I held up the Wells Fargo express."

"Now, why would you do a thing like that?"

"Because I got tired of putting my life on the line for thirty dollars a month and food. And because I got sick of working for John Slaughter."

"I see. So you were once a lawman, and now you are a wanted man."

"There's paper out on me."

"Is that so?" Chacon came closer, halving the distance between them. Cradling the Springfield in the crook of his left arm, he reached under the *chaqueta* and took out the wanted poster that Miguel had brought back from the border. At least Cochran had to assume it was the same one. And he also had to assume that it was Miguel's blood that stained the paper. Chacon held the poster up for him to see. "This is you, eh? Not a very flattering likeness."

"I didn't think so, either."

"What are you doing here?"

"I'm no rustler, if that's what you're thinking. I don't

ride with this bunch. I'm just hiding out here for a spell."

"Well," said Chacon, "you gave me a scare back in Tombstone. Maybe I should shoot you for that."

Cochran was thinking that if he hoped to take Chacon down now, this was his one chance. The man had the wanted poster in his right hand. It would take him precious seconds to bring the Springfield around.

But he didn't want to kill Chacon. Not yet, anyway. Slaughter was sure Chacon had been hired by someone—someone who would still want Texas John dead even if Chacon ended up in Boot Hill before getting the job done. Cochran wanted the name of Chacon's employer. Only with that information could the threat to Slaughter—and Viola—be removed.

"Maybe you would do better to keep me alive," said Cochran.

"And why would that be better, *señor?*"

"Because I can help you get a shot at John Slaughter. And I figure, from what I've seen, you only need one."

Chacon's dark face was inscrutable. "Why would you do that?"

"Because I'm in love with his wife."

Chacon stared at him—and believed. It was obvious to him that Cochran was telling the truth. The truth was there to see in his face, to hear in his voice.

"I see," said the killer. He was intrigued. "So, with John Slaughter dead, the way is clear for you. Perhaps, even, the grieving widow would seek solace in your arms, eh? But how could you be of help to me in this thing? He is a lawman, you are a wanted man."

"I send word to Slaughter at his San Bernardino Ranch that I want to meet with him, alone. That I want to talk to him about returning the money I stole, and maybe turning myself in. He'll come."

"Hmm." Chacon racked the Springfield on his shoulder. "I tell you what, *señor.* I will let you live a little while longer and think about your offer. Besides, I do not like to kill unless there is a profit in it. And I am being paid a flat fee to take care of this little rustling problem. Now, if I was being paid by the head, I would probably kill you now and collect more money. But I will let you live—provided you do not try to shoot me with that *pistola* you have hidden behind your back."

With that, Chacon turned his back on Cochran and walked away into the rocks whence he had come.

He was back a few minutes later leading his horse, a black stallion. Cochran thought all the black was a little pretentious, but then Agustin Chacon could afford a pretension or two. Certainly there was no one in Mexico foolhardy enough to make a snide comment about his color preference.

"Come," said Chacon. "If we are going to be partners, you can start helping me now."

He went to the corral, and there Cochran helped him saddle the horses. They led the mounts around behind the adobe, where the corpses of Miguel and the other rustlers lay. Cochran did not fail to notice that in each case a single bullet, in heart or head, had done the job. Near the bodies was a stack of rifles and six-shooters.

"I am just a businessman," said Chacon, smiling, "and in every business one must take care to keep his expenses down. Ammunition costs money."

They strapped the bodies over the saddled horses with the lariats that Miguel and his men had used to lasso cattle belonging to other people. Then it was Billy Stiles's turn. This done, Chacon collected the guns and they left the canyon. Cochran took charge of a couple of the corpse-laden horses and Chacon took the others.

They did not get far before night fell, camping only a half dozen miles from the hideout. Chacon shared his food—beans and hardtack—with Cochran. Afterward the Mexican opened a pouch, took out a pipe, filled it with tobacco, and lit it.

"So what do you have to do with these bodies to collect your fee?" asked Cochran.

"Deliver them to the man who has hired me. It will only take a couple of days. Then we will go north, and you will help me kill *Señor* Slaughter, yes?"

Cochran nodded. "What I can't figure out is why you want him dead. What did he ever do to you?"

"He has done nothing to me. Absolutely nothing. But then, neither did these men."

"So what is it? You just want to be known as the man who killed Texas John Slaughter? That would be a feather in your cap, wouldn't it?"

Chacon chuckled. "I only kill for money, remember?"

"So someone hired you to kill him."

"Now you are beginning to understand."

Cochran wondered if he should push his luck. If he seemed too curious about Chacon's business arrangements, would the killer become suspicious? Would he give the game away? He decided to take the chance. It was a little late, after all, to start getting cautious.

"Who was it?" he asked.

"A man like John Slaughter makes many enemies."

"That's true. But most of them are dead."

Chacon grinned over the pipe stem. "Well, he left at least one alive."

Cochran didn't press the issue. Chacon was being elusive; he didn't want to give up the name.

Two days later, though, he had his answer—when he and Chacon rode into the *hacienda* of Don Francisco Robles.

He had heard about Texas John's problems a few years back with Robles, when the *haclendero* had tried to foist some culls on Slaughter and then had made the mistake of insisting that Slaughter pay for the cattle whether he took them or not. Texas John had suspected Robles of being behind his subsequent quarrel with a gang of bandits at

Aqua Prieta. But since then there had been no further trouble. Of course, it was possible that Don Francisco had only hired Chacon to dispense with the rustlers and knew nothing about the killer's interest in Slaughter—but Cochran doubted that. And he quickly learned that his doubts were justified.

Robles emerged from the *casa grande* when Chacon and Cochran entered the *casco* trailing the corpse-laden horses.

"Did you get all of them, Chacon?" asked the *haciendero*.

"But of course, Don Francisco."

"And who is this?" Robles peered at Cochran. "I thought you worked alone."

"This man is going to help me kill John Slaughter."

"I did not think you needed help."

Chacon leveled an impassive gaze on Robles, and for a moment Cochran thought the man was going to take offense at the *haciendero*'s remark.

"John Slaughter is no ordinary man," said Chacon. "As you have learned, Don Francisco. I am not too proud to accept help when it is offered."

"His horse carried Slaughter's Z brand."

"That is because he used to ride for Slaughter."

"I don't like it," decided Robles.

"You do not have to like it, Don Francisco. If it becomes a problem, then it is my problem, not yours. But perhaps you would prefer to kill John Slaughter yourself, eh?"

Robles stiffened. He was not accustomed to being spoken to in such a manner.

"Just do what I have paid you to do," he said curtly.

"I always get the job done. You know that is true."

They did not linger long at the Robles *hacienda*. Chacon left the bodies of the rustlers and collected a sack of gold and then he and Cochran rode out of the *casco*.

"I do not like that arrogant bastard," said Chacon as they passed through the gate and down a tree-lined lane. "The dons, they are all the same. If you are not one of them, then they treat you like dirt."

"Then why do you work for him?"

"Because he pays well."

"Is that all that matters to you? Money?"

"No. What matters to me are those things that money can buy. My father was very poor, a *campesino*, like his father before him. I swore I would not die a poor man."

Cochran wondered why Robles had waited all these years to exact revenge on John Slaughter. Del Hooper had told him how Slaughter had shamed the *haciendero* in front of his people. The memory of that day must have burned like hot coals. Perhaps Robles had not found anyone willing to try Texas John on for size—until Agustin Chacon had come along.

They arrived at Aqua Prieta the following day. Cochran found a young man willing to carry a message to nearby San Bernardino. Late the next day, the messenger returned. Cochran told Chacon that it had all been arranged; Slaughter had agreed to meet him at the ruins of the Jesuit mission right across the border at noon tomorrow. And he had promised to come alone.

Chacon listened and nodded. "That is good. I assume Slaughter is a man of his word. He will be alone. But you will not be."

By this time Cochran was having second thoughts about the whole business. He could hardly believe that a man with Chacon's intelligence and cunning would not be at least a little suspicious. Didn't the man realize that this could be a trap? Or maybe he did realize it, and was willing to take the chance to get close enough to Slaughter for one clean shot. He had not mentioned just how much money Robles was paying him to kill Texas John, but Cochran had a hunch it was a big sum. Enough, maybe, to compel Chacon to accept exceptional risks.

The problem for Cochran now was that he liked Agustin

Chacon. He couldn't explain it, but in some ways he admired the man. Yes, he was a hired killer. He seemed to have no compunctions when it came to taking human life. And he was dead set on taking John Slaughter's life—which made him Cochran's enemy. Still, he was a brave man, and one with more character and more integrity than many Cochran had met in his day. That included Don Francisco Robles.

"I think you should forget about the whole thing," he told Chacon. "Lots of men have tried to take John Slaughter and failed."

Chacon smiled faintly. "You are concerned about my welfare? I thought you wanted this man dead."

Cochran shrugged and spoke no more on the subject.

They left Aqua Prieta before dawn, and arrived at the ruins of the mission an hour before noon. It was an overcast day, cold and blustery. Chacon had wanted to reach the rendezvous before the appointed time in order to check out the lay of the land and plan his ambush of Slaughter. The crumbling ruins offered plenty of hiding places.

What Chacon hadn't counted on was John Slaughter being crafty enough to anticipate that his would-be killer would arrive early. So Slaughter had been waiting among the ruins since shortly after daybreak.

When Chacon and Cochran rode in, Slaughter showed himself, rising up from behind the remnant of an adobe wall and leveling a Winchester repeating rifle at the Mexican.

"Live or die, Chacon," he said. "It's entirely up to you."

Chacon was startled—but he did not fully realize that he had ridden into a well-laid trap until several of Slaughter's men emerged from their hiding places and aimed their long guns at him. Del Hooper, Tad Roland, and Wake Benge had Chacon covered from all sides. Only then did Chacon put the pieces together. He looked at Cochran, his features a stoic mask.

"Congratulations," he said calmly, and without rancor. "I am not easily fooled."

"Shed that pistol, Chacon," said Slaughter.

Chacon looked at the rifles aimed at him, considered his options—and slowly took the pearl-handled pistol from its holster and tossed the weapon away.

"Now the long gun," said Slaughter. "Nice and slow."

Chacon complied, drawing the Springfield Trap Door rifle from its saddle boot and letting it fall to the ground.

"Does he carry any other iron, Tom?" asked Slaughter.

"No." Chacon had sold the guns he had taken from the rustlers at Aqua Prieta.

Chacon turned his attention back to Cochran. "So tell me, my friend, I am curious—were you lying about yourself and this man's wife?"

"No. I was not lying."

Cochran glanced at Slaughter. He couldn't read the expression on Texas John's face and figured that was probably just as well.

"No," said Chacon, "I did not think you were."

Slaughter took his prisoner to Tombstone, where Agustin Chacon was charged with the murder of an American trader named Elijah Smith. Chacon did not deny that he had done the deed. Smith, he explained, had been running guns to the Apaches, and a competitor had wanted him out of the way. Smith's nefarious activities were not sufficiently mitigating as far as the jury that decided Chacon's fate was concerned. The defendant was found guilty and sentenced to death by hanging.

Several days after the execution was carried out, Slaughter rode down to Aqua Prieta to find Tom Cochran. He had suggested that Cochran cool his heels at San Bernardino while steps were taken to clear his name. But Cochran had chosen not to accept that invitation. He had been spending most of his time in the cantina, located at one end of the

old customs building where, some years before, Slaughter
and Del Hooper and Old Bat had battled twenty *bandoleros.*

"So is he dead?" asked Cochran, when Slaughter walked
up to the table in the back of the cantina that he had claimed
as his own.

"Yes."

Cochran kicked a chair out. "Have a seat. Mescal?"

"No, thanks." Slaughter settled his wiry, compact frame
into the chair. "He died game, I can tell you that much."

"You didn't need to tell me that. I already knew."

"He said, 'I consider this the greatest day of my life.'
Right before they sprung the trap door."

Cochran shook his head. "I never should have done it."

"I've got everything squared away with Wells Fargo and
the territorial governor. You're not a wanted man anymore,
Tom."

"That's not what I meant. It's not that I shouldn't have
robbed the express. I shouldn't have led Chacon into your
trap."

Slaughter gave him a long appraisal. "Well, personally
I'm kind of glad you did."

Cochran took another long pull on the jug of mescal. He
had been drinking steadily for several hours since midday,
but seeing Slaughter had sobered him up. Now he had to
start all over.

"So you can come back to Arizona now, Tom. You can
have that tin star back, or you're welcome to come work
at San Bernardino."

Cochran stared at Slaughter with skepticism written all
over his face. "You can't be serious."

Slaughter fired up one of his Mexican cheroots. "I guess
you're thinking about Viola. Hell, Tom, I knew how you
felt about her long before I heard what Chacon said."

"You did?" Cochran was stunned. "And you didn't do
anything about it."

"What would I do about it? Run you off? I couldn't

blame you for falling in love with her. I did. Viola liked you, Tom, but she was never in love with you. I knew that, so I could live with the rest of it."

"I see." Cochran took another drink.

Slaughter puffed on the cheroot for a moment. The blue smoke lay heady in the still air between them. Cochran was paying undue attention to the mescal jug. He didn't seem at all interested in the fact that he was no longer wanted by the law—any more than he was interested in coming back to work at the ranch.

"Well, Tom," said Slaughter at length, "my door is always open to you. If there's ever anything you need . . ."

"I just need to be left alone."

Slaughter nodded. He considered Tom Cochran a friend, and, while he was concerned, he respected his friend's wishes.

Standing, he turned and walked out of the cantina.

CHAPTER NINETEEN

THE LAST RAID

It all started with a broken arm.

The arm belonged to a Chiricahua woman, and Lieutenant Britton Davis, in command of the army guard posted near the Apache reservation, arrested the woman's husband and sentenced him to two years in jail. Davis was a gentleman, and he could not tolerate abuse of the gentler sex, even if the woman *was* an Apache.

A few days later, Davis was confronted by all the Chiricahua leaders. Among the Indians was Geronimo, the Bedonkohe Apache whom Davis believed was nothing but a malcontent and a troublemaker. The Chiricahua chiefs insisted that Davis had no right to interfere in the domestic affairs of an Apache man. If a wife misbehaved, then it was the husband's prerogative to punish her as he saw fit. Davis would have none of it. He proceeded to lecture the Apache headmen, chiding them for their uncivilized customs. It was Nana who ended the meeting, rising abruptly and turning to the army scout named Mickey Free and speaking sharply to him.

"What did he say?" Davis asked Free, who was acting as interpreter.

Mickey Free was reluctant to translate Nana's words into English, but Davis insisted.

"He says to tell you he had killed many men before you were out of baby grass."

"We all drank tiswin last night," said Chihuahua, another of the leaders. "What are you going to do about that? Put us all in jail? You do not have a jail big enough."

The manufacture and consumption of tiswin on the reservation was forbidden; Davis was convinced that the potent brew only encouraged bad behavior among the Apaches. But he did not arrest the Chiricahua leaders. Instead, he sent a wire to his superior, General George Crook, asking for instructions on how the general wanted him to deal with the troublesome Indians.

Before Crook's reply could reach him, an Apache breakout had occurred.

Davis blamed Geronimo for it, and he was right to do so. The army scouts had been telling the soldiers that Geronimo was continually stirring the embers of discontent among his people. Aware of this, Geronimo feared that he would meet the same fate as Kaytennae, who had been dragged off to Alcatraz Prison, caged like an animal in a stone cell. Or perhaps the *pinda lickoyi,* the white eyes, would murder him, as they had the great Mangas Colorado. So Geronimo ran, and with him went Nana, Naiche, and Chihuahua. Also there was Lozen, the woman warrior— plus forty bronchos, and one hundred women and children, about a fourth of the entire Chiricahua population on the reservation.

They had gone twenty miles before Britton Davis managed to organize a pursuit. The Apaches reached the rugged Mogollon Mountains and there broke up into small groups and scattered. Geronimo and Naiche led their bands south into Mexico. Other groups circled back to the north, hoping to throw the "blue wolves"—the army's Apache scouts, led by the likes of Chatto and Mickey Free—off the scent. If they succeeded in eluding their pursuers, these bands would drift south later and rejoin the others.

Notified of the breakout, General Crook dispatched twenty troops of cavalry and over one hundred scouts from five forts to find and catch the fugitives. Within a week, two thousand men were hunting the fugitives. Sometimes the trail was easy to follow—one had only to ride for the plumes of black smoke that marked the burned-out ranches. The Apaches killed seventeen settlers and stole one hundred and fifty horses. They spared no one, not man, woman, or child. Sometimes their trail simply vanished. The Chiricahua Apache was the most elusive prey of all. They did not spare themselves, either. Two Apache women gave birth during the flight; the infants were left by the trail to die, for they could not be cared for under the circumstances, and nothing could be permitted to slow the fugitives down.

Panic reigned in every community in Arizona and New Mexico. The army was severely criticized for its inability to keep the Apaches on the reservation and then to catch them promptly once they had "jumped." Posses were formed as private citizens armed themselves and rode out to teach the bluecoats how to deal with hostiles. In Cochise County, a family of settlers were found murdered. John Slaughter took Lorenzo Paca with him to investigate, and when he got back to Tombstone he found the town up in arms. He confirmed that the Apache renegades had done the killing. A posse of sixty men formed, and the reaction to Slaughter's refusal to lead it was, predictably, one of keen disappointment and anger. John Clum paid a call on the sheriff, finding him at his house on the edge of town.

"I've been expecting you, John," said Slaughter when he answered the door. "How about a drink?"

"No, thanks. Texas John, you know the people are angry at you. They don't understand why you won't ride with them to catch the savages who killed that family. Frankly, I don't understand it, either."

"Most if not all of the renegades are south of the border

by now, John. I'm not inclined to lead a bunch of trigger-happy shopkeepers into Mexico. Crook is trying to seal off the border and it is my understanding that he plans to send columns south to locate and capture Geronimo and the others."

"We have a right to protect ourselves. You can't expect these men to simply sit by and wait for more people to be massacred."

"We wouldn't see a single Apache if we rode around out there until next Christmas, John. The only thing those men will get for their trouble is saddle sores." Slaughter adamantly shook his head. "With all those posses and cavalry troops roaming these parts, there must be at least five thousand men looking for the renegades—all forty-two of them. Leave it to the army, John. Leave it to Crook. He knows the Apaches better than any general in the army. And most importantly of all, he's got his Apache scouts. When it's all said and done, they'll be the ones who bring Geronimo and his people to heel."

Slaughter's information turned out to be accurate. Crook did try to seal off the border to prevent the renegades from returning to the United States, and he sent two columns, one led by Britton Davis and the other by Captain Emmet Crawford, into Mexico to find and corral the Apaches. The panic had spread into Mexico's northern provinces, with the result that one of Davis's Apache scouts was shot and killed by a farmer near Oputo, who mistook him for a broncho. The "blue wolves" wanted to ride into Oputo and exact a terrible vengeance, and it was all Davis and lead scout Chatto could do to prevent that from happening.

As Slaughter had told John Clum, it was the scouts who ultimately made the difference. They found a renegade camp and captured fifteen women and children. A few weeks later another camp was located, this one deeper in the Sierra Madres. As in the first case, the Apache bronchos were off on a raid, but again women and children were taken into custody—including a wife and son of Geronimo himself. General Crook had high hopes that these events might so discourage the renegades that they would turn themselves in. Instead, Geronimo led a daring raid back into Arizona, slipping past the border patrols and recapturing his family, who were being held with the other prisoners in an encampment at Fort Apache. Geronimo and his raiders then struck deep into New Mexico, kidnapping some Mescalero women. Crook was humiliated. But it soon got worse. Chihuahua's brother, Ulzana, led another raid into Arizona a month later. The renegades were desperately short of ammunition, and Ulzana was determined to solve that problem. His raiders killed forty people, rode twelve hundred miles, and attacked Fort Apache itself, killing twelve White Mountain scouts and making off with horses, mules, and plenty of cartridges. Not a single broncho lost his life.

Crook resorted to a desperate measure. He gathered together one hundred of his best Apache scouts, placed them under Captain Crawford's command, and sent them after the renegades, who were again holed up in the Sierra Madre. Crawford was a good choice—mentally and physically tough, he was admired by the men under his command. He pushed them hard; a two-day march took them deep into Mexico, moving so quickly that he almost caught Geronimo napping. While the Apaches escaped deeper into the mountains, Crawford seized food and horses that the renegades desperately needed.

Then tragedy struck. Mexican troops attacked Crawford's command, mistaking the "blue wolves" for Apache wild ones. Crawford was shot in the head. Enraged, his scouts attacked the Mexicans, killing some of them and forcing the rest to surrender. Captain Crawford died from his wounds several days later.

For a while it looked as though the incident would lead to an outbreak of hostilities between the United States and the Republic of Mexico. Washington demanded reparations. The Mexican government claimed that the Apache scouts had fired first, and that in fact Crawford had been shot by one of his own men.

But Crawford had not died in vain. His attack had convinced many of the renegades that death or capture was inevitable, and that not even the Sierra Madre could provide them with sanctuary. When the column returned to the United States, the soldiers had some Chiricahua women and children in tow, as well as two warriors, one of them Nana. Better yet, they brought Geronimo's promise to meet with General Crook in two moons.

Geronimo kept his word, and the meeting took place in the Cañon de los Embudos. Crook kept his promise, too, showing up without soldiers, apart from his aide John Bourke, Lieutenant Marion Maus, and several interpreters. Also accompanying Crook was Camillus Fly, the Tombstone photographer whose shop stood adjacent to the vacant lot where the Earp brothers and Doc Holliday had confronted Ike and Billy Clanton and the McLaury brothers.

The talk took place beside a stream in the shade of sycamore and willow trees. Two dozen Apache bronchos appeared, and Fly, undeterred and determined to capture the meeting for posterity with his camera, ordered them around into the poses and groupings he desired without any apparent concern for being in such close proximity to well-armed hostiles.

Crook allowed Geronimo to speak first. The Bedonkohe launched into a lengthy harangue, contending that he had been falsely accused of being a troublemaker and that he had fled the reservation only because he had feared for his life. He then went through the usual litany of Apache complaints about their treatment at the hands of the *pinda lickoyi*. Finally he suggested that he and his followers would consider surrendering and, furthermore, give their solemn promise never to raid again, if they were given complete amnesty for the crimes they had committed since the breakout.

Geronimo became increasingly agitated as he spoke because to him it seemed that Crook was aloof and unfriendly in his demeanor. Finally the general interrupted the Bedonkohe.

"You are talking nonsense," said Crook sternly. "I am no child. You have two choices. Surrender unconditionally or remain on the warpath. If you choose the former, I can make no promises. If you choose the latter, I will keep after you and kill every last one of you—even if it takes fifty years. And that *is* a promise."

Crook then informed Geronimo that he and his people had two days to make up their minds. The Apaches returned to their camp, Crook to his. The general had low expectations. His superior, Phil Sheridan, commanding general of the army, had insisted on the unconditional surrender terms. Crook seriously doubted that Geronimo would accept them.

So when they met for the second time, two days later, Crook sweetened the pot on his own initiative. He took the chance because he felt obliged to do whatever he could to save the lives of those who would otherwise die in the weeks and months to come if the renegades remained at large. He assured the Chiricahuas that they would be sent east for a period not to exceed two years, after which they would be allowed to return to their homeland. As, one by one, the Apache leaders lay down their weapons and gravely shook Crook's hand, the general prayed that his government would accept the arrangement he had just made.

Geronimo was the last of the Apaches to make a decision. He sat, brooding, under a tree on the banks of the stream. Finally it was his turn. All eyes were on him. Wearily, the Bedonkohe rose and shook the general's hand.

"I give myself up to you," he said. "Do with me what you please. Once I moved about like the wind. Now I surrender to you, and that is all."

But it wasn't over.

That night the Apaches got drunk on mescal. Crook had already left the meeting site, in a hurry to get back to Fort Bowie so that he could send a telegram to General Sheridan, explaining what had happened and what had been agreed upon. This left Lieutenant Maus with the responsibility of bringing in the fugitives—virtually by himself. The party made only four miles on the first day, getting a very late start as the Apaches procrastinated. That night the Apaches were drinking again. Maus had a bad feeling about the whole affair. But there was precious little he could do without troops to back him up and keep the renegades under close guard. When dawn came, he found that his worst fears had been realized. Some of the renegades had had a change of heart. Eighteen warriors had vanished, along with thirteen women and six children. They were led by Geronimo and Naiche.

Maus was furious when he learned that the Apaches had gotten their mescal from a man named Tribolet, who operated a tent saloon on the border. The lieutenant suspected Tribolet of having told his Apache clients that the army planned to hang them all as soon as they crossed over into the United States. It was Tribolet whom Maus very much wanted to hang.

Accompanied by a handful of scouts, Maus gamely pursued the fugitive Apaches. The renegades made sixty miles on foot before splitting up and slipping into the Sierra Madre in small groups. Short on rations and riding trail-worn mounts, Maus and his men wisely opted not to venture into the mountains.

At Fort Bowie, Crook received two pieces of bad news on the same day. A wire from Sheridan informed him that the government would under no circumstances accept the arrangement he had made with the Apaches. Their surrender had to be unconditional. Sheridan added that the hostiles could not be allowed to escape once they were in custody. A short while later, word arrived from Mexico that the hostiles had done just that.

At his own request, General Crook was reassigned. General Nelson Miles replaced him.

A few weeks later, an army officer showed up at San

Bernardino looking for Texas John Slaughter.

The officer introduced himself as Captain Henry Lawton. He was a tall man, standing six feet four, brawny and keen-eyed, and had the appearance of a capable and experienced soldier.

"General Miles sends his compliments, Mr. Slaughter," said Lawton. "He would appreciate your coming to see him at Fort Bowie at your earliest convenience."

"What does he want to see me about?"

"He would like for you to participate in the campaign against Geronimo, sir."

"I'm the sheriff of Cochise County, Captain. I have responsibilities here."

"Yes, sir. But the general told me to tell you that your help in capturing Geronimo and his band would be much appreciated."

"I don't see how I could be of much help, frankly," said Slaughter.

"You know this country as well as anyone, and better than most, sir. Or so they say."

"I reckon that's true enough."

"And you are familiar with the province of Sonora, too."

Slaughter nodded. "I've done some business down there. But if it's a scout your general is looking for, well, he has plenty of Apache scouts who can do a better job of it than I ever could."

"That's just it, Mr. Slaughter. We no longer have the services of the Apache scouts to rely on."

"Why not? What the hell happened to them?"

"General Miles has taken almost all of them off the payroll, sir."

Slaughter stared at the captain. He could scarcely believe his ears. "Why would he do something like that?"

Lawton grimaced. "In the general's opinion, sir, the cavalry can do the job quite well. And, um, well, frankly, he doesn't trust an Apache to catch another Apache."

Slaughter had to laugh at that. "By God, that's just about

the only way to catch a renegade, Captain. You look like a man with some experience in Indian fighting. Am I wrong?"

"No, sir, you are not wrong."

"Then you must know that your new general has made a big mistake."

"That's not my place to say, sir."

"You're right. Of course not. Well, Washington has made a mistake, too, in replacing Crook. The man knew what he was doing. Probably the only general that knew how to fight Apaches."

"Yes, sir. What message should I convey to General Miles, sir?"

Slaughter grimaced. "So Miles proposes to make war on the bronchos without Apache scouts to help him. My God. There will be some lives lost. How many run with Geronimo now? I've heard anywhere from three to three hundred. What's the truth of it, Captain?"

"About forty, sir. All the rest gave themselves up and came back."

"Who are they?"

"Naiche. Lozen, the woman warrior. Chapo, Geronimo's son, and Geronimo's cousin, Perico. And then there is Yanozha."

"Yanozha. Yes, I know about him. He once stole some of my cattle. Where are they now, do you have any idea?"

"We're fairly sure they're in the Sierra Madre. The Mexican government has more than three thousand soldiers in the field to locate them."

"You can forget about the Mexican army. The units assigned to the northern provinces are filled with convicts and other riffraff. You know, Captain, that Geronimo may decide not to surrender this time. He and his followers are diehards. They would rather die free than live in chains. And you and I and Geronimo know that would be their fate if they give up."

"Yes, sir. However it turns out, I think it's safe to say

that this will be the final Apache campaign. I guess that makes it the last Indian campaign in the West. We've dealt with all the other tribes."

"But not always fairly, have we?"

"I'm just a soldier, Mr. Slaughter. I go where they send me and do what they tell me to do."

Slaughter nodded—and relented. "I apologize, Captain. You're just doing your job. And I reckon part of my job is to help you corral those bronchos. Without the Apache scouts, General Miles is going to need all the help he can get. I'll help you get Geronimo because if I don't, he may decide to carry out another raid or two into this county. Stay for supper, Captain, and I'll ride back with you in the morning."

When Slaughter informed Viola of his decision, he saw the deep concern in her eyes. Chasing horse thieves and road agents was dangerous enough, but it amounted to horseplay compared to chasing Apache bronchos. And yet she did not give voice to her fears or try to talk him out of it. She had never done that before, and wouldn't now. She respected her husband too much.

Slaughter sent word to Jeff Milton in Tombstone. He felt comfortable leaving Milton in charge of things while he was gone. The man had earned his complete confidence a dozen times over. The following morning he kissed his wife and hugged his children goodbye and rode out of San Bernardino with Captain Lawton, bound for Fort Bowie.

CHAPTER TWENTY

THE SURRENDER

When Slaughter reached Fort Bowie, he expected to find the army ready to launch its campaign and promptly march out after Geronimo. Word was that the last band of Apache bronchos were engaged in a frenzy of raiding that had claimed dozens of Mexican lives, and the Mexican army seemed powerless to halt the butchery. None of this surprised Slaughter. Geronimo and the Apaches who followed him knew that they were doomed and intended to go out in a blaze of glory, inflicting as much damage as they could on their enemies before the end came. And the fact that the Mexican army units were ineffective was hardly unexpected news. The worst conscripts were shipped off to the northern provinces and most of the officers assigned to posts in Sonora and Chihuahua were there because they were being disciplined.

It seemed to Slaughter that General Miles would be concerned that Geronimo might begin raiding into the United States again—and if his activities below the border were any indication, then he would likely cut a bloody swath through Arizona and New Mexico. And yet Miles was apparently in no big hurry to get under way. He had requested substantial reinforcements and intended to wait until they arrived before acting. "That will give me five thousand men," he told Slaughter. "With a force that size, I will be able to guarantee that wherever Geronimo turns, he will find the United States waiting for him."

Slaughter kept his opinions to himself. Miles had fought with distinction in the War Between the States. He was no West Pointer; he had volunteered for action and worked his way up through the ranks. Conspicuous for his valor and wounded twice, he was a brevet major general by 1864. Only George Armstrong Custer had managed a more meteoric rise.

With the war over, Miles had sought and been given assignment on the frontier, fighting the Sioux and the Nez Percé. In Slaughter's judgment the general just didn't comprehend how different the Apaches were from the plains tribes. You could not fight the Apaches in the same way that you fought the Sioux or the Cheyennes or the Arapahos. He shared this outlook with Al Sieber, the army chief of scouts, and Sieber heartily concurred with his assessment.

"We're just damned lucky that we ain't up against more than a handful," said the bearded, wiry Sieber. "If we had to tangle with the whole Chiricahua band, it would be a bloody mess and there's no two ways about it. But Geronimo and his bunch are on their last legs now. They're getting shorter every day on food and ammunition and places to hide out. It's just a matter of time."

"And every day Miles waits for his reinforcements, more innocent people die."

Sieber grinned sardonically. "Yeah, that's true. But see, they ain't American citizens, Texas John, so the general doesn't have to worry about that."

"Well, I'm worried about it. I'm worried about a whole lot of this. You and I both know an army of five thousand men isn't what is needed to end this business. When Crook sent Crawford and a hundred scouts down after Geronimo a while back, look what happened. Most of the renegades gave up. Try that once or twice more and I'm betting Geronimo would be finished."

Sieber nodded. "I'm right with you on that score. The problem is, we don't have a hundred scouts anymore."

The German-born chief of scouts sounded a little bitter, and Slaughter figured he had every right to be. More than any other individual, Sieber deserved the credit for turning the Apache scouts into the most effective fighting force General Crook had had at his disposal. Sieber had fought right alongside the "blue wolves" on numerous occasions, and admired them greatly, just as they had looked up to him. Now most of them were gone—dispatched to the misery of the reservation without so much as a thank you from the government they had served, treated now just like any other Apache—that is to say, with contempt. Worse, many of their own people were contemptuous of them as well, scorning them for having ridden with the enemy, the *pinda lickoyi*.

Slaughter became acquainted with the handful of scouts that were still available. There was Mickey Free. And then there was a young half-breed known only as the Apache Kid. The latter was a moody and taciturn character, who largely kept to himself and spurned any offer of friendship. But Sieber vouched for him without reservation.

"Yeah, I know he's meaner than hell with the hide off," Sieber told Slaughter. "But he fights like a devil, rides like the wind, shoots better than I ever could, and can track an ant over a rock. For some reason he just doesn't get along with anybody—neither white nor Apache. But he's the kind you want fighting on your side—and you sure as hell don't want him against you!"

Slaughter considered returning to San Bernardino until such time as Miles could get his campaign under way, but the general insisted that he stay, and Slaughter didn't kick up much dust about it. He knew a lot about the Apaches but wanted to learn more, and he spent his time productively, talking to Sieber and Mickey Free and some of the officers—those who had had experience in previous campaigns against the Apaches.

He was also fascinated by the general's pet project, a heliograph system. This utilized large mirrors that reflected sunlight to flash Morse code signals. Miles established nearly thirty stations on mountaintops across the width and breadth of southern Arizona. He believed the heliograph system would be an effective tool in the struggle against the hostiles, should Geronimo dare venture back into the United States. With it, proclaimed Miles confidently, he could be in rapid and continual contact with his various columns, so that once Geronimo was spotted, all the columns could quickly converge on his location. Always before, when the army had responded to a sighting of Apache raiders, they had arrived on the scene far too late to engage the enemy—too late, usually, to do anything but bury the latest victims.

Two weeks passed. Sharing a bottle with Sieber one night, an exasperated Slaughter asked the chief scout what Miles was afraid of. "You'd think he was scared to tangle with the bronchos."

"I reckon he's more scared of failure." Sieber leaned forward, lowering his voice to a conspirator's whisper—for dramatic effect and nothing more, since they were alone in a stable stall. "I hear tell Miles has his sights set on the White House. What do you think about them apples, Texas John?"

"He wants to be President?"

Sieber nodded. "To be the man who captures Geronimo—well, that would be a real feather in his cap. Make him a national hero. But if Geronimo gets the better of him, like what happened to Crook . . ." The chief scout shook his head. "No, Miles would rather die a thousand agonizing deaths than fail this go-round. So he is going to wait until he's got all the cards in his hand."

"I just hope we're not all too old to even climb into the

saddle before he decides to get moving," said Slaughter dryly.

Then it happened. The renegades embarked on a raid north of the border. An isolated ranch in the Santa Cruz Valley was the first to be hit. Several cowboys were killed, as were the rancher's wife and daughter. The rancher himself was out on the range at the time. He was captured by the bronchos later, only to be released—and warned not to go home. A miner in the Whetstone Mountains was the next victim. Then there was a sheepherder in Happy Valley. A doctor was ambushed and killed near the San Pedro River. A young white boy was kidnapped, and a ten-year-old girl. All of Arizona was up in arms. Remarkably, all the fear, all the devastation, was caused by a mere seven bronchos.

Slaughter blamed Miles for the deaths of the innocents in Arizona, but one good thing came of it all. The uproar spread quickly from the Southwest clear across the nation to Washington, and Phil Sheridan pressured Miles to move at once. The general finally put his army into motion. Five thousand soldiers—more than a quarter of the entire United States Army—was now in action. The enemy numbered a grand total of eighteen Chiricahua warriors.

Miles placed troops at every water hole along the border. Bluecoats guarded every ranch, mining camp, and way station. No one could say where or when Geronimo would turn up next. He and his followers were like ghosts. You seldom saw an Apache until he was in the process of killing you. Eventually, though, it became apparent that the renegades were once again back in Mexico. Miles sent a hundred experienced soldiers under the capable command of Captain Lawton to pursue them.

Slaughter was not chosen to accompany Lawton's command, and he wasn't sorry. He considered Lawton a good officer, one of the best in the army, but the fact remained that the men with him were white soldiers, not Apache scouts. Hardened veterans though they were, they could not last long under the hardships of a pursuit in the heat of summer across the burning wastelands of northern Mexico. Their ordeal was terrible—rumor had it that at one point their thirst was so overwhelming that some of the men resorted to cutting open their veins so that they could drink their own blood. And after several months on the trail, they had nothing to show for all their suffering. Not a single Chiricahua was killed or captured.

By the time Lawton had returned from his failed excursion into Mexico, John Slaughter was back at San Bernardino. He had helped Miles locate the water holes to be watched and the mountain passes to be guarded throughout southern Arizona, but after that there wasn't much more for him to do, and one day he informed the general that he was going home. This time Miles did not try to make him stay.

At the end of the summer, when the campaign was five months old, General Miles reluctantly came to the conclusion that Crook had been right all along when it came to employing Apache scouts. He ordered Al Sieber and Lieutenant Charles Gatewood to reorganize the "blue wolves."

"Well, then, that's it," Slaughter told Viola when he heard the news. "It may take a little while yet, but Geronimo is done for now."

But the cunning Geronimo was not finished quite yet. He had a few more tricks up his sleeve. He sent two women into the Mexican town of Fronteras to inform the authorities there that the renegades wanted to surrender. All they asked for was assurances that the Mexicans would not resort to treachery—as they had done many times before—when the meeting to discuss the surrender took place. In a show of good faith the Mexicans sent the women back into the Sierra Madre with ponies carrying plenty of food and mescal. Of course, they heard no more from Geronimo. Slaughter had a good laugh when word of this reached him. He imagined the bronchos were having a good laugh, too. Who would really believe that Apaches would surrender themselves into the custody of the Mexicans? Geronimo was no fool; he would never trust the word of a Mexican. Once again Geronimo had pulled the wool over the eyes of his enemies. It was soon revealed that, in fact, the Mexicans had hoped to lure the renegades into an ambush—two hundred *federales* slipped into Fronteras under cover of darkness in anticipation of Geronimo's arrival.

When Slaughter rode out to Fort Apache to pay a call on Al Sieber, he learned that Miles was sending Gatewood and a handful of Apache scouts into the Sierra Madre under a flag of truce.

"Looks like he thinks Geronimo really does want to give up," said the chief scout, "and would have surrendered to the Mexicans, only he found out what they were scheming. So the general is hoping he'll surrender to us. Two of the scouts are Kayitah and Martine. Lieutenant Gatewood thinks Geronimo will listen to those two."

"Is he right?"

"No officer in this army knows the Apaches better than Gatewood, Texas John. Martine rode with Juh, and Geronimo respects him. Kayitah is Yanozha's cousin."

Slaughter was skeptical. He shook his head. "I've met Gatewood. He's a brave man. He's got to know that Geronimo might just kill him and his scouts without bothering to listen to what they have to say. A flag of truce will mean nothing to Geronimo—he and his people have been tricked too many times to put much faith in it."

Sieber nodded agreement. "You could be right. I can't imagine why Geronimo would give up. He must know that he'll be slapped in irons and hauled off to Florida, if not hanged. And even if he lives, he won't ever see his homeland again. By the way, and don't tell anybody I told you this, but I've heard that Miles plans to ship all the Chiricahuas east."

"All of them?"

"Yep. Every last one of 'em. All four hundred—men, women, and children."

"But why would he do that? Most of those people have never jumped the reservation, participated in a raid, or raised a hand in anger against us."

"I know that. But Miles is afraid Geronimo might talk them all into breaking out to join him. And since the general is well aware that some folks are making fun of him because eighteen Apache warriors have made a shambles of his grand campaign, he's downright terrified at the thought of what four hundred Chiricahuas on the loose could do."

Slaughter shook his head. "Damn it, Al, it's just not right."

"Texas John, you have earned your reputation as a hard man. You spent your early years fighting the Comanches, and I don't know that you ever shed a tear over how they were driven off their land by your fellow Texans. And yet here you sit with your heart bleeding all over the ground for the Chiricahua Apaches. You mind explaining to me why that is?"

After a moment of quiet contemplation, Slaughter smiled ruefully. "I guess I'm just getting soft in my old age."

Al Sieber sighed. "The end is near, my friend. When Geronimo gives up or gets killed, it will be the end of an era. It'll mean this country has finally been tamed. We'll have taken all the wildness out of it. And we've both of us done our fair share to see that job through. I reckon we ought to feel proud."

Slaughter grunted skepticism. "Funny, I don't feel proud. How about you?"

"Proud? Hell, no. Sad? Damn right I feel sad. Pretty soon we won't recognize this country. It will all be civilized. And we won't know how to handle that. Because you know it's the wildness that made us feel alive, that drew us out here. Just about the only thing men like you and me will have left to do is die out."

"All I ever wanted when I came out here was to live in peace. To raise cattle and love my wife."

"You wanted space. Elbow room. You wanted to live someplace where people weren't always telling you to do this and don't do that. Well, now that we've tamed this land, pard, the folks will be pouring into it. And they'll have all kinds of notions that you won't cotton to."

"If you say so."

"Well, let's drink to peace and quiet. After all, that's what we always wanted."

"Yeah," said Slaughter. "Right." But he knew he didn't sound too convincing.

Captain Lawton was back in Mexico on the trail of the renegades when Lieutenant Gatewood joined him. With the lieutenant were Martine and Kayitah and a man named George Wratten, a former store clerk who spoke fluent Apache. Only recently had Lawton received a clue regarding Geronimo's location. The ruse the Apaches had pulled off at Fronteras convinced the captain that the fugitives had a hideout somewhere in the northern Sierra Madre. Soon word came that the Apaches were camped at the northern bend of the Bavispe River. Lawton and Gatewood quickly moved in that direction.

When they were a day's march from the broncho hideout, Gatewood insisted on going on alone, taking only his small party. Lawton thought the whole idea of trying to coax the Apaches into negotiations was at the very least futile, and more than likely fatal—for his colleague. But he knew Gatewood—knew him as a man who had more experience fighting Apaches than anyone in the army, and that included himself. Gatewood was fluent in the Apache language; he knew how Apaches thought. He was cool, calm, and courageous under pressure. And, most of all, he was mule-stubborn. Lawton realized it was a waste of time trying to convince Gatewood not to go.

As they neared the broncho camp, Gatewood sent Martine and Kayitah on ahead. The renegades spotted the pair from high up in the rocks. Geronimo gave orders that they be shot if they came any closer. But Yanozha balked at this command. Kayitah was his cousin. "They are very brave to come here like this," he told Geronimo. "Let us find out why."

"When they get close enough, shoot them."

"I will shoot—the first man who raises a rifle against them."

The other bronchos had gathered around, and in scanning their faces Geronimo saw that the majority of them agreed with Yanozha—it was only right to see what their brothers, Kayitah and Martine, had to say. So Geronimo relented.

A brief council was held. Kayitah did most of the talking. "You are all my friends," he told the renegades, "and I do not want to see you all killed. The soldiers are closing in from all directions. You have been running for a long time. You sleep with one eye open. You see your women and children suffering. It is time for you to come home. Many of the soldiers who are coming after you are Mexicans. They will kill all of you, the women and the children, too. You know I speak the truth. Your people want you to live. So I want you to come down with me and talk to the lieutenant named Gatewood. You all know him—Nantan Long Nose. He is a man of his word. He would like to have a talk with you."

Geronimo agreed to meet with Gatewood—but Martine carried this news back all by himself. Kayitah was kept as a hostage. The Apaches insisted that Gatewood bring no other soldiers to the meeting. That was no problem for Gatewood. The following day, he and Martine and George Wratten arrived at the meeting place on the banks of the Bavispe.

A little while later they saw Kayitah leading Geronimo and the bronchos down out of the rocky heights. Geronimo walked up to Gatewood, put his rifle on the ground, and shook the lieutenant's hand enthusiastically. Gatewood handed out some tobacco and jerked horse meat.

"You look thin, Nantan Long Nose," Geronimo told Gatewood. "Is something the matter with you?"

"All of us horse soldiers are thin because we've been chasing after you for so long, Gokliya," said Gatewood, calling Geronimo by his Apache name.

Geronimo's knife-slit of a mouth widened into a smile. "Then you should stop chasing after us."

"I would like to. I am tired of running around. Aren't you?"

Geronimo nodded and, the smile gone, curtly asked for General Miles's terms. Gatewood told him the unvarnished truth, straight out—unconditional surrender. They would go to Florida with all the other Chiricahuas. The President would later decide if any of them ever were allowed to return to their homeland.

A grim silence descended on the scene. Gatewood's nerves were as steely as Geronimo's. He met squarely the Bedonkohe's dark gaze.

Finally Geronimo spoke. "We will go back to San Carlos and be given full amnesty for all that we have done."

"I can't negotiate with you, Gokliya. I'm just the messenger. I have given you the terms. That's all I can do."

"Take us back to the reservation or fight."

"Then I'll have to fight you, though I don't want to."

Geronimo looked away, hoping Gatewood would not see the bitterness on his face. "What would you do in my place, Nantan Long Nose?"

Gatewood leaned forward. "I would live. Only in death can the Chiricahua be conquered."

Geronimo understood exactly what he meant.

The bronchos discussed the situation among themselves—and the discussion went on for hours. At length Geronimo returned to Gatewood.

"It has been decided," he said flatly. "We will live."

The last of the wild Apaches surrendered to General Nelson Miles in Skeleton Canyon, located just north of the border

in Arizona. Thanks to Captain Lawton and Lieutenant Gatewood, the renegades got there alive. A force of two hundred
vengeful Mexicans tried to take the Indian captives away
from the cavalry and kill them. In past months Geronimo
and his raiders had claimed over five hundred Mexican
lives.

From Skeleton Canyon the prisoners were escorted back
to Fort Bowie, where Miles learned that President Grover
Cleveland wanted to have the Apaches turned over to the
civil authorities. Miles knew what that meant—Geronimo
and the other warriors would be tried, found guilty of various atrocities, and promptly hanged. Though he had no
fondness for the Apache, Miles could not go along with the
President's scheme, and said so in no uncertain terms. The
renegades had surrendered with the understanding that they
would be deported to Florida, not hanged in Arizona.
Cleveland relented; the government would abide by the
terms Miles had dictated at Skeleton Canyon.

On September 8 Geronimo and his followers were
hauled by wagon to the railhead at Fort Bowie. They were
loaded on to a train bound for Florida. The windows of the
railroad cars had been locked shut and the bronchos were
under heavy guard. Geronimo took one last look at his desert homeland through those windows—he would not live
to see it again.

The rest of the Chiricahua Apaches—four hundred and
thirty-four men, women, and children—were also trans-
ported eastward on a separate train, packed like cattle into
boarded-up passenger cars. Among them were Kayitah and
Martine. Their reward for the role they had played in bringing the Apache Wars to a conclusion was treachery; they
had expected the gratitude of the *pinda lickoyi*—and Martine swore that General Miles had personally promised him
a three-thousand-dollar award. But they, too, were shipped
off to Florida.

A single warrior escaped from the train, a man named
Massai. He was hunted for many months, but never recap-

tured. And there was talk that a handful of renegades still prowled the Sierra Madre for many years thereafter.

Unlike most of his contemporaries, John Slaughter was saddened when he heard of the fate that had befallen the Chiricahuas. Nearly all the whites in Arizona and New Mexico were overjoyed; the Apache scourge had finally been dealt with, once and for all. General Nelson Miles took the lion's share of the credit. He scarcely mentioned Lieutenant Gatewood or Captain Lawton in his official reports. Kayitah and Martine and all of the Apache scouts were promptly forgotten. The latter were disbanded and dispatched to the reservation without so much as a thank you from the government they had served so ably. Slaughter thought that was a real shame. He knew how instrumental the scouts had been in bringing the war to a close.

As it turned out, one Apache scout did not go quietly into oblivion. The one called the Apache Kid—the brooding young killer Slaughter had met at Fort Bowie—slipped away into the mountains, refusing to give up his guns and his freedom. In their jubilation over the defeat of Geronimo, most folks overlooked the Kid. John Slaughter didn't. He could vividly remember the uneasiness he had felt in the Apache Kid's presence. He knew trouble when he saw it, and he had a strong hunch that Arizona had not heard the last of the Kid.

CHAPTER TWENTY-ONE

THE APACHE KID

WHEN JOHN CLUM PAID A VISIT TO SAN BERNARDINO, IT wasn't just to see how Texas John and his family were getting along. He had an ulterior motive. But he kept that to himself until after supper. Viola insisted that he stay over for the night, and Clum could not resist. The Slaughters' Chinese cook was the best in the territory, and no one could ask for better company. Addie was there, bright and vivacious as always. So was Willie, dark-haired and compact in build just like his father, and with that familiar glint of mischief in his eyes. Viola claimed that Willie was the spitting image of John, and in more ways than one. For one thing, the youngster was forever roaming the countryside, shirking his studies—not to mention his chores—just like his father had done as a boy back in Texas.

"He causes me no end of worry," said Viola, her tone of voice a scolding one as she looked across the table at Willie, even though a tolerant smile curled her lips.

"Willie can take care of himself," said Slaughter.

"Well, it certainly is a lot safer these days, thanks in no small part to your husband's efforts, Viola," said Clum. "At least Willie doesn't have to worry about running into a gang of Mexican bandits or a pack of Comanche raiders like Texas John did back in his wild youth."

Viola smiled at her husband. "Yes, John did a good job cleaning up Cochise County, as I always knew he would."

Clum nodded. "As we both knew."

"But I'm glad he's not doing that kind of thing anymore," she continued. "I'm glad he's home and no longer wearing a badge. I'm glad he lost that last election, frankly. These past few years have been the happiest and most complete of my life."

"And mine," said Slaughter, reaching out to place his hand over Viola's.

Clum experienced a twinge of guilt. But it passed quickly enough.

The conversation moved on to other topics, and when the meal was over and the table cleared away, Viola sent Willie off to bed while she and Addie retired to let the men drink their bonded whiskey and smoke cigars. Clum accepted Texas John's offer of a Mexican cheroot. He puffed on the cheroot for a moment, savoring the bite of the pungent tobacco, then peered at Slaughter through a veil of acrid blue smoke.

"You know, Texas John, I don't think you get the credit you deserve for bringing law and order to Cochise County."

"I didn't do it so I could get credit. I did it because it needed to be done."

"I know. But still, it was a remarkable job you performed. In four short years you shut down most of the rustling gangs. You broke up the Cowboys once and for all. You brought more men to justice than all of your predecessors combined. Hell, you did something not even the Earp brothers could do. Now, that's saying something."

"Ah, well. Thing is, John, the Earps weren't all that interested in law and order."

Clum let that one pass. He knew by this time that he and Slaughter would never see eye to eye when it came to Wyatt Earp and his brothers. And he knew it bothered Texas John a little that the Earps had received such renown as champions of justice because of the way the events surrounding the gunfight at the O.K. Corral had been glorified by eastern news correspondents and dime novelists.

"Still, it concerned me, some of the things that were said about you when you ran for re-election," said Clum.

"You mean how I preferred to dispense justice from the barrel of a gun? How for every criminal I brought before the court I left one lying dead in the dust? Hell, John, why does it concern you so much? That's all true."

Clum shrugged. "People have notoriously short memories, don't they? They so easily forget how bad it was before you became sheriff. They forgot all the many times you risked your life to rid this country of the lawless element."

"Well, I hate to tell you this, John, but I didn't do it for all those other people, so I really don't care what they remember."

"I know, I know." Clum chuckled.

Slaughter leaned forward and put his elbows on the table, looking squarely at Clum with the cheroot clenched between his teeth. "I say, John, will you be getting around to what you wanted to talk to me about anytime soon?"

Clum sighed. "Damn it. Is it that obvious?"

"You keep bringing up my being sheriff, and it's for a reason. And as I recall, the *Epitaph* was not exactly standing four-square behind me in that last race. But don't get me wrong. I'm glad it happened. Didn't really want to keep that job. I was ready to lay it down."

"I understand, Texas John, believe me I do. But, well, fact is, you did such a damned fine job of law-dogging that one day we all took a good look about us and realized that you were the most dangerous man left alive in Cochise County!"

"And politics had nothing to do with it."

Clum laughed. "Thing is, we were wrong. You're not the only dangerous man left, after all."

Slaughter shook his head. "I spent too many years away

from this place, from these people. I missed a lot of the growing up my children have done. I spent too many nights hunched over a campfire that I could have spent in the arms of my wife. I am not going back to the way it was before. I will not wear a badge again."

Clum thought it over for a moment, then said, "It's the Apache Kid."

Slaughter felt a chill slide down his spine.

"He has killed once again," said Clum. "This time it was Ben Williams, the sheriff over at Bisbee."

"Damn." Slaughter knew Williams as a conscientious lawman—and a husband and father.

"The Kid ambushed him in Guadalupe Canyon. Of course, a posse was put together. But they didn't find any sign to follow. The Kid is like a ghost, Texas John. You know that."

"Yes, I know," said Slaughter. "He always had to be. You sure it was him?"

"Yes, quite sure. He left his calling card. They found an empty shell casing in Williams's mouth. Fired from a Sharps Big Fifty. One shot at long range."

"Well, I was hoping the Kid was gone for good."

"I think it's safe to say we were all hoping that."

When the army had shipped the Chiricahua Apaches off to Florida and disbanded the "blue wolves," the Kid had gotten into trouble and was thrown in jail. But no jail could hold him long. Recaptured some time later, he was dispatched to San Diego, but a jurisdictional battle brought him back to Arizona, where he was sentenced to seven years in Yuma Prison. The Kid led another jailbreak. Several guards were wounded. Leading a gang of hardcases, all of them Indians, the Kid embarked on a murder spree, killing a number of whites, then fled into Mexico, finding sanctuary in the old Apache haunts—the Sierra Madre. On a few occasions he slipped back over the border to steal a woman from the reservation. When he grew weary of the squaw, he killed her so that she could not betray him, and then stole another one to replace her. He lived like a bron-cho, and was as bad as any renegade who had come before.

A year had passed since anyone in Arizona had seen the Kid, and Slaughter had hoped against hope that he would never resurface, that he had met his death down in Mexico.

"Guadalupe Canyon, you said," muttered Slaughter. "That's pretty close to San Bernardino."

Clum nodded. "Texas John, several posses and the United States Army are looking for the Kid. Do you think they'll find him?"

"No."

"Do you think you can?"

Slaughter gazed bleakly at John Clum. He was thinking about Willie, about how his son loved to take off alone on horseback to avoid his chores and book-learning. What he didn't want to think about was what would happen to Willie if he ran into the Apache Kid.

"Do me one favor, Texas John," said Clum. "This time don't go alone."

"Alone is the only way I'll catch him."

Slaughter spent weeks looking for some clue to the whereabouts of the Apache Kid. He asked everyone that he thought might have some idea, and made the effort to check out every rumor as long as it seemed remotely possible. Eventually he was pretty sure that the Kid was down along the Animas River somewhere, probably in the breaks. And he was also fairly sure that the Kid was no longer riding with his gang of Indian renegades and half-breed cutthroats. Most of those gentlemen had been captured or killed, and word was that the rest had decided to quit the Kid because by now he was the most wanted man in the Southwest, not to mention all of northern Mexico, too. So being around the Kid was extremely hazardous. Based on the most reli-able accounts he could unearth, Slaughter believed that the Kid was alone now except for an Indian woman, one who had only recently been abducted from the Mescalero reservation. The kidnapping had all the trappings of something the Kid would do. It had been swift, daring, and brutal. The girl's father had been killed.

Combing the badlands along the Animas was not a business for the impatient or the faint of heart—there were a hundred perfect hiding places and a thousand excellent sites for an ambush. But Slaughter kept at it, completely undeterred as one long and fruitless day piled on top of another. He figured it was really just a matter of time before he found the Kid or the Kid found him. He could only hope that the former would turn out to be the case.

For days he saw no sign of another human. This land of arid sandstone ridges and dry gulches was desperately short of good graze and water, fit only for rattlers and horned toads. Slaughter did not know it very well. He didn't know of anyone who did. Not even Lorenzo Paca. Still, there were times when he wished he had brought Paca along. Lorenzo had gotten married—something Slaughter had thought would never happen, not least because Paca had sworn he would never fall into that trap. Lorenzo was nothing if not an independent thinker, and firmly set in his bachelor ways. Or so Slaughter had thought. Now Paca was hitched, and gone into retirement at the behest of his bride. It wasn't solely out of respect for Mrs. Paca's wishes that Slaughter had refrained from asking Lorenzo to join him in this last manhunt. It was also because the prey was none other than the Apache Kid—the most dangerous man Slaughter had ever hunted. He simply did not want to put his old friend in harm's way. He knew he would never forgive himself if the Kid killed Lorenzo. And he also knew that Paca would have come along. He wouldn't have been able to resist, no matter how much his bride complained.

Days turned into weeks. And then, at long last, Slaughter got the break he had been praying for.

He came to a water hole located at the intersection of three canyons, and there he found some tracks. They were several days old, but clearly captured in the now-dried mud

rimming the small pool of green, brackish water. A barefoot
child or woman had led a pair of horses, one iron-shod and
the other not, to this water hole, then returned up the canyon headed north. Slaughter followed the sign about a quarter of a mile up the canyon. Then his instinct for danger
took a firm grip on him and made him pull up short. If the
footprints belonged to the Mescalero girl that the Kid had
taken, then he was riding straight into a death trap. He
turned around and went back to the water hole and let his
horse drink. Sitting on his heels in the shade of the tall
gray, he pondered his next move.

The foremost question on his mind was whether the Kid
was fool enough to trust the Mescalero girl with his horses.
Had he won her over? Slaughter doubted that. He'd killed
her father, after all. That meant the Kid had shadowed her,
and she knew it—knew it would mean certain death if she
attempted to flee. Slaughter scanned the barren rocky
heights. No, the Kid was no fool. He knew that a water
hole was a dangerous place for a wanted man. So he was
letting the girl water the horses and watching her from
somewhere up there.

The girl—if indeed it was the Mescalero girl—had
brought the horses at least three days ago. Had she taken
much water back with her to the Kid's hideout? How soon
would she return to the water hole? Slaughter thought it
would likely be pretty soon, and decided to stake out the
water hole for a day or two. If that didn't work, then he
would be forced to proceed up that canyon and locate the
Kid's camp. That was a last resort because he wasn't at all
sure he would come out of that canyon alive.

He picked his spot carefully—on a rock-strewn ridge-
top east of the water hole, overlooking the intersection of
the canyons; from this vantage point he could see up the
north canyon several hundred yards. But more importantly,
his was the highest point around, and if the Kid took up a
position on the heights anywhere near the water hole,

Slaughter figured he would see the renegade and, with any luck, get a clear shot at him.

Settling down among the rocks, Slaughter waited. He kept his long gun, a Winchester repeater, near at hand. His canteen was full and he had some hard biscuits and jerked beef to tide him over. The sun blazed in a sky of brass, and there wasn't any shade to speak of. He slept in fits and starts, afraid he might miss his prey if his eyes remained closed too long.

She came the next morning, at dawn, when the shadows were still deep in the canyon bottoms, and at first he did not see her—had no idea she was there until she emerged from the north canyon, a black-haired, skinny girl wearing an old tattered gingham dress and leading two horses.

Slaughter searched the high ground. Where the hell was the Apache Kid? A moment later he saw movement across the canyon, and strained to see more in the uncertain light. The Kid knew how to use whatever cover was available, was an expert on how to blend into his environment. He knew—like any Apache broncho knew—how to remain invisible until it was time to kill.

Curbing his impatience, Slaughter decided he had to have better light. He would stay low until the Mescalero girl had finished her task at the water hole and was on her way back up the canyon. The Kid wouldn't go anywhere until then.

I'll only get one shot at him, thought Slaughter. *I have to make it count.*

The minutes seemed like hours. The sun climbed higher, banishing the shadows that lingered down in the canyons, and throwing the heights into sharper relief. Finally the Mescalero girl was done. She had let the horses drink all they wanted, and she had filled the two large water bags joined by short lengths of stout rope and carried on the back of the unshod horse like saddlebags. Slaughter kept his eyes glued to the high ground where he thought the Kid was hiding.

Suddenly he saw him—a slender figure dressed in Apache garb, a calico shirt, a breechcloth, and *n'deh b'keh,* the desert moccasins. A red bandanna was tied around his head.

Slaughter jumped to his feet, raised the Winchester to his shoulder, and drew a bead on the Kid as the latter moved across the skyline in an effortless, ground-eating lope. He adjusted his aim for range and windage, leading the Kid slightly—and squeezed the trigger.

The gun's report shattered the morning stillness. The Kid went down—and then was up and running again, faster now. Slaughter swore under his breath. He was pretty certain that he had hit his mark. But he just hadn't hit it in the right place.

The Mescalero girl was trying to get the horses to move faster, pulling on their halters, but they were waterlogged and one started to balk at this rough treatment. Slaughter saw his chance. He ran to his horse, not bothering with the saddle that lay on the ground, and rode hell for leather down a steep game trail. It was a miracle that he made it to the canyon bottom in one piece. Once there, he kicked the responsive gray into a gallop. The Mescalero girl saw him coming. She leaped aboard the horse that was not burdened with the water bags and tried to flee up the canyon, leaving the other animal behind. Slaughter was in hot pursuit and closing on her—until the Kid killed the gray.

Slaughter heard the shot and felt the horse give one massive shudder. As the animal's front legs buckled, Slaughter swung his right leg up and over its neck and dismounted on the run, stumbled, fell, came back up quickly on one knee, rifle still in his grasp, his eyes scanning the skyline. Seeing nothing up there to shoot at, he swung the rifle around and fired, killing the horse the girl was on, the shod horse, the horse that he believed was the Kid's.

It was the horses, after all, that he was after, not the Mescalero girl. The horse went down, the girl went flying through the air. Slaughter broke into a hard run. Another gunshot sang out from above, and the Kid's bullet kicked up dust between Slaughter's legs. Spotting the powder smoke from the Kid's Big Fifty, Slaughter fired one round, then started running again. Reaching the girl, he thought for a moment that she was dead, killed by the fall. But as his shadow fell across her, she sprang to her feet and lashed out at him with a knife. She was quick and agile, but he was quicker, and he struck the blade from her grasp with the butt of his rifle. She launched herself at him, trying to claw his face, but he knocked her down before she could do any damage.

"Stop that," he snapped, speaking in Spanish, hoping she knew enough of the language to understand, since he didn't know nearly enough about the Apache tongue to communicate effectively. "I mean you no harm. Run. Get out of here. Take that other horse and get out of here. Now!"

She stared up at him, and he saw comprehension dawn in her eyes, and then she glanced apprehensively up at the high ground.

"Don't worry about him anymore," rasped Slaughter. "He's a dead man. Now move it!" He picked up her knife and handed it to her.

She looked at him again, big dark eyes in a gaunt, dirty face—and then she was up and running, making for the only horse left alive. Slaughter craned his neck to watch the skyline, and just as he did, the Kid appeared, standing right there on the rimrock, in full view, if only for an instant. The Kid was about to get off a shot—at the girl, not Slaughter, for in a glance the renegade could see what was happening down below. Either he did not want the girl to leave here alive, or he wanted the horse for himself; either way, it didn't matter to Slaughter. He fired the Winchester. Again the Kid seemed to vanish in midair. Slaughter fired several more rounds at the rimrock. The Mescalero girl had reached the horse. She grabbed a handful of mane and vaulted onto its back. With one last look, she cut the ropes with her knife and let the water bags fall to the ground.

One burst open. The thirsty earth sucked up the moisture. With one last look at Slaughter, the girl spun the horse around and left the canyon at a gallop.

Slaughter ran to the base of the cliff directly below the spot where he had last seen the Apache Kid. There he sought momentary refuge, a little time to catch his breath, settle his nerves, and reload the Winchester. Glancing across the barren canyon floor, he felt a twinge of sadness at the sight of the gray gelding lying dead. That horse had been a faithful companion, carrying him down many a trail.

He waited for over an hour, wondering if the Kid would come down after him, hoping he would. When that didn't happen, he walked up the canyon two hundred yards to a steep draw. Climbing to the rim was an arduous task—twice the sandstone crumbled under his weight and nearly plunged him to the bottom of the canyon. It was also a nerve-wracking ascent, for he felt very exposed, and if the Kid reappeared above him, then he was done for. Finally reaching the top, Slaughter found cover behind some rocks and rested a few minutes. Was the Kid still around, or long gone? There was only one way to find out. Slaughter darted for another cluster of rocks, crossing thirty feet of open ground at a crouching run. No shot rang out. No bullet chased him. The Kid was gone. But where?

In no time at all Slaughter located the blood trail. He was elated. He *had* hit his mark. The Kid was hurt. Best of all, the blood would lead him to his prey. Slaughter thought things were beginning to turn in his favor.

Feeling terribly exposed on the ridge-top, knowing that at any time the Kid might turn at bay and find a place of concealment from which to kill him, Slaughter followed the blood for a quarter mile. The Kid was leaking badly but still making good time, and Slaughter felt a grudging respect for the renegade. The Kid was tough as they came— tough and smart and as game as a rooster. He was also a cold-blooded killer. *You cannot fail in this,* Slaughter told

himself. *And you sure as hell can't quit. The Kid has got
to be put down. And if you don't do it, who else will?*

The trail of blood led him to the edge of a ravine. Down
below was a seep, which nurtured a little grass and a thicket
of scrub trees, and somehow Slaughter knew that the Kid
was down there, hiding in that brush, and he dove for some
rocks just as the Kid fired. The bullet hit Slaughter in the
calf, knocking him off balance. He fell behind the rocks,
and a second bullet whined off a stone disconcertingly close
to his head.

Wincing at the pain, Slaughter muttered a string of
curses.

"My God, Clum," he muttered, exasperated, "this is *absolutely the last damned time!*"

The Kid wasn't wasting any more ammunition. But
Slaughter chose to waste some, shooting down into the ravine every twenty or thirty minutes, just to let his adversary
know that he was still alive and ready to kill him if he
broke cover. He prayed that the Kid was hurt bad enough
that he would stay put. Slaughter tied a bandanna around
his leg to stanch the flow of blood. The wound was painful,
but the bullet had missed bone and artery. It wasn't going
to kill him. But Slaughter was well aware that the next one
might.

Lying there, his body hammered by the merciless sun,
and trying to ignore the throbbing pain in his leg, Slaughter
waited for the day to run its course. It seemed like a small
eternity before the late afternoon shadows began to stretch
across the Animas badlands. A wind picked up; the sigh of
the parched land as the burden of the sun's heat dissipated.
Still Slaughter waited, until the last light had bled from the
sky. Only then did he move, crawling on his belly down
into the ravine. He left the Winchester up in the rocks; now
all he had was his side gun. He moved slowly, trying not
to make a noise that would betray his position. He could
not be certain that the Kid was still in the thicket, but he

had to work on that assumption, not caring to even contemplate the choices he would have to make if the renegade had managed to slip away.

Reaching the bottom of the ravine, Slaughter crawled another twenty-five feet until he was at the edge of the sparse, sun-browned grass. Checking the wind, he struck a match on his belt buckle and set the grass ablaze, then crawled away. The fire was quick to spread, shoved by the wind closer to the brush. Slaughter got up, six-shooter now in hand. Ignoring the dull pain in his leg, he ran to the downwind side of the thicket, just as the first of the scrub trees caught fire and seemed to explode into flame. In moments the entire thicket was ablaze. Slaughter's hopes began to fade. The Apache Kid wasn't in there. He had slipped away after all! No, wait. Slaughter saw movement—then the shape of a man silhouetted starkly against the leaping orange flames. The roar of the fire filled the ravine. Eyes narrowed against the smoke, Slaughter advanced as the Kid stumbled out of the brush. His left arm hung limp and useless at his side. Slaughter realized then that his bullet had crippled the Kid. And the fact that the Kid had only one good arm explained why he had missed when he'd fired down into the canyon at Slaughter. Because otherwise he would not have missed.

The Kid saw him, raised a pistol as he turned to run along the edge of the thicket. Slaughter ran in the same direction to cut him off. Thirty feet apart, they blazed away at one another. Slaughter had a slight advantage—he could see the Kid clearly against the flames, while he himself was shrouded in darkness and smoke. The Kid stumbled, nearly fell, and pulled up short, bending over at the waist. *I have hit him again,* thought Slaughter, who straightened, drew a bead. The Kid raised his gun as though it were almost too heavy for him. Slaughter squeezed the trigger. The Kid was hurled backward into the flaming brush.

Heaving a deep sigh, John Slaughter lowered the Colt and stood there for a while, his mind empty, watching the fire burn ferociously. Eventually he turned away. The Apache Kid was dead. It was over. All of it. Time to go home, and this time it was for good. He had done what needed doing.

A DANGEROUS MAN

1921

"I THINK WE'RE ALMOST THERE," SAID THE MAN DRIVING THE buckboard. "As I calculate it, the ranch is maybe two miles farther on."

"I just hope you know what you're talking about," replied the man who sat beside him, a double-barreled shotgun laid across his lap. "That would be a change."

"Go to hell, Drake."

"I'm waiting on you, Sam," said Drake laconically. "And you had better be right about this whole business or we'll both be making that trip soon."

"Stop worrying so much. This will be so easy we could do it with our eyes closed. I'm telling you, it's just an old couple who live there with a few cowboys who are as old as they are. You're not afraid of a few old waddies, now, are you, Drake?"

Drake didn't say anything. As far as he was concerned, Sam's comment was not worthy of a response. Sam talked too much, and he had a tendency to talk even more when he was nervous. Drake wasn't at all nervous. He never got nervous about anything. He didn't mind danger, didn't give killing a second thought. Those who knew the two of them also knew that Sam was the one who thought up all the jobs and Drake the one who made them succeed through a combination of audacity and brutality. That struck observers as odd, since Drake was a small, thin, rat-faced man while Sam was a big, brawny fellow. Others believed that Drake was just too stupid to be nervous, and too lacking in conscience to mind dispensing death. But none of them were foolish enough to suggest this in Drake's presence.

Drake half turned to see if their companion was still conscious in the back of the buckboard.

"Hey, Tom, did you ever work around here?"

The third man sat with his back to the bench on which Sam and Drake were sitting. He was facing the three saddle horses tied to the rear of the buckboard. Sam's idea had been that they would leave the stolen buckboard at the scene of the crime and make a quick dash for the border using the horses. The third man looked to the left. Then he looked to the right. Not that he could see much of the passing countryside. It was close to midnight and dark as sin.

"Hell," he drawled, his words slurred by whiskey. "I'm not even sure where we are."

Drake shook his head and snorted. "Sam, tell me again why we brought this drunkard along. He's worthless. I ought to blow his head off."

"That's your answer to everything," complained Sam.

"Well, it's worked for me so far."

"Tom is along because he is a friend of mine. If it weren't for him, I would still be in that hellhole they call a jail in Monterey."

"Oh, yeah, that's right. You spend too much time in crossbar hotels, Sam, did you know that?"

"Don't be a wiseacre, Drake."

"Sometimes I can't help myself. Now, you're sure we're gonna find plenty of cash at this here ranch?"

Sam sighed the sigh of the long-suffering. "Damn it, Drake. When are you going to learn to trust me? Have I ever been wrong about these things?"

He looked at Drake. Drake was looking at him, smirking.

"Okay, okay. There was that one time in Kansas City. But I'm right this time. The old codger used to own half of Arizona. Ran tens of thousands of head of cattle. He doesn't put his trust—or his money—in banks. Fair enough?"

Drake nodded. "And we kill everybody there. We don't leave any witnesses."

"That's right," said Sam. "But you don't have to sound so happy about that."

"I'm not happy," said Drake. "And I'm not unhappy. I'm not anything."

"He just doesn't give a damn who he has to kill or how many," remarked the third man.

"You haven't fallen out yet, Tom?" asked Drake. "What's the matter, still on the first bottle?"

"The blaze-faced sorrel. That your horse, Drake?"

"Yeah."

The third man waited until he was sure Drake wasn't looking, then spat a stream of cheap whiskey into the sorrel's face. The horse snorted and jerked its head violently. He felt bad about treating the horse that way; he liked the horse a lot better than he did Drake. But maybe the animal would be harder for Drake to manage when the killer got into the saddle. After all, Drake was a lot of things, most of them bad—but he was no horseman.

"What's the matter with that nag?" asked Sam.

"Nothing," said Tom. "Probably a coyote nearby, that's all."

"I see a light up ahead," announced Drake, leaning forward to peer into the darkness.

"That must be it," said Sam, elated. "Must be San Bernardino."

"What did you say?" asked the third man.

"I said that's it, San Bernardino. Boys, we're about to be good and rich." Sam stopped the buckboard. "Okay, Tom. Here's where you get off. Now, remember, bring the horses as close as you can without being spotted, and wait until you see us come out of the big house, then bring 'em up the rest of the way. You clear on that?"

"Sure. I'm just a little drunk; I'm not stupid."

"Why are we doing this, again?" asked Drake. "This business with the horses, I mean."

Sam heaved a sigh. "Because we're down on our luck, drifters looking for some kind of work. We're broke and we're hungry. So we don't own any saddlehorses, Drake. Jesus!"

"Getting religion, Sam?" asked Tom as he climbed gingerly out of the buckboard. Feet more or less firmly planted on the ground, he put away his pocket flask and untied the three horses. The blazed sorrel jerked against the reins, but Tom held it fast.

"Okay, here we go," said Sam tensely. "You ready, Drake?"

Drake stifled a yawn. "I'm ready for something to happen."

Tom watched the buckboard pull away down the road. When it was a few hundred yards on, he let go of two of the horses and pulled himself into the saddle on the third. So much for making Drake's sorrel ornery. Two words had changed everything. *San Bernardino.* Tom smiled bitterly, thinking about how life had a way of playing tricks on a man.

The hull beneath him was an old Texas rig. Like its owner, it had seen much better days. But being in the saddle again, on this range, brought back a flood of memories to Tom. He tried to block them, but without success. Taking a deep breath, hoping to clear some of the cobwebs out of his head, he tried to focus on the distant bead of light far off across the flats. He felt a twinge of something in the vicinity of his heart. Then he kicked the horse into a gallop across the flats, stretching the animal out and heading straight for the light.

When he reached the ranch buildings, he slowed the horse to a walk. The ride had cleared his head. He looked back along the road, wondering how long it would be before the buckboard arrived. Sam and Drake were city-born hoodlums who had come to Arizona only because the Midwest had become too hot for them. They were wanted for armed robbery and murder in places like Chicago and St. Louis and Kansas City. They weren't used to the wide-open spaces, and Sam was a lousy judge of distance. When he'd seen the speck of light and stopped the buckboard, Sam had guessed that the ranch was only a mile or so away. In fact, it had been closer to five or six miles.

Dismounting, Tom left his horse behind the main house and walked around to the front. The bunkhouses across the hardpack were dark and quiet. If they were occupied at all, then the occupants were sound asleep. Every day started early for a cowboy.

The light they had seen far across the flats issued from a window of the adobe main house. Tom knocked softly on the door, listened intently for any sound from within. Was someone still up? Was that what the light meant? He knocked again, a little harder this time, then looked around to check the road again. He was running out of time. He raised a fist to knock a third time, but before his knuckles could connect with wood, the door swung open. Tom turned to find himself staring down the barrel of an old Colt Peacemaker. The end of the barrel hovered steady as a rock about an inch from his right eye.

"It's a little late to be making a social call," said the man behind the venerable six-shooter.

Tom looked past the gun at John Slaughter.

"Hello, Texas John. You remember who I am?"

Slaughter's dark eyes narrowed. "The voice sounds awful familiar. But it has been some years since I heard it last."

Tom smiled wistfully. "About thirty years. I didn't sport a beard back then, either. You haven't changed all that much, Texas John. Though, as I recall, your hair used to be black as the ace of spades, not white."

"Yeah, well, thirty years ago I didn't have arthritis and asthma like I do now, either. Wait a minute. Could it be? My God, is that you, Tom?"

Tom Cochran nodded. "It's me."

"I'll be damned," breathed Slaughter, lowering the Colt. "Come in! What the hell are you doing here?"

"You said your door was always open."

"I meant what I said."

"I've come to tell you that two men are on their way up the road. They plan to rob and kill you, Texas John. You and everybody else here."

Slaughter looked at Tom, digesting this surprising news, then stepped out to peer up the road into the night. "Do tell," he said flatly.

"They'll be here in a few minutes."

"Okay, then. Gives us time for a drink."

Slaughter herded Tom inside and shut the door.

As he stood there gazing at the main room, Tom Cochran was struck by how so little had changed. A flood of memories left him a little weak in the knees.

"How is . . ." He caught himself, and experienced the old shame again. Even after all these years, it still burned hot.

"She's doing just fine, Tom. Sound asleep." Slaughter had put the Colt under his belt and moved to the sideboard to pour two shot glasses full of bonded whiskey. "What have you been doing? Where have you been keeping yourself? I confess, I had you figured for dead by now."

"Pretty much dead," replied Tom morosely. "Spent a dozen years down in South America, doing odd jobs like riding shotgun on mine shipments, that kind of thing. These

last few years . . ." He shook his head. "I've lost them,
Texas John. They may be at the bottom of an empty whiskey bottle somewhere."

"You never settled down, then."

"No. Never had reason to," said Tom, thinking about
Viola, sleeping like an angel nearby.

"I should go wake Viola up. She'd be thrilled to death
to see you."

"No, don't." Tom was suddenly embarrassed. He didn't
want Viola to see him looking the way he did—like a bum.

"Time enough for that later. So who are these two men?"

"Hoods."

"What are they carrying?"

"Two pistols and a shotgun between them. The little one,
with the shotgun, his name is Drake—he's a dangerous
man."

Slaughter smiled. "It's been a while since I've seen one
of those in these parts."

"You see one every time you look in the mirror, Texas
John. You have a telephone here?"

"I do. But I dislike the contraption. Only got it because
Viola wanted it."

"Then we should call the sheriff. And wake up the men
in the bunkhouse."

Slaughter leaned casually against the sideboard, sipping
the whiskey. "They'll wake up when the shooting starts, I
reckon. So tell me, Tom. How did you fall in with these
two?"

"How did I ever get into anything? Just lucky, I guess."

Slaughter nodded, put down the shot glass. "I think
you're friends are pulling in."

Tom listened intently, but didn't hear anything. He
watched Slaughter go to the gun case. When Texas John
turned around, he had a sawed-off shotgun in hand. Breaking it open, he loaded both barrels.

"You've still got that old scattergun, I see," said Tom.
"The one you took off of—what was that man's name? The

one that came after you all the way from Texas because you caught him trying to cheat you at cards?"

"Gallagher."

"How many men have you killed, Texas John?"

"Enough."

"What about that feller, Robles? The one who hired Agustin Chacon. Whatever happened to him?"

"I have no idea."

"You mean you never went down there to settle the score? That's not like you."

Slaughter smiled pensively. "I just never got around to it, Tom. Always seemed to have better things to do."

Tom nodded. He knew what those "better things" were. The same things he had never had—a loving wife, a family, a home to call his own.

He heard the buckboard then, rattling across the hard-pack in front of the house.

"I'd like to back you on this, Texas John, if you'll have me."

Slaughter was moving toward the door. He stopped in front of Tom and looked him straight in the eye, judging him, measuring him. They were eyes, thought Tom, that had seen many years come and go, and yet they were still eagle-sharp.

"That would suit me," said Slaughter. "And when we're done, you can stay over, and in the morning, we'll ride out and see if we can't scare up some quail for breakfast. How does that sound?"

Tom looked around the room. It didn't look like anything had changed in thirty years.

"I'll settle for that," he said, and followed John Slaughter out into the night.

AUTHOR'S NOTE

JOHN HORTON SLAUGHTER WAS BORN ON OCTOBER 2, 1841, in Sabine Parish, Louisiana, right across the river from Texas. It was to Texas that his father Ben was moving the whole family, and John always thought it one of the great misfortunes of his life that the first breath he took was not filled with Texas air. He spent his formative years on the edge of civilization, the Texas prairie, first at Lockhart and then at Friotown. His youth is as described in this novel, and they were years that made him the man he was, a hard man, bold and fearless, sometimes merciless but never cruel, who lived by the frontier code and expected everyone else to do the same. He was cut from the same cloth as his father. A story that is a favorite of his descendants has Ben Slaughter attending a cattlemen's luncheon at San Antonio's Southern Hotel. He came in off the range wearing an old Mexican blanket over his shoulders, and the hotel manager adamantly refused to allow him entry in such a dusty and deplorable condition. Ben reluctantly exchanged his blanket for a Prince Albert coat and went in to the luncheon. After it was over the hotel manager wanted his coat back, but Ben refused to give it up. "No, you damned Indian giver," said Ben. "You shamed me into wearin' it and now I'm going to keep it." The hotel manager wisely decided not to argue the point with a man who had a Remington revolver stuck in his belt—especially when that man was a Slaughter.

Ben and his three sons, Billy, Charles, and John, all became successful cattlemen in their own right, and at one time claimed a large portion of the land in two counties as their own range. John Slaughter fought Comanches, enlisted in the Confederate Army, and served for a short spell as a Texas Ranger in the 1870s. He married Eliza Harris in 1871, and by her had two children, Addie and Willie. The details of her tragic death are as described in this book and occurred during that period when Slaughter was seeking a new beginning in the Southwest, as were other Texas cattlemen. On his way to Arizona, Slaughter met with some trouble in New Mexico when Governor Lew Wallace targeted Texas cattle outfits in the belief that they were largely responsible for a wave of lawlessness sweeping the territory in the late 1870s. A warrant was issued for Slaughter's arrest, and hundreds of his cattle were confiscated. Slaughter wisely moved his outfit to Arizona and settled near Tombstone on the old San Bernardino land grant.

Don Francisco Robles is a fictional character, and the conflict between Robles and Slaughter that is one of the themes of this novel never occurred. The facts are this: Slaughter rode into Mexico with $12,000 in silver to buy cattle, accompanied by Jean Baptiste—Old Bat—and his foreman John Roberts (whose place, in the novel, is taken by Del Hooper). They were set upon by a band of forty bandits, and the *vaqueros* Slaughter had hired fled the scene. Slaughter and his men were confronted by the bandits in a small village but managed to slip away; the bandits followed and rode straight into a night ambush, which discouraged them sufficiently to allow Slaughter to continue on his cattle-buying excursion unmolested. Word reached his new wife, Viola, that her husband had been killed, and she drove a wagon south to recover his body, meeting him on the trail. Later Slaughter would say it was "the only time I remember having been murdered."

John Slaughter had no part in the Earp–Clanton feud that culminated in the gunfight at the O.K. Corral. He did on one occasion find some of his Z brand cattle in the possession of the Clantons, but apparently his stern warning was taken to heart by Old Man Clanton, whose crew left the San Bernardino herd alone from then on. It seems clear that Slaughter did not have a very high opinion of the Earp brothers or the Clanton crowd, so it was not hard for him to remain neutral during that conflict. He focused his attention on building a cattle empire, going into partnership with a neighbor named George Lang, and running cattle as far as California.

In 1886 Slaughter was persuaded by his Cochise County acquaintances to run for sheriff. A man who had no faith in the efficacy of posses or vigilante committees, he often tracked down the lawless, all by his lonesome, occasionally relying on a handful of (usually) dependable deputies, represented in the novel by Jeff Milton and Lorenzo Paca. There were others—Enoch Shattuck, Ed Barker, Burt Alvord (who went bad), and even Tommy Howell, Viola's cousin. Slaughter had a no-nonsense approach to bringing law and order to Arizona. As his friend Milton once said, "John was noted for reading his warrants to the culprits *after* the shooting was over." Another acquaintance said of Slaughter, "He didn't like to shoot people. He did it simply because it was in the day's work and was for a good purpose." It appears that during his career as a lawman Slaughter killed about twenty men. One of these was Geronimo Baltierrez, who paid for taking the life of one of Slaughter's deputies with his own. Baltierrez was not involved in an attack on Viola Slaughter—such an attack never occurred—but he did meet his end on a night when he visited a señorita in a tent a half mile outside the town of Fairbank. Baltierrez cut a slit in the back of the tent with his knife, hoping to slip away in the darkness, but Slaughter was there waiting for him, and a moment later the criminal's career came to a bloody end.

Agustin Chacon is a historical character, and his first meeting with Slaughter—in a tent on the outskirts of Tombstone—occurred pretty much as described in this book. However, he was not hired to kill Slaughter; he came up with the idea on his own. He escaped Slaughter, but was later captured thanks to the efforts of Arizona Ranger Burt Mossman. The daring Mossman infiltrated Chacon's gang, which included ex-deputy Burt Alvord. Mossman persuaded Alvord to aid him in his deception, and when the time was right got the drop on Chacon, arrested him, and brought him to justice. Chacon's last words, as he stood on the gallows with a noose around his neck, were, "I consider this to be the greatest day of my life." It is said that Slaughter fervently agreed. Chacon was one of the two men that made John Slaughter nervous. The other was the Apache Kid.

How the Apache Kid died is still a matter of some controversy. John Slaughter did participate in the massive manhunt that resulted from the Kid's various depredations, but he did so with the assistance of his deputies and the United States Cavalry. The elusive Kid slipped through their grasp on several occasions. It is possible that Slaughter did kill the Kid in the Sierra Madres in 1894, with the help of a cavalry officer named Benton. But Tom Horn, who knew the Kid from the days when both scouted for the army, insisted that the Kid died of tuberculosis. Others believe he was finally tracked down and dealt with by a posse in 1907.

Slaughter was Cochise County sheriff until 1890, after which he spent most of his time managing his thriving business concerns. He served a brief stint in Arizona's twenty-fourth territorial legislature, but politics were not for him. As the years went by he was occasionally called upon to strap on his guns and ride off in search of an outlaw—the careers of longriders like Peg Leg Finney and Little Bob Stevens were brought to an abrupt end thanks to Texas John

and his proclivity for dispensing justice from the barrel of
a gun.

In 1921, a year before Slaughter's death, four men arrived at San Bernardino intent on robbery and murder. One
cowboy lost his life, but the robbers fled the scene rather
than face the wrath of John Slaughter. Such was his reputation that even at the age of eighty his name could strike
fear in the hearts of scofflaws. That incident forms the basis
for the events described in the epilogue. As to Tom Cochran, there was a man by that name who worked for Slaughter, and who had at one time frequented the owlhoot trail.
But there is no evidence that Cochran fell in love with
Viola—that particular thread of this story is entirely fictional.

Texas John Slaughter played a crucial role in bringing
law and order to Cochise County, for many years one of
the most lawless places in the American Southwest. He was
a man of few words, a staunch friend to some, a relentless
foe of the outlaw element and as brave a man as the Old
West ever saw.

The author is indebted to the following works: *The
Southwest of John H. Slaughter* by Allan A. Erwin (Glen-
dale, CA: Arthur H. Clark Company, 1965) and Robert
Barr Smith's "Texas John's Odyssey," which originally ap-
peared in *Wild West* magazine and later in the anthology
Best of the Wild West, published in 1996. Another work
which proved invaluable is *Once They Moved Like the
Wind: Cochise, Geronimo and the Apache Wars,* by David
Roberts (New York: Touchstone, 1993).

THE TRAIL DRIVE SERIES
by Ralph Compton

From St. Martin's Paperbacks

The only riches Texas had left after the Civil War were five million maverick longhorns and the brains, brawn and boldness to drive them north to where the money was. Now, Ralph Compton brings this violent and magnificent time to life in an extraordinary epic series based on the history-blazing trail drives.

THE GOODNIGHT TRAIL (BOOK 1)
_____ 92815-7 $5.99 U.S./$7.99 Can.

THE WESTERN TRAIL (BOOK 2)
_____ 92901-3 $5.99 U.S./$7.99 Can.

THE CHISOLM TRAIL (BOOK 3)
_____ 92953-6 $5.99 U.S./$7.99 Can.

THE BANDERA TRAIL (BOOK 4)
_____ 95143-4 $5.99 U.S./$7.99 Can.

THE CALIFORNIA TRAIL (BOOK 5)
_____ 95169-8 $5.99 U.S./$7.99 Can.

THE SHAWNEE TRAIL (BOOK 6)
_____ 95241-4 $5.99 U.S./$7.99 Can.

THE VIRGINIA CITY TRAIL (BOOK 7)
_____ 95306-2 $5.99 U.S./$7.99 Can.

THE DODGE CITY TRAIL (BOOK 8)
_____ 95380-1 $5.99 U.S./$7.99 Can.

THE OREGON TRAIL (BOOK 9)
_____ 95547-2 $5.99 U.S./$7.99 Can.

THE SANTA FE TRAIL (BOOK 10)
_____ 96296-7 $5.99 U.S./$7.99 Can.

THE OLD SPANISH TRAIL (BOOK 11)
_____ 96408-0 $5.99 U.S./$7.99 Can.

THE DEADWOOD TRAIL (BOOK 12)
_____ 96816-7 $5.99 U.S./$7.99 Can.

TERRY C. JOHNSTON
THE PLAINSMEN

THE BOLD WESTERN SERIES FROM
ST. MARTIN'S PAPERBACKS

COLLECT THE ENTIRE SERIES!

SIOUX DAWN
92732-0 _____$5.99 U.S. _____$7.99 CAN.

RED CLOUD'S REVENGE
92733-9 _____$5.99 U.S. _____$7.99 CAN.

THE STALKERS
92963-3 _____$5.99 U.S. _____$7.99 CAN.

BLACK SUN
92465-8 _____$5.99 U.S. _____$6.99 CAN.

DEVIL'S BACKBONE
92574-3 _____$5.99 U.S. _____$6.99 CAN.

SHADOW RIDERS
92597-2 _____$5.99 U.S. _____$6.99 CAN.

DYING THUNDER
92834-3 _____$5.99 U.S. _____$6.99 CAN.

BLOOD SONG
92921-8 _____$5.99 U.S. _____$7.99 CAN.

ASHES OF HEAVEN
96511-7 _____$6.50 U.S. _____$8.50 CAN.

CAMERON JUDD
THE NEW VOICE OF THE OLD WEST

THE GLORY RIVER
Raised by a French-born Indian trader among the
Cherokees and Creeks, Bushrod Underhill left the dark
mountains of the American Southeast for the promise of
the open frontier. But across the mighty Mississippi, a
storm of violence awaited young Bushrod—and it would
put his survival skills to the ultimate test...
0-312-96499-4___$5.99 U.S.___$7.99 Can.

SNOW SKY
Tudor Cochran has come to Snow Sky to find some answers
about the suspicious young mining town. And what he
finds is a gathering of enemies, strangers and conspirators
who have all come together around one man's violent
past—and deadly future.
0-312-96647-4___$5.99 U.S.___$7.99 Can.

CORRIGAN
He was young and green when he rode out from his family's Wyoming ranch, a boy sent to bring his wayward brother home to a dying father. Now, Tucker Corrigan was enter-
ing a range war. A beleaguered family, a powerful landown-
er, and Tucker's brother, Jack—a man seven years on the
run—were all at the center of a deadly storm.
0-312-96615-6___$4.99 U.S.___$6.50 Can.